Campfires in the Night Sky

Campfires in the Night Sky

Ian Kennedy

Copyright Notice

Cover illustration by: George Cotronis

Author Website: ikennedyauthor.com

Author email: ikennedyauthorquestions@gmail.com

CIP: A catalogue record for this book is available from the National Library of Australia

ISBN: 978 0 6459747 3 7

To all those lost on the tide.

Chapter 1

"Look up, young one, and what do you see?" said the old man. He stood unsteadily leaning on his walking stick. His limbs were worn; his mechanical augmentations creaked; his face creased with age and experience. He looked up into the night sky. There were so many memories up there.

"Stars," said the young child, fresh and without years. He looked skywards too with trembling eyes.

"Out there, there are wonders and horrors beyond imagining," said the old man.

"How do you know?" asked the child. He gripped the old man's hand tightly, as if never wanting to let go, lest he become lost in the vast inky black space above.

"Because, I have seen them…"

"When?" The child looked with a face full of promise from the sky to the old man.

"Let me tell you a tale; a tale of wonderful and terrible things, of war and death, of hope and life; a story of humanity." The old man looked down at the young child and smiled. The child looked at the old man with wide eyes.

"What are the stars?" asked the child.

"They are the campfires of the dead waiting for us to join them," said the old man with a smile.

"There are so many!" The child squeezed the old man's hand.

The old man squeezed back, his hand creased with age and life's troubles. He felt the child's small and innocent hand in his own. "Let me start, from the beginning."

***

"First, we colonised the planets and moons of our solar system. We spread across the worlds out there enthusiastically and energetically. We transformed the barren wastes of the moons of the planets into habitable zones. We made sure that we had the resources that we harvested from these worlds and used those resources to make them more and more habitable. We grew trees and crops. As we spread we invented machines, Artificial Intelligences that could help us in our conquest. We named them after the gods of old times. The most comprehensive and master AI was called Zeus. It, or he, some gave the AIs genders, ruled over and managed all the other AIs.

"In order to make the AIs more relatable to us humans, we made them in our image. We gave them emotions and feeling; desires and wishes. It made them more independent and less needing of constant monitoring. They could perform on their own and do what they were programmed to do. We thought that this was a good idea.

"As time went on, we realised that this was a mistake, but it was too late to go back on what we had done. The AIs dictated human existence, and it was too late to shut them down.

"And because we made the AIs in our image, they had the same flaws as us. They became jealous, vindictive, and fought amongst themselves. And they dragged humans into the conflicts with them. We became their pawns and play things.

"And yet, many of us worshipped the AIs as they wanted us to. They demanded to be treated like gods, and we obeyed.

2

Temples and altars sprung up across the solar system to the god AIs. Any failure to pay tribute to the new gods was punished.

"And so, with worship and war, the AIs controlled human lives. We were pawns to their whims.

"And yet, the AIs also knew that they needed humans to worship them and keep them running. Without humans, the AIs were nothing. So, it was a symbiotic relationship.

"Different groups of humans supported different AIs and they went to war with each other. This led to a ten year war on the soils of Titan, one of the moons of Saturn. We had terraformed this foggy world decades earlier and now it was torn apart.

"But I am getting ahead of myself. First, the Cerv forces had to land on the moon of Titan. They wanted to take the Citadel by force, but did not want to deploy nuclear weapons as the Citadel was shielded and their prize was within it."

**

"We're landing in twenty minutes!" said the intercom inside the belly of the landing craft.

The Cerv soldiers stood in rows inside the craft, all facing the large door at the end of the craft which would lower and allow them to spill onto the Plains of Titan.

In the front was Arakus, young and headstrong, he would lead his soldiers, the Kiyerons, to many victories. It was said that he was immortal. That would be tested.

What was clear was that Arakus had the most advanced cyber implants of all the soldiers. He could see further, hear clearer, and run faster than any of them thanks to these implants.

All the soldiers had implants of some sort. Some had half their heads replaced with machinery. Others had mechanical limbs. Some even had brain implants.

Arakus checked his sword and force shield. They both buzzed with power. He looked down at his armour. All the troops wore armour that glittered in the lights of the assault craft. The armour would keep them alive on the surface of Titan. Not so much from a harsh atmosphere that had been tamed decades earlier, but from the attacks of the Titans who they were going to pacify. Their helms were metal with a slit for the eyes and a slit downwards for the face. Many helmets had long plumes on top. They had breastplates and shields too, forged with skill and care.

Turning to his men, the Kiyerons, the most skilled of all the Cerv forces, Arakus shouted over the noise of the engines, "What do we do this day?" He saw the soldiers armed with shields, spears and some with bows and arrows.

"Take back our honour and glory!" shouted the soldiers.

"A-hoo!" shouted Arakus, banging his shock spear on his force shield. The shield looked like a normal metal shield until the spear neared it then there was a fizzing and crackling of energy as the two repelled each other. The electric discharges illuminated the interior of the craft.

"A-hoo! A-hoo!" shouted the soldiers, doing the same.

The craft rang to the buzzing and fizzing sound of their spears and shields colliding. The soldiers stamped their mechanical legs in unison and the craft reverberated.

"Five minutes," said the intercom.

Arakus breathed hard and turned back to the front of the craft. He knew that all around them were similar craft that were on course to land on the Plains of Titan. Each one held many soldiers. Each soldier brave and true.

His implants told him details of the battlefield they were about to land on. He could 'see' the terrain before him outside the walls of the craft.

"One minute!"

"30 seconds!"

"5, 4, 3, 2, 1…"

There was a loud crash and the soldiers jostled each other in the craft. Then the landing ramp smashed down and ahead of them were the verdant fields of the Plains of Titan.

"Here we go!" shouted Arakus. He thundered down the ramp, each footfall echoing in the humid air.

Arakus ran up the beachhead and up a small hill. He looked around and saw thousands of fellow Cerv warriors doing the same. They raced up the small rise and looked around.

Ahead of them was an army, armed in similar fashion to them. They had armour and force shields along with energy swords and spears. They were arrayed in blocks along the plains.

Arakus looked back at his soldiers. He grinned. He turned back to the foe, and charged.

***

Arakus ran across the soft soil of the Titan Plains. His mechanically enhanced limbs powered him forward. The chem dispensers in his brain and spine discharged and filled his natural muscles with the power of the AIs. All around him his fellow warriors were doing the same, and felt the same. But Arakus' own implants were special. They were said to be made from the same circuits as the servers of the AI Zeus. They made him feel invincible.

Arakus heard the shrill whine of shells being fired from the landing craft and impacting and detonating on the force shields of the Citadel of Titan and the surrounding troops. The explosions were blocked and deflected by the force shields built to protect the massive server farm within the Citadel. This would have to be done the old fashioned way, Arakus smiled to himself.

The Cerv soldiers raced up the Plain, each trying to beat the other to combat first.

To Arakus' chagrin, there was a soldier who had outstripped him in the race up from the landing. This stung his pride and he redoubled his efforts to make it to the front line.

As he watched, the soldier, unknown to Arakus, leapt at the front line of Titans, his great force spear blazing with energy in the light filtering through the thick clouds. But it was not to be. This heroic Cerv would not have praises sung to his bravery, only his demise. The Cerv soldier, in his haste, was cut down by one of the Titan arrows. The Cerv soldier fell and lay, propped up by his spear.

Arakus smirked. Glory would still be his. He screamed his battle cry and crashed into the force shields and weapons of the Titans.

The fighting was fierce. Shields clashed and weapons sizzled. Arakus cut down Titan soldier after Titan soldier. He was unstoppable. His rage unquenchable. His wrath unbounded. Soldier after soldier fell.

The Titans fought back hard. They were fighting for their home. Arrows filled the air. They made sure that they defended it with all they could. And yet, under the fierce onslaught of the Cerv soldiers, the Titans were pushed back, slowly but surely, they were pushed back.

Arakus' cyber implants told him his kill count projected on his vision. His augmented eyes also told him who and what he was looking at. As he stood there, breathing hard, in a lull in the fighting. He saw Sius running over to him. Sius was one of the Cerv commanders. They stood there, together, breathing hard.

"We're driving them back!" said Sius, running up to Arakus.

"Good," said Arakus with a grin. Sius grinned back.

Arakus knew that Sius was a wily commander. He led his soldiers well and he was a hero with high praises sung of him in his own right, but not as great as Arakus. That Arakus also knew. He grinned wider.

"Why don't we raid that?" said Arakus, pointing his force spear towards a small black building on an outcropping below the walls of the Titan Citadel.

Sius stayed silent in the din of battle for a moment, cocked his head to the side and said, "All right. What is it?" His eyesight was not as augmented as Arakus'.

Arakus turned and began running towards it. "A server node for Apollo!" he shouted over his shoulder. He did not look back to see if Sius was following him.

Reaching the server node, Arakus saw Sius right there beside him. They tried the door. It was locked.

"Wait," said Sius and attached a lead from his head implant to the wires of the locked keypad. He closed his eyes, and in a few seconds, the door slid open with a hiss.

Arakus smiled again. "You're always useful," he said.

Sius grinned and put away the lead. "Being a man of ideas can be a curse."

"Come on!" said Arakus. They shouldered their way into the inner rooms of the server node.

The priest was still there, tending to his computers. Arakus gutted him where he stood. The crimson gore of his intestines stained the bright flooring.

"What do we do?" asked Sius.

"Tear it down," said Arakus calmly. He thrust his force spear into the nearest server stack. Sparks flew and Sius joined him in defiling the server node. After a few short minutes, the whole of the server farm was shorting out and destroyed.

In the moment of calm that followed, Arakus wondered if he had done the right thing, but the thought was gone in a second.

The two of them raced out of the server node and back into the battle.

***

Hours of fighting went by, and the two armies ground each other to a stalemate.

***

Arakus and Sius returned to their camps along the edge of the Plains of Titan. They needed to recharge their shields and weapons. They left the fight.

As they jogged back to the landing craft, their mechanically augmented limbs sank a little in the soft Titan sand. It made the going just a little bit harder.

Returning to their camp, the pair saw that the slaves had been busy, building camp structures, hospitals and mess halls. The landing craft had been turned into makeshift dormitories and even some of the larger craft from the invasion fleet in orbit around the small moon had landed and acted as large staging posts for new warriors to join the fight. The angular ships towered above the Plains and the light filtering through the thick clouds reflected and glinted off their steel and white armour.

Arakus and Sius stopped for a moment and admired their warships, then the hubbub of the camp drew their attention, and they snapped out of their reverie. They headed back to their landing craft to recharge their shields and weapons.

As Sius saw Arakus break off and head in his own direction, he smirked. He knew that Arakus was destined for greatness. All Sius wanted was to return home, alive. He had tried to get out of going on this war. He had posed as a simple peasant. And yet, he had been dragged along. How had it happened? He had been acting like a simple farmer back on Earth. And then they had come for him. He had acted crazy, and they had seen through it. They had placed a child in the way of his plough machine. And he had stopped. That damn child. He might die because of that damn child.

But he was here now. He would try to survive. What else could he do?

Sius had been walking to his soldier's landing craft and was lost in his thoughts. He reached the craft and plugged in his shield and weapons. They recharged quickly, only a few minutes. Then he disengaged and felt the slight fizzing feedback as the batteries in his system were at maximum charge. It made a slight tang on his tongue and a buzzing behind his augmented eyes.

He walked through the camp, slowly. He did not particularly want to return to the fighting. He was sure that Arakus was already half way back there. That man was destined for things, he knew.

He walked, carrying his shield, spear, and sword. He watched the slaves assembling the structures. They were almost totally machine. Or at the very least, mind wiped humans who were reprogrammed to be loyal servants. They could not fight, they were too slow, but they were useful. They talked to each other in computer noises and with strange transmissions. They could speak the Cerv language, but to each other they communicated in much more efficient ways.

Sius saw a group of slaves man handling the hover horses that the chariots would use. They were just managing to ride and direct the large machines that hovered a few feet off the ground and pulled the chariots for the great warriors. Arakus' chariot was there, decked out in gold. But he had opted to fight on foot and get into the fighting quickly, rather than wait for the hover horses to be unloaded and fuelled.

Sius saw a priest of the network. He seemed troubled. Sius went over to see what was wrong.

The priest was in a small alcove of one of the hastily assembled structures in the camp. He was looking perplexed at a computer screen.

"What's wrong?" asked Sius.

"Sir, the computer says something…"

Sius waited, then added, "What?" as the priest failed to continue.

"The computer predicts a long war. A long siege!"

Sius laughed a nervous laugh. That was not possible. Already the Cerv forces were routing the Titans.

"That's wrong, clearly," said Sius.

"Clearly," said the priest. "We're already winning. I can hear it." The man pointed at the sky and the two of them heard the clash of battle nearby on the Plains.

"Well, keep trying," said Sius. He was not sure what was worse, the slaves or the priests. He left the man pondering the signs in the network. He did not want to ask what the AIs thought of all this.

Then, while almost reluctantly exiting the camp, Sius ran into Oreson, leader of all the Cerv forces coming back from the battlefield, presumably to recharge his systems.

The two men exchanged nods and Sius asked how it was going on the Plains outside the Citadel.

"We almost have them routed," said Oreson. He nodded again, and headed towards his landing craft.

Sius grinned wryly. That priest was clearly wrong.

Sius returned to the battle, his circuits pumped up with energy. He killed many Titans.

***

"They're retreating inside the walls!" called out Arakus. He ran after the retreating Titans.

Looming up out of the Plains of Titan was the Citadel. It had massive walls and was for all intents and purposes a giant stronghold that was used to protect the server nodes for the AIs in that area of the Solar System.

For all the Cerv soldiers' alacrity, the Titans fought a good rear guard action and were able to retreat most of their forces back inside their Citadel walls.

Arakus raced up to the walls of the Citadel, just as the giant black doors were closing. He pounded on the doors with his fists and spear. He shouted for them to come out and fight, but to no avail.

Sius stepped up and put a hand on his comrade's shoulder. "We'll get them," Sius said.

Arakus fumed. He was denied the ultimate victory.

"We'll just have to wait," said Sius.

"Wait...I don't want to wait," snapped Arakus, still staring at the black doors.

"Sometimes we have to," said Sius.

"Not me, never," said Arakus.

Sius snorted a laugh. "One day you'll learn patience. Come on, we'll return to the camp. I'm sure Oreson will have something to say about his glorious victory."

Now it was Arakus' turn to snort a laugh.

They, and the rest of the Cerv army, retreated back to their camp on the Plains of Titan.

Arakus knew that the Titans would have to come out of the Citadel eventually. There would be more death, more killing, and he welcomed the thought.

As they walked, they noticed the riverbed that had been terraformed. In times past it would have run with methane, now that had long since evaporated, but the humans had made it run again, with blood.

***

The Cerv army reached the camp. They tried to rest, but each soldier was both tired from fighting, and yet invigorated by the adrenalin and electricity that powered through their cybernetically augmented systems.

Sius knew that his mechanical joints would need servicing. He had taken an energy spear in the leg, but the damage was not bad, so he could wait before seeing to his injury.

The slaves had been busy. Sius saw that the slaves had been building a rampart around the Cerv ships and camp. They had erected something that looked not unlike the Titan citadel wall. It was shorter, but it had the same purpose.

Sius swallowed hard. This was meant to be a short war. Most of the time was meant to be in travelling from and to the Earth. The actual fighting on Titan was not meant to take very long. The Cerv forces were clearly superior. But now, with the Titan forces safe inside their Citadel, and the same ramparts being built around the Cerv camp, Sius had a sinking feeling in his mechanical stomach. This might take time. This might take a long time. And a siege is not what they had in mind.

Chapter 2

"It's been ten years," said Sius to Oreson. "You said this would be short. You said this would be easy!"

Oreson paced in his quarters in the middle of the Cerv camp. The quarters had become more and more permanent as the years dragged on. Now the Cerv camp was akin to a small city. It had all forms of buildings constructed out of metal panels and wood harvested from the trees that had been planted on Titan when it was terraformed.

"Did you hear me?" snapped Sius.

"Yes, I heard you," said Oreson in a low growl.

Sius knew he should not be talking to the leader of the invading forces with such distain, but it had been a ten year siege, something none of them were prepared for.

"Well?" Sius said.

"Well what?" snapped Oreson. He turned to face the insolent man in his quarters.

"What are we going to do?" said Sius. "There's a plague ravaging our soldiers. It's some sort of virus that works its way through their implants. It's killing and incapacitating hundreds if not thousands of our soldiers. What are we going to do about it?"

"What can I do about it?" said Oreson. "You raided the node of Apollo years ago."

"But you took the girl as a dataslave. The corruption started from then," said Sius.

"I can't give her back. I refuse!" snapped Oreson.

"Then we will all fry," said Sius. He stormed out of the quarters.

Sius marched along the rows of buildings and quarters that made up the Cerv camp. He came to Arakus' quarters and knocked.

"Come," said Arakus.

Sius stepped inside and saw, in the dim light of a few bulbs, that Arakus was there, eating, and also sitting at the table was his companion and lover, Drebus. They both turned to face Sius, but remained seated.

"Ah, Sius, come, eat," said Arakus.

Sius nodded and sat down. He helped himself to the plate in the centre of the table. There was bread, and some different fruits.

"Any news?" asked Arakus.

"No, our 'glorious leader' is as stubborn as ever. He wants to keep his dataslave and damn the consequences," said Sius.

Drebus snorted a laugh.

"And so, the virus will keep spreading," said Arakus.

"Indeed. We have angered Apollo, you and I. But Oreson refuses to return his dataslave…" said Sius.

"We did nothing of the sort!" snapped Arakus. "That server node was fair game!"

Sius shrugged. "We're still here ten years later," he said. He stared absent mindedly at the table.

"We can't lose," said Drebus carefully.

"We're not going to," said Arakus.

"But we might not win, either," said Sius.

"Do you remember how this all started?" asked Arakus.

Sius nodded.

"Xos was chosen by the AIs to win the affection of the most beautiful construct," said Sius. "Fria was the most elegantly coded, most intelligent, and most beautiful AI construct there was. She was a new form of AI that was manifested in a real body. She was beset by programmers, when one of them won her affections in a simple lottery—"

"And you still call it a 'she'," said Arakus with a smile.

Sius smirked and said, "Well I prefer to think of her as a 'she' rather than an 'it'."

"Always the romantic," said Arakus. "Go on."

"Why? We all know the story. We're here, and that's what counts. Ten years later. Ten years! It took that long to get here from Earth. We'll be old men by the time we go home," said Sius. He looked at Drebus who had said nothing and was simply eating. Sius thought that the man had the best idea.

"Just tell me the story. I want to hear it again," said Arakus. He tore off a slab of bread and ate it.

"Well, we all pledged to protect the winner of the lottery. And Verius won. So we pledged to protect his union with the AI construct," Sius said, pausing to eat some fruit.

After a few minutes of chewing, Sius continued, "And then came Xos. He barged his way into our court with silken words. He bewitched the AI with his charms. He then stole her from Verius and fled here."

"And so we all came here, to get Fria back, and win glory in battle," said Arakus.

"Speak for yourself," said Sius.

Arakus and Drebus both gave Sius an odd look.

"Well, I'm not here for glory or honour. I just want to go home. It was meant to be a quick operation. In and out. Now it's taken a ten year siege. What are we doing here?" said Sius.

"We're fighting for glory and honour!" said Drebus with a grin.

Arakus said nothing through a mouthful of food, but grabbed Drebus on the shoulder enthusiastically.

After a few more minutes Arakus jumped up. "Let's go raid something," he said.

Drebus jumped up and fetched Arakus' force shield and shock spear. Arakus made sure his shock sword was fastened to his waist.

"Come on Sius. Oreson has raided a number of the nodes around here. He's brought back some young priestess of the AI and he's having all the fun. I want some fun too!" said Arakus. "You're fully charged?"

Sius sighed. He stood and retrieved his shock spear, shield, and sword from the entrance to Arakus' quarters.

The three of them set off at a brisk, mechanically augmented pace out of the camp. They headed towards one of the server nodes that dotted the Plains of Titan and that broadcast the AI information throughout the outer Solar System.

The three reached the door of the node. They burst in and they impaled the guards who had no idea they were coming.

The priestesses screamed and ran. The priest begged for his life.

Sius looked around the black structure. It had many lights blinking in the darkness. There were cables running everywhere. The floor was slick with blood. More blood was added when Arakus impaled the priest on the end of his shock spear. The man collapsed and gurgled his last as his hot intestines mingled with the cool air of the server node and began to steam on the floor.

Arakus slung his shield over his back and grabbed one of the priestesses who was cowering at the altar of the server. He was about to stab his spear into the server racks, but Sius grabbed his arm.

16

"Don't. We don't know what will happen. Don't anger the AIs," he said.

"Pfft," said Arakus. He broke free from Sius' grasp and stabbed the spear into the servers. They sparked and fizzed. There was a flash as the shock spear discharged it's energy into the computers.

Sius sighed. There would be consequences from that, he knew. But Arakus was already gone. He had left the server node with the priestess.

Sius turned his attention back to the other priestesses around the altar. They were still cowering. He indicated with his head that they should run.

The priestesses hesitated, but then ran. They ran out of the server node and away, to where, Sius did not know. He did not really care. All he knew was that the AIs should not be angered.

This was a server node to Apollo, the same AI he had raided the server node of on the first day of the war. Now, ten years later, Sius wondered if that was why it had taken so long. And what would happen now that they raided another server node to the same AI.

Sius looked down at the eviscerated priest spoiling the floor, and then up at the sparking racks of servers. He shook his head.

He turned and ran out. He could see Arakus dragging the young, female priestess along in the distance. He was moving slowly due to her protestations. Sius smiled.

Catching up with the pair easily, Sius fell in step with Arakus.

"Nothing for you?" Arakus said.

"No, I have someone at home," said Sius.

Arakus snorted a laugh, but said nothing.

They both ignored the screams and yelling of the priestess that Arakus was dragging along by one of her arms.

Chapter 3

Oreson paced in his quarters. The High Priest was with him. Oreson's footfalls made muffled clicks as he paced back and forth across the rug covered metal floor. His dataslave was standing in the corner of the room. She was trying to be submissive.

"What do you mean, 'it's my fault'?" snapped Oreson as he made one revolution and started marching the other way in the room.

"Sire, it's the will of the AIs. You have taken a dataslave as your own. She did not belong to you. You are the reason that the virus is spreading through our networks and infecting our soldiers!" said the High Priest desperately.

Oreson stopped pacing and regarded the Priest coldly. He glared at him. Oreson could see that the High Priest was definitely nervous and uncomfortable. He looked down and fidgeted with his robe. His mechanical implants clicked and whirred.

"So, in the case that I don't give back the dataslave, what then?" said Oreson, still rooted to the spot.

"Then we all catch the virus, sire. All our soldiers will be rendered incapable of fighting. We will lose." The High Priest kept looking at the ground. He shuffled his feet.

"Look at me," said Oreson.

The High Priest did not comply. He kept looking at his feet.

"Look at me!" shouted Oreson.

The High Priest flinched. He then looked up at his commander. Slowly, hesitatingly, his eyes crawled across the floor, up Oreson's mechanically augmented legs, up his armoured and gilded torso, and finally settled uneasily on his half machine face and eyes. "Sire?" he said meekly.

"Find another way!" said Oreson. His words clicked in his mouth as his mechanical jaw spat the words.

"Sire," said the High Priest.

"Don't you dare," said Oreson.

"Sire, I am a messenger of the AIs. I cannot lie in that regard. There is no other way. You will have to give back the dataslave to save our soldiers," the High Priest said. "There is nothing else to do. Believe me I would love for you to keep her. It would give me all the joy in the world, but your troops are dying. The virus is sent by the AIs. They do not like the sacrilege of their temples. There is no other way, sire," said the Priest.

Oreson sighed. He began pacing again, but less angrily. He had seen the virus' effects on his soldiers. Many had been laid low by the virus. He knew that if it continued, there would be no army left.

"All right," said Oreson. "All right."

"Sire?"

"Return the dataslave. Send some warriors to return her to the server node where she was taken." Oreson waved a hand and dismissed the High Priest.

"Yes, sire!" said the High Priest. He scurried out of the room, clearly eager to be away from the gaze of his master.

Oreson was left in the tent with the dataslave. He turned to her. She looked at him. In those eyes, Oreson saw, was a combination of pure hatred, and utter terror.

"I hope the virus kills you, and all your damned soldiers," she said. She spat the words.

Oreson walked over to her, and slapped her across the face. "I am warlord of all these soldiers. I'm not going to let some small dataslave bring down my entire battleforce.

"We will win. You cannot breach our walls," said the dataslave. She looked defiantly up to the man who towered over her. Her fleshy cheek now growing red and blemished from the slap from the mechanical arm.

"We'll see about that," said Oreson. He grinned a toothy, mechanical grin.

"In ten years you haven't been able to, and now your soldiers are falling thanks to the great AIs. You will fall too. I know it. One day, you will fall, and it will be when you least expect it." The dataslave looked defiantly into those mechanical eyes.

Oreson, in that defiant stare, saw embodied the resistance that he had encountered all these years. Perhaps she was right. Perhaps she knew something, told by the AIs to her, that he did not know. Or perhaps she was just insolent and bluffing; pleased to go home. He did not know, but in those eyes, he saw hate, and it made him pause.

Then, a couple of soldiers appeared at the door to Oreson's quarters. They stood to attention.

"Take her back to her server node. Take her back," said Oreson, without looking away from those defiant eyes.

The soldiers moved into the room and grabbed the dataslave by the arms. She did not resist. She simply glared at Oreson and then she was gone.

"How dare she!" whispered Oreson.

And then he heard some shouting and cavorting outside. He walked to the door to his room and looked out over the ash ground towards Arakus' quarters. He could see that there was the warrior with his own dataslave. She was being ogled by

20

Arakus' soldiers. And yet Arakus, seemed to be protecting her from his soldiers' advances. He shepherded her inside his quarters.

"How dare he!" snapped Oreson. "How dare he have a slave when I cannot. I must deal with this!"

And so Oreson, warlord of all the Cerv forces, who had led his soldiers here and fought hard for ten years, grew jealous and plotted to take Arakus' dataslave.

***

Verius stormed into Oreson's quarters and slumped down into a chair. "How much longer?" he said.

"How dare he," said Oreson.

"Huh?" said Verius, looking at his brother with confusion, eyebrows raised.

"How much longer of this damn siege?" snapped Verius, not looking at his brother, but scissoring his mechanical fingers open and shut with a menacing click.

"Pfft," said Oreson. He shook his head at his younger brother. "Here I am, making decisions that affect the entire army, and all you can do is complain about the siege."

"Fria is my wife," said Verius, quietly and with menace.

"And you lost her," said Oreson. "Yet don't make out that that is the only reason we are here. If we lose this war, then our trade routes with the outer planets might be in jeopardy."

"You and your damn trade routes. The planets move in orbits at different rates. Find another way to connect them," said Verius, waving a dismissive hand.

"I am supreme commander of this venture. You will not talk to me like that," shouted Oreson.

"And I'm your brother, and my wife was stolen by some young bastard," shouted Verius.

"Don't forget what I've given up for us to come here," said Oreson, dropping his voice to a furious whisper.

"You sacrificed your daughter, like the priests decreed. It gave us favourable solar winds out here, so we could save fuel for when we have to burn our engines on the way home. Believe me, I understand," said Verius.

As he said this, Oreson moved to the table Verius was sitting at and towered over his younger brother.

"My daughter!" snapped Oreson. "I cut my daughter's throat so that we could get a favourable solar wind so that we could take back your damn wife who couldn't keep her legs together!" Oreson snapped. He banged his hand down on the table, sending the cups and food flying.

Verius did not flinch at his brother's anger. "Finished?" he said, looking up at his brother. "You have to give up a slave. It's no big deal. We can get another."

Oreson fumed. He said nothing. Verius could see his mechanically augmented face was twisted with rage.

"I have a plan," said Oreson, releasing his clenched fists.

"Oh, that's new," said Verius, almost encouraging more rage from his brother.

Oreson paused, marched a few paces away from the table, and turned back to his brother. "I'm going to take Arakus' slave," he said with a smirk.

"Arakus has a slave?" Verius looked up at his brother.

"Now he does; soon he won't" said Oreson.

"Do you think that's wise?" said Verius. He reset a cup upright on the table and poured himself a drink.

"I am the supreme commander of—"

"Yes, yes, and you know best, of course," said Verius, watching the fluid run into the cup.

"Do you have to be so insolent?" said Oreson.

Verius said nothing and took a drink. After a moment, he spoke, "When are you planning to do this?"

"Soon," said Oreson.

22

"Good, because you know how headstrong Arakus is. If he gets attached to the dataslave, he'll throw the most awful tantrum."

"He can do that. I don't care. I am going to have a slave." said Oreson.

"You know best, supreme commander," said Verius, regarding his brother carefully.

"So, I have your support?" Oreson walked over to the table and sat down. He reset another cup from its side and poured himself a drink.

"You are my brother, of course I will support you," said Verius. He raised his cup and took a drink.

Raising his own cup, Oreson took a drink too. "Good."

*＊＊

Sius and Arakus dragged the dataslave through the camp to Arakus' quarters. Many of the soldiers stopped what they were doing and watched the trio as they moved through the Cerv camp. Arakus and Sius threw her onto the floor of Arakus' quarters. The rich carpets absorbed her fall. The quarters were constructed out of the side of one of the Cerv ships that Arakus had used in the first invasion.

Arakus and Sius slumped down into different armchairs on either side of the carpet. The dataslave's eyes twitched back and forth between the pair. She looked like a caged animal, terrified, yet ready to gore anyone who touched her.

Arakus reached out towards her, defying her motions. She clawed at him with her fingernails. They scratched a trail down Arakus' forearm that was not mechanical. He withdrew in pain.

Sius laughed. "You'll have to teach her manners," he said.

Arakus fumed and slapped the girl with a mechanical hand. She whimpered and withdrew from Arakus scurrying over to a corner of the quarters.

23

"And you need to control your anger," said Sius to Arakus with a chastising tone.

Just then Drebus entered the quarters. He saw the slave in the corner, a red mark developing on her face, and Arakus cradling his wounded arm.

Sius poured and raised a glass to him. "Welcome to the circus," Sius said.

Drebus moved to Arakus' side and began to inspect the wound.

"Relax," said Arakus. "My nanites will fix me."

Even as they watched the flesh that had been gouged was repairing itself. The gouges healed and left only faint scars on the surface.

"I really need some of those," said Sius. Drinking from a glass.

"Not possible," said Arakus with a smirk. "They're mine and mine alone. I am blessed by the AIs."

"But anyone could take your blood and use them, couldn't they?" said Sius.

Drebus finished inspecting Arakus' arm and walked over to the table, he poured a glass and tore off some bread. He walked over to the dataslave and offered them to her. She refused. He shrugged and put them on the floor in front of her. He then went back and sat on the arm of Arakus' chair. The two of them entwined hands and sat there, playfully.

Sius watched from behind his glass. He watched the slave; he watched the two warrior lovers. He watched everything.

"No, if someone injected my nanites into themselves with the hope of eternal life, they would die in minutes. The little things would kill them," said Arakus, still toying with Drebus' fingers. "Lots of people have nanites, no one else has mine."

"I see," said Sius carefully.

"I'm not sure you do. I am the greatest warrior there is. I am immortal." Arakus closed the sentence with a laugh. It was a laugh of warriors born in battle. It was a laugh of defiance. It was a laugh that defied the AIs and echoed around his quarters.

Sius looked over at the dataslave. "What about her?" he said, pointing with and extended finger from the hand holding the glass.

"I will keep her safe, if she agrees not to attack me," said Arakus. There was not a smile in his voice. "Eat," he said to the dataslave. She still had not touched the food that Drebus had given her. "Eat, you must be hungry. It's been ten years of rations."

The dataslave hesitated, then her resolve cracked and she lunged at the food and drink. She devoured it all quickly. She began coughing from the exertion.

Sius laughed.

Arakus smiled. "Slowly, not even I can inhale food."

"What's your name?" asked Sius quietly.

The dataslave, now fed, flashed a gaze of fear between the three men in the quarters in front of her. She said nothing.

"What is your name?" demanded Arakus.

"Softly, softly," said Drebus.

Arakus sighed. "Your name?" he said calmly.

"Krysi," the dataslave said with a cracked voice.

Sius gestured with his hands. "There you go. A start. Her name is Krysi!"

"Softly," said Drebus, gripping Arakus' mechanical hand, and then extricating himself from the grip and walking out of the quarters.

"He's a good lad," said Sius.

"Yes, I do love him so," said Arakus. "And as for, 'lad', he's about the same age as I am."

"I know, I know," said Sius with another laugh. He stood up. "I'll let you get acquainted with your new slave." He winked and left the quarters.

25

Sius breathed deeply as he exited the quarters. The clouds were thick overhead and the light that filtered through cast eerie glows around the camp. Much of the camp relied on the electricity generated from the ships that had landed on the Plains. There were lights rigged up at regular intervals and fires to keep warm in braziers dotted everywhere.

Some of the plague that had affected the circuits of the soldiers had started to abate thanks to the returning of the dataslave that Oreson had stolen.

Sius rubbed his face. He was getting older. This war had to end soon. It was supposed to end within a year, now it had been ten.

He walked through the camp to clear his head.

Chapter 4

"You can't do this!" snapped Arakus. He threw a glass across the room in his quarters and it smashed somewhere in the corner.

"I can, and I will. I, Lord Oreson, must have a personal slave. And, as you are part of my army, I can take yours, so I will!" Oreson grabbed the arm of the dataslave that Sius and Arakus had brought to the Cerv camp only hours ago.

"But I'm your greatest warrior. You can't treat me like this!" Arakus searched for another glass to throw, but found none.

The dataslave squirmed and wriggled in Oreson's grasp, but his mechanical arms never let her go. His guards also prevented any escape by blocking the exit to Arakus' quarters.

"She's mine!" shouted Arakus.

"Not anymore," said Oreson. A smirk crossing his face.

Arakus reached for his sword. Oreson's guards drew theirs.

"Think very carefully," said Oreson with quiet fury. "Or we will test how immortal you are supposed to be."

Arakus' will faltered. He looked across at Drebus, who had been sitting at the table the entire time. He now had his hand on his sword.

"What's her name?" said Arakus quietly.

"What?" said Oreson, clearly already bored with the tantrum.

"What is her name?" said Arakus more forcefully.

"How should I know? 'Slave' is what I will call her. Her name is meaningless now," said Oreson.

Arakus fumed. He threw himself down in a chair. He glared at the table. "I won't fight for you then. I won't fight for anyone. My Kiyerons will stay with me, here, in the camp. You will lose."

Oreson grinned and dragged the dataslave out of the room. His guards went with him after a short delay.

Arakus got up, stomped around, sat down, grabbed a glass, went to throw it across the room when Sius entered the quarters and caught the glass as it flew across his path.

"What's happened?" Sius said. He moved to Arakus' side and put a hand on his shoulder.

Arakus shrugged off the hand and simply stared at the table. He began to pick at its surface.

"Is this some in joke?" said Sius. He sat down next to Arakus.

"Oreson took his dataslave," said Drebus.

"Krysi? Why?" said Sius. He leaned closer.

Arakus said nothing. He simply boiled with quiet rage.

"Look, Arakus. I might be able to help. Just tell me. I'm older than you, maybe Oreson will listen to me," said Sius. He slapped Arakus on the back as they all sat at the table.

"He stole her. He stole her from me. I can't believe it. He did not even know her name. He stole her!" shouted Arakus. He banged a fist on the table.

"Why did he steal her?" said Sius.

"Because he lost his, therefore he took mine. His great Lordship must have a slave, and he saw mine, so he took her. He took Krysi. She was mine. She was mine!" snapped Arakus. He banged the table again.

"Can we get her back?" said Drebus, looking at Sius.

Sius said nothing but looked carefully at Arakus.

"Before you say, 'don't do anything stupid,' yes, I know you Sius, that is something you would say," said Arakus.

"What have you done?" said Sius.

"I have decided not to fight. I will not commit my troops to battle, until Krysi is returned to me. I know my soldiers are the best fighters in the Cerv army, and I will not let them draw blood while his Lordship has my dataslave." Arakus said carefully, a childish grin came across his face. "Let's see how he likes it when his forces start to lose."

"I'm not sure we're winning now," said Sius offhandedly. "We've been here ten years."

"Then we will be driven off the moon," said Arakus. "All because of his greed. Drebus, let the soldiers know that we have no reason to fight anymore. They are to stand down and let their weapons discharge. Power everything down. We will sit here as long as it takes."

Drebus nodded and left Arakus' quarters.

"I'm not sure this is wise," said Sius. "It's only one slave. You have others. We can get someone else."

"Oh, Sius, you really think this is about one slave? I've been treated like a child all the time I've been here. I am the greatest warrior in this army, and I'm treated like I'm fourteen years old. Hell we've been here for ten years and still I'm treated like a boy. Oreson lords it over me and I'm sick of it. I've had it. I am far more glorious than he is. I should be leading this army. Not him. My skills are far beyond his. He got us into a ten year siege. My forces would have stormed the Citadel and ransacked the AI drive bays in the first year of the war easily if he'd let me do what I wanted. And so, he will pay for his arrogance." Arakus slumped, all rage vocalised and expended.

"Finished?" said Sius.

"Don't you treat me as a child too," snapped Arakus.

"Sorry," said Sius. He paused, then continued, "Are you sure this is the best way to go about this?"

Arakus snapped his mechanical fingers open and shut a few times. "I don't care if it is the best or worst way, I will do it my way, and Oreson will feel the consequences."

"I know you well enough that in this mood you cannot be dissuaded," said Sius. "So, I will leave you to stew. I think you're making a mistake." He got up from the table and walked towards the exit. "Tread carefully, Arakus," he said over his shoulder and left the quarters.

Arakus raged to himself. All the nasty thoughts in the world crossed his mind. How dare he. How DARE he. Oreson had it coming to him. Arakus knew that with his forces stood down, there was no chance of victory, and he smiled to himself.

Drebus entered the room and sat down by his lover.

"Well?" said Arakus.

"It is done. We will not fight. We will let our weapons discharge. We will sit here…and lose," said Drebus.

"Good."

"Do you think this is wise?" said Drebus.

"Now you sound like old man Sius," said Arakus.

"Eat something," said Drebus.

Arakus pushed the food and drink away. He stood and paced his quarters. He snapped his mechanical fingers back and forth. He waited for the end.

Chapter 5

Xos stood alone on the battlements of the walls of the Citadel. He looked out over the Plains of Titan. He saw, in the distance, past the wreckage of previous battles, the glittering lights of the Cerv invasion fleet that had landed and set up camp on the edge of the Plains. He stood there for what seemed like hours. He simply watched, and dreaded.

"What happens if they breach the walls?" he said to himself. "What if?"

There was no reply. His words were simply whisked away on the light wind that blew across the Plains and over the walls of the Citadel.

There was nothing he could do. He knew this. He knew that he and Fria had started this war by escaping Verius' palace and fleeing to this end of the Solar System.

"What can I do?" he said to himself.

"Be my husband?" said a voice behind him.

Xos turned sharply and confronted the intruder into his innermost thoughts. He put a hand on his sword. His mechanical augmentations whirring into action. Even before he realised who the voice came from, even though he had heard it a thousand times, he prepared to strike down the bearer of the voice.

"Easy, easy," Fria said. She put a hand on her husband's chest.

Xos felt ashamed all of a sudden. He could be angry over nothing and almost strike down his wife, yet he could not confront the real enemy. His mechanical augmentations calmed down and the stimulants in his blood abated and were absorbed back into their receptacles.

"I'm so sorry," Xos said. He hugged his wife. He felt her circuit infused body. Her warmth. Her softness. She was an AI made flesh. He knew her intelligence was vast, beyond the confines of this small moon, but somehow, as a physical being, she was small, perfect.

"What for?" She hugged him back. Even with his mechanical augmentations in his arms and chest, she hugged him tightly.

"For everything. For all this. For this war. For your captivity here," Xos said exasperatedly. He kept hugging the woman he loved with all his soul.

"Come back to bed. The war can wait for tomorrow. We have enough to worry ourselves with now," Fria said, breaking the embrace and taking Xos by the hand.

Xos felt her supple fingers and palm through the sensors in his mechanical hand. He knew it would feel hard and cold to her, but he thanked her silently in his mind that she did not flinch; that she did not let go.

"All right, all right," Xos said. He glanced back at the Cerv encampment far away, too close all the same, and walked along the city walls with his wife.

They retreated through the city. As they walked, they saw some people going about their business. Traders were trading. Businesses went on.

One thing neither of them spoke about anymore, was the daytime and night time cycle. The moon of Titan had such long day/night cycles. Each full 'day' took 16 Earth days.

Therefore the light that filtered down through the clouds illuminated the Plains for 8 days, and then there were 8 days of night. At the moment it was night. And they had another few Earth days to go before light came back. Originally, the Sun never reached the surface of Titan many centuries ago. Now, thanks to the terraforming that the Corporations did, the clouds were made thinner, the air breathable, and the Plains farmable. Then the people came. They came with water, and they grew life on the moon that was once a choked, cold, toxic wasteland.

Xos and Fria walked through the people. Even in the night they still worked. Most people still observed old Earth times, Xos mused to himself.

Turning his head skyward, Xos saw no stars. The clouds were thinner, it was true, but they were still obscuring. Light filtered through, when it was day, but at night there were no stars. Xos missed the stars. He had seen them in his travels. Titan rarely had a night sky, just cloud. Sometimes the clouds broke and the sky filtered through, but it was rare. He knew that the Cerv soldiers would notice the lack of stars too. They were from Earth. They had a sky.

"What are you looking at?" asked Fria. She tugged on Xos' arm.

Noticing that he had stopped walking and was simply staring skyward, he said, "Oh, nothing. Just remembering the stars."

"Hah, that should be my job. I am from Earth. I should mourn the lack of stars, yet I do not, because I have you. And you have me. Forget the stars. We are here now," Fria said, pulling on Xos' mechanical arm again.

Xos smiled. He knew she meant it too. He started walking again. They moved through the city streets to the nods and bows of many of the citizens going about their tasks.

They returned to their bed chamber and lay down together to very little sleep.

***

Zoriam sat on his throne in the palace of the Citadel. Beside him sat his wife, Oricula. In front of them paced Brior.

"I do wish you would sit down," said Zoriam.

"How can I sit when the city is besieged?" said Brior.

"It's been besieged for ten years, my son," said Zoriam. "We have held out this long. We will continue to hold out."

"I must go and fight them. You have me here, organising defences all the time, yet I am never able to go and fight," said Brior. He stopped pacing and looked at the king. "Father, please!" His tone was pleading.

"If you end up dead, the Citadel will fall. We cannot hold out without your training and expertise," said Oricula. Her tone was calm and measured. She sat upright in her throne, head held high.

"Mother…" Brior said, reaching out to his mother and imploring her to be on his side.

"Enough!" said Zoriam. "You will fight when necessary and not before. When the Cerv forces threaten our walls, then you will fight. As you have fought before. But while they cower in their camp, you will not fight them. You are not immortal. If you fall, your mother and I will never forgive ourselves."

Brior looked from his father to his mother. They both had resolute looks on their faces.

Zoriam knew what was pulsing through his son's veins and circuits. The same feeling had flowed through his own many times many years ago. The will to fight. The desire to kill those who threatened his home. The need to rid the world of enemies. And yet, Zoriam knew that the young man who stood before him had only a fleeting idea of the world of death. Yes, Zoriam knew that his son had fought well in the war so far and had avoided most injuries, but he was young and headstrong. His circuits were newly wrought and implanted.

Zoriam had seen war before. He had fought off enemies to his Citadel before. He had killed men before. He had won wars before. He had seen his friends and family die before. And now, in this time of renewed war, he wanted his sons, both Brior and Xos and the others that were stationed around the palace, to live. And if keeping them inside the walls was the way to have them live. And if having the Cerv forces batter themselves to pieces on his walls, while a virus gripped their camp, was the way of having his sons live, then so be it. Even if they viewed him as a coward.

Brior kept pacing in front of the thrones. He marched up and down the throne room.

"Son, please, sit," said Oricula.

"While my people die, I cannot sit. How do you sit?" he turned and snapped at his parents.

"We are safe here," said Zoriam. "They cannot breach our walls. We will ride out this war."

"Bah!" said Brior throwing up his hand.

"When you've quite finished!" said Zoriam. His voice boomed around the chamber and was absorbed by the rich tapestries and old wooden furniture that adorned the throne room.

Zoriam could see his son visibly pause at the shout.

"What does Pyrakra say, your daughter?" said Brior turning carefully and cautiously to face his parents.

"You know she is disturbed," said Zoriam. "We do not trouble her with such things."

"But she knows things. She sees things. She knows when bad things will happen," said Brior.

"She is disturbed," repeated Zoriam. "It was the result of a poor melding of machine and flesh. She sees things yes, but they are all imaginary. It is because her circuits did not join properly in the melding process. Her brain is not quite right."

Brior looked sideways at the old man. "And yours are?"

Zoriam controlled his anger. He heard his wife draw a breath through her teeth. "I will pretend I did not hear that. Now go, take your insolence with you, and go back to your quarters. We will deal more with the defence of the Citadel tomorrow."

Zoriam saw his son fume a little, then bow, then leave the throne room.

"Are we too hard on him? You know how headstrong you were, like him, in your youth," said Oricula. She turned her head to her husband. She smiled faintly.

Zoriam turned in his seat to face his wife. His wife of so many years. He felt his mechanical implants in his arms, legs, and chest belying his age. The flesh around them had withered and aged. The machine parts had grown stiff. "My love," he said. "My love, I know exactly how he feels, and yet, I know what he does not. That death is final, and comes too soon for us all." He reached across the small gap between the thrones and grasped his wife's slender, unaugmented hands. "I must keep us all safe, no matter how much he hates me for it. One day he will know, that I have done the right thing. And that he will thank me for it."

"And what about what Pyrakra says? She comes out with the most horrid sayings," Oricula said. Her face creased with worry.

"She is deranged. And that is my fault I made her join with the machine too early. It scrambled her circuits and mind. All she can do is be a priestess. And we hide her away from the public," Zoriam said. His voice cracked and he choked back a tear. It had been his fault that she was like this. And yet, he knew, that she did say some things that seemed to come true, but he could not believe them. He must not believe them.

"My love, that is the end of our work for the day, let us return to bed," said Oricula. She rose and Zoriam followed her out of the throne room and back to their quarters.

As they walked through the quiet palace, with its stone and brick corridors and walls, with people sleeping in their rooms for the night, Zoriam heard the defences of the city being constantly readied from outside the palace walls. He heard soldiers patrolling and clanking in their armour and the buzz of shock weapons. He knew that the Citadel's outer walls had held all this time, ten years, and he insisted that they would win, but he also doubted. If the Cerv forces were as tenacious as they were, could there be any winner in this fight?

When they reached their quarters; rich and opulent in furniture and tapestries; they waved the dataslave away, and settled down to sleep.

***

Brior moved through the sleeping palace. He was one of the few members of the royal household that was still awake. The corridors were empty, save for the few guards stationed here and there for the night shift. They nodded to the prince as he walked past them. He nodded back.

Brior should have been heading to his rooms to sleep. He should have been preparing for the next day in the war. He should have been honouring his father's wishes and preparing for another day of the siege; another day of hardship; another daylight raid to the edges of the Cerv camp. But he was not.

Brior headed towards the temple compound within the palace. He had to see his sister. He had to see Pyrakra. He had to find out what she thought.

He kept walking through the palace. It was large. It contained many rooms for the hundreds of court staff and also it held many of the princes and princesses of the royal household.

37

Brior came to a fork in the corridor. In one direction, was his sleeping quarters and the sleeping quarters of the Prince Xos. Their suites of rooms were next to each other. In the other direction was the way towards the temple complex.

Pausing at this junction. Brior thought to himself. He could go left, towards sleep; towards rest; towards his father's wishes. Or he could go right, towards knowledge and perhaps, understanding.

There were no guards at this fork in his path. There was no one here to judge him. He had the time to decide.

He looked down the left corridor. It stretched away, darkened for the sleep cycle. He looked down the right corridor. It was still lit. There were no sleeping quarters down that way.

Brior turned on his heel and walked down the right corridor. He headed towards the temple complex. He needed to talk to his sister.

***

Reaching the temple complex, Brior stood outside the imposing doors in the front of the building. He paused again, but this time, only for a short time, and pushed the heavy metal doors open.

He stepped inside and immediately his nose was alerted to the smell of incense. Whisps of the spiced smoke were snaking their way amongst the stone pillars that held up the large and high vaulted ceiling. The smoke gathered and hung in the vaults above, shrouding the ceiling in mystery.

Brior looked around from where he stood in the entrance to the temple. He could not see anyone. It was night cycle after all, he reminded himself. But he knew that his sister would be here somewhere.

He walked down the long rows of seats that were gathered in the temple for anyone who might be passing by to sit and take stock of life. He moved between pillars. Some he touched with his mechanical hands as he passed. He felt the rough surface of the grey stone through the sensors that were implanted in his mechanical hands.

Moving to the front of the temple. He saw the representation of the large servers that filled the space behind the altar. The black structures were covered in flashing green lights. Brior paused again, here, looking at the representation of the servers. On the altar were the incense burners that filled the temple with their holy incarnation. Brior knew that the servers he saw here were simple representations of the massive bank of servers and AI broadcasting equipment that was stored below his feet in the basement of the church. The real servers needed a smoke free, temperature regulated environment. That was not the case in the body of the temple, with people coming and going and incense being burned to honour the AIs.

Brior moved to right next to the altar and picked up an incense stick that was unlit. He moved it through one of the many inextinguishable flames that was nearby. The stick coughed and spluttered in the flame, but it lit. Brior blew on it to extinguish the naked flame and then placed the smouldering stick into some sand that was in a bowl on the altar.

He took a step back and bowed his head to the great AI generating machine that stood there, thrumming and bleeping quietly, in the stillness of the temple.

Brior felt his augmented heart beating in his chest. It's rhythmic thumping seemed to be mirrored by the flashing of the lights and the hum of the fans.

"Now, where's my sister?" he said quietly to himself.

Nodding his head to the server again, he turned and moved through the temple in another direction. Perhaps she would be in the quarters provided by the temple to its priests and staff.

He walked along some side corridors in the temple and came across his sister. She was sitting and reading in an alcove.

Brior stood out of sight behind a pillar and observed her. She was slight, and small. She was not military augmented. She did not have the arm, leg, chest and head implants that he had. She had brain implants, he knew, but there was not a mark on her externally. Her dark hair spilled down over her shoulders. She wore a white robe which spilled down over her frame and pooled around her feet on the floor. She seemed calm, at peace. She was reading something, Brior did not know what it was. He almost turned around and left her peacefully there. She was not peaceful a lot of the time now, thanks to the war. He hated to break her concentration, but he had to hear from her what she thought.

He coughed deliberately.

She jumped slightly and looked around.

He hated to interrupt her.

She saw him, and smiled a sad smile. The mouth moved, but the eyes did not. There was an eternal sadness in those eyes. She saw things, Brior knew, she saw terrible things.

"Brother!" she said quietly in the space, but it echoed around the alcove and corridor.

"Sister!" said Brior. He smiled.

"If I'd known you were coming, I would have been more prepared," Pyrakra said, closing the book and putting it on the seat in the alcove as she stood up and moved towards him.

They embraced. Brior felt her tremble as his mechanical form enveloped her slender frame. Then they held each other at arms' length.

"I don't come here enough," said Brior.

"I like it when you do," said Pyrakra. "Why are you here?" her voice changed, as if she sensed something.

Brior grinned wryly and said, "Nothing gets past you."

A look of worry crossed Pyrakra's face.

"I want to know what you've seen," he said.

"Don't," she said, breaking away from his arms. She walked back to the alcove. She stood with her back to him. She did not sit down.

"Tell me!" he said, his voice echoed around the corridor.

She flinched. "I see your death. I see all our deaths. I see it all, in vivid crimson gore. We will all die. Since Xos is here. Since his whore is here. Since you fight. I see it all. We all die!" she said, her voice getting more distressed as she spoke.

"That's not possible. That means the Cerv troops win. That's impossible. They cannot breach our walls," he said.

"You don't believe me, I know. No one believes me. It is my curse. But I have seen it. I know…"

"At least I know something," Brior said. He moved to stand by her. She was still facing away from him. He put both hands on her shoulders.

"What?" she said, she turned to face him, and his arms fell by his sides.

"I won't die. I won't let myself die!"

The look she gave him broke his heart.

"See? you don't listen. No one listens. But I've seen it!" Pyrakra clawed at her scalp. "I have implants. I see what the AIs see. And no one ever believes me!"

"Hey, hey," said Brior. He grabbed for her scrabbling hands. "You'll hurt yourself." He stopped her.

She gave in to his mechanical hands. "Just go and let me read. One day you might believe me." She shrugged herself free and went back to sitting in the alcove and went back to reading her book.

Brior grimaced. He regarded her for a few seconds, but said nothing. He then turned on his heel and marched out of the temple without a backward glance towards the altar.

As he left through the large metal doors he said to himself, "I cannot die. We will win. She'll see."

Now, he had to sleep and rest; recharge his circuits. Tomorrow would be another day of the war.

Chapter 6

Oreson slept. He lay in his quarters on his camp bed. He tossed and turned. He dreamed.

He saw, in his dreams, the battlefield ahead of him. He had his shock spear in his hand and his shield in the other. He was in full battle armour. His mechanical arms and legs tensed and readied for the fight.

Ahead of him, through the mists and fog of his unconscious, he saw the great walls of the Citadel. They towered to the swirling, boiling sky of Titan's clouds. They seemed impregnable. Around him, the Plains of Titan stretched on and on to the hills on the horizon.

Looking around, Oreson saw that he was alone on the battlefield. There were no Cerv allies. There were no Titan enemies. There was no camp. There was nothing, other than the Plains and the Citadel.

"Hello!?" Oreson called out. His voice echoed around the vast Plains and bounced off the impossibly high walls of the Citadel.

Oreson took a few steps towards the Citadel. His augmented heart raced. It pumped blood and chemicals around his body, preparing him for the fight. But there was no fight. There was nothing. There was no one.

"Hello!" he called out, angry this time. He did not know what was going on. He did not know that this was a dream. It seemed so real.

He felt the soft soil beneath his armoured feet. He took a few steps, so as not to be swallowed up by the ground. He planted the end of his spear in the ground and threw down his shield.

"HELLO?" he called out again. This time, he was furious.

"Yes."

The voice came from behind him. Oreson spun around, grabbing his spear and shield in the process. He brandished the shock spear at the now new apparition.

"Who are you?" said Oreson, spear poised, shield ready.

The old man who now stood in front of Oreson smiled. "You need to take the fight to the Titans," he said.

"Who. Are. You?" Oreson laboured the words.

"Oh, you know me," the old man said.

Oreson could see that the old man was old, but not frail. He seemed to be muscular beneath his old armour. He had a white beard, and a proud chin. The man carried the most exquisite shield and spear: gold, and shining in the light that filtered through the boiling clouds above.

"You seem too old to be a warrior," said Oreson. He cocked his head to one side.

"Don't judge me on appearances," said the old man.

"Then how am I to judge you? I have seen nothing of substance from you, other than a few words," Oreson said. He was getting annoyed again. "Now what's going on?"

"You are dreaming," said the old man.

"I see, then why can't I wake up? Why am I dreaming of you?" Oreson said.

The old man took a step towards Oreson. Oreson brandished his spear and shield.

44

"I'm not here to harm you. I want you to fight," said the old man.

"Have you seen their defences?" Oreson pointed his spear behind him and at the walls of the citadel.

"I will help you," said the old man. He smiled. His teeth were perfectly white and straight.

Oreson chuckled. It was all too absurd. This old man in his dream would help him conquer the walls of the Citadel?

"And how will you do that?" Oreson scoffed.

"Don't doubt me. I can be cruel to those who mock," said the old man. His tone was suddenly very serious. He took another few steps towards Oreson.

Oreson raised his shield, but then heard a sound behind him; a sound from the Citadel. He turned, and saw a full army of Titans stretching from horizon to horizon in front of the Citadel walls.

"Men! Men! To arms!" Oreson called out. But there was nothing; no one. "Help me, old man," Oreson hissed between his teeth.

The Titans looked ready to charge.

"Old man! Help me!" Oreson cried out and turned back to where the old man had been. There was no one. "Damn you, old man!" Oreson yelled.

"I will help you," came a voice from the heavens. It was the old man's voice, strong now, and everywhere.

Oreson spun around. The Titan army was cowering around the walls of their Citadel. As Oreson made a full revolution, he saw his own army, thousands strong, arrayed where there had, moments before, been nothing. They shouted and yelled. They were ready for war.

"Who are you?" said Oreson quietly.

"I am The AI."

"Zeus?" Oreson nearly dropped his shield and spear.

"The very same," said the voice which echoed around the Plains.

"How are you speaking to me?"

"Through your implants. All my type can communicate with you through your implants. It's how the priests see us and interpret our wishes. We can talk to you, as if you were machine."

"Then we cannot lose," said Oreson. A grin crossed his gnarled and scarred face. "The AI Zeus is with us. I must tell the men!"

And then, there was nothing.

Oreson tossed and turned throughout the sleep cycle. He slept a fitful sleep. But he knew, that he would win, with The AI backing his forces. They would surely be unstoppable.

As the lights came on to signify a new awake cycle, Oreson awoke. He sat up quickly on his camp bed. He rubbed his eyes. He had a strange feeling something important had happened in his sleep. That somehow there had been something.

"Take the fight to them," a voice echoed in his head. He flinched. He knew that voice. It was the voice from his dream. It was The AI. It was Zeus!

"I must tell my soldiers!" Oreson said as he jumped up and donned his armour. "I must talk to my High Priest."

Oreson stormed out of his quarters and towards the High Priest's quarters. He needed some divine interpretation.

***

"And you say that the main AI appeared to you?" said the High Priest. He narrowed his eyes and scrunched up his nose while looking at the leader of the invasion.

"It did! I swear!" said Oreson emphatically. He paced back and forth across the rich carpeted floor of the High Priest's rooms. The walls were draped in cloth and the metal surroundings were covered in lush and decadent tapestries and rugs. But Oreson was too busy to comment on the Priest's living quarters. His mind raced with the dream.

"And you saw armies?" said the Priest. He was dressed in his night attire and, although his implants were keeping him awake, he yawned but tried to hide it behind a hand.

"Yes, yes!" said Oreson. He kept pacing. "I told you the whole dream. Just tell me what it means?" Oreson kept flicking glances to the Priest. He ran a hand through his own hair and seemed to have trouble deciding where to lay his vision. Sometimes he stared into the distance, sometimes at the floor, and sometimes, nervously, at the Priest.

"Sire, if you stop pacing, I can run a diagnostic," said the Priest. "Please, sit."

"There is no time. I must have an interpretation now!" snapped Oreson.

The Priest sighed. "It will only take a moment. And you know that this will be an interpretation. Please, sire, calm yourself. You don't want to overload your circuits."

Oreson paused and took a deep breath. He stood there and closed his eyes. "Yes," he said. "Yes, run a diagnostic. I must know what this dream means."

"Sire, sit over here," said the Priest. He brought out a computer that had a lead attached to it.

Oreson moved to the table in the centre of the room and sat down at the Priest's computer. He rolled up a sleeve and prepared for the sting of the needle.

"This will only hurt a bit," said the Priest. He put the needle into the pre-prepared jack in Oreson's arm.

Oreson took a sharp intake of breath, and then he saw numerous symbols appear on the screen.

After a few seconds the Priest said, "Interesting."

"What's interesting?" snapped Oreson. His arm had begun to twitch with the current as it lay on the table.

Now it was the Priest's turn to inhale sharply.

"What is it!?" snapped Oreson.

"I believe you," said the Priest.

"What do you mean, you 'believe me'?" Oreson went to pull the jack out of his arm. "This is stupid. Damn priests making work for themselves. I should have kept that dataslave. Then Arakus would still be fighting… It was just a dream. It was stupid. Why are you looking at me like that?"

"Don't log out, sire. I detect markers on your circuits. Markers that indicate you came into contact with a very powerful force," said the Priest.

"What are you babbling about, man?" said Oreson. He grasped at the jack.

The Priest's hands clamped around Oreson's arm with such force that Oreson let go of the jack and did not pull it out.

"It was real!" is all the Priest said. His eyes wide. His mouth open.

"It was a dream," said Oreson.

"No, no, it was real. You were touched by an AI. The AI!" The Priest shut down the computer and withdrew the needle from Oreson's arm.

"Zeus!" said Oreson. He stared at the table.

"The very same," said the Priest. "And it wants you to do as it said!" The priest sat down at the table opposite Oreson. The computer and jack sat impotently on the table.

"Then what do I do?" asked Oreson, looking up from the table to the Priest, his eyes wide.

"What did it tell you to do?" said the Priest. It was clear to Oreson that they were both shocked by the revelation.

"Take the war to the Titans. Make sure I fight them outside the Citadel walls."

"Then do that. Now. This moment. The Sun is coming up. We have many days' worth of light after the many days of night. It is time for war. Muster your troops, sire. It is time to fight!" The Priest salivated.

Oreson nodded. He stood up and turned to go. Then he paused and half turned back to the Priest. "Thank you, Priest," he said.

"Sire," said the Priest, standing and almost knocking his chair over.

Oreson exited the quarters and marched towards his quarters. He shouted as he went for his generals. He shouted for Sius and Arakus. He shouted for Verius. He needed to prepare for another attack!

The camp sprang to life around him as he marched. The soldiers could see that a new attack was in the works. They could see their ruler was in control again. They could see that they were going to win this time. After ten years, they were going to mount an assault that would be unstoppable.

***

A shout went up among the Cerv soldiers. It was infectious with Oreson at the centre. He grabbed his shock spear; girded on his sword; and strode out to the mouth of the Cerv camp. He gazed across the Plains of Titan. A cool wind whipped at his hair. He smelled the smells of the Cerv camp behind him: the fires burning in the braziers, the food just consumed for morning meals, the anticipation of the soldiers.

Oreson saw the walls of the Citadel in the distance with rising towers of broadcast beacons stretching into the clouds high above. This was the day, he thought. This was the day!

He turned to see the light of the Sun filtering down through the clouds. It's faint rays shining and bursting through the thick cloud cover. The rays glittered off his armour and shield.

"Soldiers of the Cerv Army!" Oreson bellowed to his fighters. They were forming up in ranks at the entrance to the camp. "Soldiers of the Cerv Army!" he called out again. "Now is the time! We march out this day and take back the Citadel! We get our AI back! We burn the Citadel to the ground!"

The soldiers, who had waited silently in anticipation suddenly burst out in shouts and cheers.

Oreson looked across their number. He saw Sius and his soldiers, along with many of the other commanders and their fighters; but there was no Arakus.

Arakus and his men were missing. Oreson scowled at Sius, who simply shrugged, obviously understanding Oreson's anger.

"Oh well, we'll go to glory without him," said Oreson beneath his breath. "Come soldiers of the Cerv Army. We march!"

Oreson even saw Sius start shouting and banging his shield. Oreson smirked. He turned and marched out ahead of his army towards the Citadel. His orderlies brought his chariot behind him.

The ground reverberated with the marching soldiers. Oreson thought to himself at the head of his force, that never had there been a more proud and impressive army amassed in this part of the Solar System. He would make the Titans pay for their insolence. He would, personally, spear Xos and take back his brother's AI.

***

Arakus lounged on a chair in his quarters. He ate some rations.

"There they go," said Drebus, standing at the entrance to his lover's quarters.

"Let them go. They'll lose, and then he'll beg me to fight for him," said Arakus calmly. He swallowed some bread.

"What if they don't?" said Drebus, turning from the doorway.

"Don't what?"

"Lose."

"Hah, of course they'll lose. I'm not there," Arakus said, letting out a chuckle.

"Your men are restless. Many of them believe we should fight," said Drebus, leaning on the doorway.

"I'm in charge. I give the orders to my men. Not that fat oaf," snapped Arakus.

"I know, I know. But is this anger wise? Is it…sound," said Drebus, cocking his head to one side against the doorway.

"You doubt me now?" said Arakus. He patted the chair beside him.

Drebus straightened up and walked over to the chair and sat down. "No," he said. "I simply think that the sooner this war is over, the better. It's been ten years. We're getting old. Put your pride away and fight with your men."

Arakus slapped Drebus lightly on the knee. "We will fight, when he returns my slave. We will fight, when he begs me to. We will fight, when we need to and never before. I want the fat oaf Oreson to think he will win, and then not. I want him brought low. I will have my revenge on him. He will regret the day that he wronged me. I will never let him win on his own."

"That all seems rather petty. What about what Sius said?" Drebus said, moving his knee out of range of Arakus.

"Sius is an old fool. He acts like he knows what's going on, but really he is just an old fool. No one is as glorious as me," said Arakus, reclining in his chair.

"I still think this is a bad idea," said Drebus.

"Think all you want, but I'm not moving. And without me, my men don't move either."

***

Lining up on the Plains of Titan, Oreson's forces faced down the walls of the Citadel. Oreson had mounted up on his war chariot, pulled by a couple of large hover horses. He was in the process of riding back and forth in front of his massed forces who were beating their force shields with their shock spears and swords. The cry that went up was deafening. So

51

deafening that Sius could hardly hear what his commander had to say.

But Sius knew, that this was a critical time. This battle might end the war. The war that had gone on for ten years. Sius felt old. He had grown old in the time of the war. His mechanical implants were in need of a service. His arms felt stiff. This could not go on much longer, could it?

"…And on this day we…" Oreson rode past again, and was drowned out by his forces shouting again.

"Something about fighting, something, something," whispered Sius. He brandished his spear and shield.

"…To take back my AI!..." There went Verius on his own chariot and hover horses. He followed Oreson around in a loop.

"For you we all will die," said Sius quietly. None of his soldiers around him heard him. They were all too busy shouting insults at the walls of the Citadel.

The Citadel sat there, with its walls protecting the Titan city, towering into the sky.

Sius watched the walls. There was a gate a few hundred metres ahead of them. It split open and, with a grinding that could be heard above the shouts of the Cerv soldiers and commanders, it retreated into the walls as it split down the middle.

The Cerv forces fell silent. They watched with anticipation as the Titan soldiers filed out and took up positions in front of their city walls.

Both forces stood there, silently, watching, waiting. Even Verius and Oreson fell silent and stopped doing laps in front of their army.

***

Brior stood at the front of the Titan forces. They had marched out of the Citadel gates and formed up in front of the walls. There were thousands of them, and thousands of the enemy.

Brior's eyes scanned the Cerv forces that were arrayed a few hundred metres away. They were all armed like the Titans. They had their shock spears, swords, and force shields. Each warrior of the Cerv forces was mechanically augmented. There were a couple of commanders, Brior assumed one was Oreson, riding up and down on a chariot pulled by hover horses. They were shouting something to their own forces. The words were snatched away by the winds, so all that filtered through to the Titans was the sound of the enemy army.

Flexing his hand around his spear, Brior looked along the line of his own men. They stood proudly and steadfast in the face of the enemy. He saw Poiy, Lord of his hundreds of men standing there, armour glinting in the faint Sun. He saw Greol with his massive axe, swinging it around in front of his men. There was no shield for him, simply his axe, big enough to cleave any augmented soldier in half. There were dozens of them, Lords of war who stood at the front of their squads and forces that made up the Titan forces.

Brior could see in the Cerv forces ahead of him, Lords and masters doing the same with their men. Each brandishing their weapons ahead of their forces. There was Creatus, famed with the sword. And there was Sius, Lord of his men, brandishing his spear, just like Brior.

Scanning the Cerv forces with his mechanically augmented eyes, Brior could not see one particular enemy commander. He could not see Arakus. He knew that Arakus was one of the greatest warriors in the Cerv forces. And that he had brought a full contingent of his men with him from Earth. And yet, he was not here. He was not here on the battlefield. Brior wondered why he was not there, and grinned. Any advantage that his forces could get would be welcome.

Turning to face his men, but saying no words, Brior looked up at the Citadel walls and the giant gates that had sealed as the Titans had marched out. He could see, on the top of the walls, the form of Zoriam, his father, and Oricula, his mother, watching, waiting. Fria was not there. She was safe inside the palace, Brior knew. But Pyrakra was there, her hair wild, her eyes wide, she did not cry out, but Brior saw her face was strained and she was trying to tell Zoriam something.

Brior smiled and waved to the people gathered on the top of the walls. The people gathered, to watch the slaughter.

Just then, Xos shouldered his way through the men to stand by Brior's side. He carried a shock spear and a force shield, and had a proud sword on his waist. His armour gleamed in the half light. His mechanical augmentations strained for the fight.

"Get back inside," said Brior tersely. He indicated the gates of the Citadel with his head.

"Never. I'm here to fight, brother. You will not get rid of me," said Xos with a grin.

Brior sighed. "Fine, just don't get yourself killed."

"I wouldn't give them the satisfaction," said Xos, grinning wider.

"Men of the Citadel," bellowed Brior, turning to his forces. "Today we fight for our Citadel. We fight for our people. We fight for our AIs. We fight for glory. We fight to the death!"

A shout went up at the conclusion of the words. It rippled through the Titans and swelled to a roar. Then there was silence. Both armies stood poised, waiting, watching.

***

For a horrible moment, both armies stood, facing each other, and silent. Then a shout went up somewhere, and it was followed by another and another. Then the entire Plain reverberated with the shouts of soldiers from both sides. Even Sius shouted. He banged his shield and spear. The sparks from

54

the shock weapons caused sparks to fly across the front line as both sides rang with the sounds of clashing arms.

"This day we go to victory! Charge!" called out Oreson as he manoeuvred his hover horses and chariot towards the Titans. He was followed by his brother.

Sius yelled with his men. They charged. Across the Plains of Titan, they charged. And then there was chaos.

Chapter 7

Sius' mechanical legs pounded on the soft ground. He ran. He ran hard. He ran headlong with his men into the Titan forces. They yelled as they ran. They screamed with anger built up of a decade in waiting. They screamed their hatred of the Titan forces. They screamed. They screamed.

Brandishing his shock spear, Sius' mechanical arm swung the spear in a wide arc and it connected with the body of one of the poor unfortunate Titan youths. He was impaled as the spear pierced his armour and discharged its energy inside the man's body. He fell, dropping his own spear and shield on the dirt. His body convulsed as Sius pulled the spear free. Blood poured from the wound, staining the ground a darker shade.

Turning, Sius fended off a blow from a sword with his force shield. There were sparks as the blade reflected off the metal and energy surface. Sius' mechanical left arm absorbed the blow. His eyes scanned the Titan soldier for a weakness, then, as the man staggered back from the shock of the blow that he himself had given, Sius swung his spear up and, deflecting the man's own shield, pierced the neck of the man with his spear and discharging its energy in the soldier's neck.

The soldier's eyes exploded as the shock from the spear seared through his head and shoulders. He collapsed on the ground, and as Sius withdrew his spear, there was more blood from the wound and it soaked the ground.

And so it went on and on. Sius killed. Sius lived.

Behind him, his soldiers formed a protective guard and they fought hard. They killed many, and some died. But they killed many.

***

Oreson rode his chariot across the Plains. He readied his spear. His hover horses, guided by his controls, powered his chariot over the ground, smoothing out all the bumps and imperfections in the terrain with their hover motors.

As he crashed into the Titans, some managed to get out of the way, yet others did not. He swung his spear in a wide arc and killed Titan after Titan. He guided his chariot around and around.

Near him was Verius. He guided his chariot to protect his brother, yet also he struck out with hatred at those who had taken his AI from him. He made sure the Titans paid a heavy price for their insolence.

Oreson watched his brother follow him in a rampage through the Titan forces. He smiled. Zeus had come to him. He knew that now. Zeus had come to him, and as such, Oreson knew, that they would be victorious and it would be glorious.

Scanning the battlefield in one of his long loops around on the chariot, as he positioned himself for another charge, Oreson looked across the Plains of Titan, and he thought he saw, in the midst of all the fighting and killing, an old man, standing, unharmed, and in armour almost too heavy for him, yet he held it with grace. There was a slight mist around his feet.

Oreson blinked. He took one hand off the controls of his chariot and rubbed his eyes. They were mechanical. They would not deceive him. He could definitely see the old man from the dream appearing before him. Yet this was no dream.

Spurred on by this, Oreson redoubled his efforts and pulled the chariot in a tight turn to plough back into the Titan ranks.

**

Sius stood with his men. Even his mechanical arms were fatigued and tired. He hefted his shield and swung his shock spear. He and his soldiers fought hard and pushed the Titan soldiers back. Swinging his spear in a wide arc, Sius opened up a gap in the lines in front of himself.

The Titan soldiers moved back out of the way of the humming, thrumming spear. It's dangerous point carving a line through the atmosphere. It crackled faintly as it moved.

Looking around, Sius saw that Oreson was becoming bogged down in his chariot. The Titan forces had surrounded him and he was having trouble directing his hover horses with the controls.

Out on another flank, Sius, with his mechanically augmented eyes, saw Verius trying to fight through the Titan soldiers with his chariot to reach his brother.

The Titan soldiers were fighting back hard. They had been re-energised by something, Sius knew not what, but they all suddenly started to resist with great strength.

Men fell around him. Sius could see that the line was beginning to falter. He could see that the fight was not going well.

Had the AIs abandoned them? Sius did not know. Oreson had claimed that he had seen the AI Zeus appear to him and urge him to attack. Then how would Zeus allow this?

All of a sudden, a shout went up amongst the Cerv soldiers, then a cry, then they began to move back towards the Cerv camp and stronghold. Oreson had fought himself free but was making his way back towards the Cerv camp, whether it was to re-energise his circuits or whether it was out of cowardice, Sius could not tell, but it was the wrong thing in the wrong time. It sparked fear in the hearts of many of the Cerv soldiers.

"Where are you going, soldiers of Earth?" Sius shouted across the din of battle. He knew that if he did not stop this fear, then the whole army could rout.

No one heard him. The Cerv army started to fail. It began to break and run back towards the camp.

Sius stood with his few personal guard in the way of the whole Titan forces. He stood there, spear sparking and shield humming; armour gleaming in the fickle light.

"Men of Earth!" he bellowed. "Stand and fight! Not for your lord, not for your planet, but for your honour. Men of Earth, fight!"

Sius brandished his spear. The Titan forces paused in front of him and his few personal guard. They did not know what to do in the face of such bravery.

Sius stood there, and the Cerv army did not rout. It saw his gallantry and turned back to the fight. Even Verius and Oreson drove their chariots back to the front line.

Sius stood, and the army held.

With the army behind him, the rout was stopped, and the Titan forces paused in their advance. Both sides did not know what to do exactly, and so they stood there, yards apart, brandishing their weapons, with a lull in the killing.

Oreson and Verius rode up beside Sius. They nodded to him. He nodded to the two commanders. Everyone knew who was the true commander.

Both armies stood there, in the middle of all the carnage and screams of the fallen, for a time. Each not wanting to back down. Each not wanting to take a step forward, lest it result in another rout.

***

Xos stood in the front line next to his brother Brior. They had both been fighting hard and their energy supplies were drained. But he stood there, the cool Titan wind whipping at his hair. He had his spear and shield and sword.

Looking up at the battlements of the Citadel walls, he could see his father, his old frame propped against the Citadel battlements, and Pyrakra, eyes wide with fear. But he could not see the shape of his AI. He could not see Fria. She was not there.

Partially hurt by this snub, he looked back towards the Cerv forces, only a dozen or so metres away from his lines.

He looked towards his brother Brior on his right. Brior smiled and nodded towards him.

Suddenly, a strange mist began to curl up from the ground. It enveloped the feet of the soldiers, yet only Xos seemed to see it. The other soldiers simply stared out at their enemy in front of them.

"Do you see…?" said Xos to his brother.

"Shush," said Brior. "I'm thinking what to do here."

Xos looked along the line of men from Titan. They all were oblivious to the mist curling around their ankles. Then he saw her. It was definitely a she. She was standing, between the two battlelines. He felt so affected by emotion. He was almost spurred to tears. She held a golden computer chip in her hand. And Xos knew that it was the AI Aphrodite. He was protected. He knew. He must do something.

And then, Xos had an idea. He took a step forward.

"What are you doing?" said Brior.

The Cerv soldiers in front of Xos readied their weapons.

"People of Earth and Titan," Xos called out. There was silence from everyone else as he spoke. "I am the cause of all this. I must end this." He looked down at the ground. The mist was still there. He looked up. The AI had disappeared. "I took the AI called Fria and brought her here. You have travelled far to take her back. My proposal is this: I fight her previous master, Verius, for her. I fight him here and now. The winner takes the AI and goes home, the loser dies. Whatever the outcome, I want the Cerv forces gone from Titan and my family left in peace."

Falling silent, Xos scanned the soldiers of the Cerv army. They looked from soldier to soldier. They did not know what to make of this proposal.

"I accept!" shouted Verius as he dismounted from his chariot and stepped into the gap between the two armies. He hefted his shock spear and shield. On his waist glinted a keen sword. His armour shone in the filtered light. He stood a few paces ahead of his forces.

Xos took a step forward, looked back at the battlements at the nervous face of his father and the terrified Pyrakra. He felt a hand on his arm. He looked down and into the face of his brother.

"You don't have to do this," said Brior.

"Yes, I do," said Xos. He smiled, and shook off his brother's concern.

Xos turned back to his adversary. They brandished their spears. They saluted each other, then they marched towards each other.

***

Xos bent low and held up his shield with the spear protruding over the top. Verius took a more aggressive stance and remained upright but kept his body well protected behind his shield.

The two combatants circled each other, each looking for a weakness in their opponents posture.

Xos felt the soft sands of the Plains of Titan beneath the soles of his boots. His eyes narrowed in an attempt for his augmentations to scan his adversary. His computer implants analysed Verius' stance and aggressive positioning. Thousands of calculations scrolled across his vision. And Xos knew, that Verius was doing exactly the same thing.

Suddenly, Verius arched his back and hurled his spear straight and true. In a split second, Xos raised his shield and the shock spear sparked and fizzed as it smashed into the round shield and landed in the sand near Xos.

Xos staggered back at the force of the impact. His stance interrupted; his posture broken, for an instant.

Verius drew his sword and charged at Xos. Xos tried to parry the attack with his spear, but he was still stunned by the force of the impact of the shock spear.

Rolling to one side to avoid the blow, Xos regained his posture and began again, circling his opponent. He could see Verius smiling beneath his helmet.

Verius moved to where his spear was in the dirt and picked it up again, after sheathing his sword. Xos knew that hit had plenty of energy left for many more concussive blows.

The two men circled each other. Xos' arm felt rather numb from where the spear had hit his shield. He noted that his reactions from that arm were a little more sluggish due to the energy discharge.

The diagnostics across his vision told Xos that his shield arm implants were a little damaged.

"There's time to repair those later," said Xos under his breath.

"Stop circling and fight me, coward!" called out Verius.

The two men closed on each other. The circle got smaller and smaller.

Xos felt the sweat of the moment trickle down his brow. As cold as the moon of Titan was, he felt hot now. It was the fact that his implants were working at full power. They generated heat. And his body was stressed. He knew that Verius would be the same. His implants would be pushed into overdrive for maximum speed and power.

Xos felt his augmented heart beating rapidly. It pushed chemicals around his body to make him faster, more accurate, stronger.

Their spears were almost touching at this moment. Sparks flew when the tips encountered each other.

And then, Xos lunged. He struck out with his spear. Verius however managed to deflect the blow with his shield. The explosion of energy made both combatants stagger back a few paces.

But this time there was no renewed circling. This time Verius struck with his spear and The blow slid over Xos' shield and imbedded itself in his shoulder.

The spear discharge and flung Xos back a few steps. He dropped his shield and spear in shock. His left arm, his shield arm, was rendered useless.

Xos lay on his back, dazed. He saw Verius, in slow motion, drop his spear and pull out his sword. The man was walking towards him, blade drawn, with a crazed expression.

Xos' world stopped. His implants pushed stimulants through his body so that things looked like they were moving very slowly. He heard people crying out to him. One voice may have been his brother, he could not tell. There was Pyrakra, from the battlements, she was crying out something too.

Grabbing for his sword, Xos managed at the last second to parry the blow of Verius' sword that was upon him. Xos rolled away from the enemy blade and scrambled to a standing position. His sword was held in his right hand, his left arm was numb and damaged. He had no shield.

Verius was laughing. Xos saw this. Beneath his helmet, Verius was laughing.

Verius sheathed his sword and picked up his spear. He marched towards Xos, who was scrabbling backwards on his feet to try to get away.

63

"Come back here, coward," shouted Verius.

The Cerv soldiers were jeering and taunting. The Titan soldiers were deathly silent. Even Brior had fallen silent. He had stopped calling out to his brother. Perhaps in an effort not to distract him.

Verius threw the spear again, but not at Xos. It landed in the dirt a few paces ahead of him. This made Xos stop and pause. He turned to face his opponent. Then Verius was upon him, raining blow after blow on Xos, who parried it time after time with his sword. But it was in vain.

Xos tripped over backwards under the weight of the ferocious attacks. He saw the crazed eyes of the man whose AI he stole.

Verius was frothing at the mouth. His eyes were wide inside his helmet. He struck out madly with his sword. Blow after blow; stroke after stroke.

Xos tried to deflect each blow as he lay there on his back in the dirt. One final blow from Verius smashed the sword from Xos' hands. It spun away and landed in the dirt out of Xos' reach. Xos raised his one good arm to try to protect himself from the final fatal blow.

Xos could see that Verius looked elated in triumph. And then, he saw that there was a strange mist rising from the ground. It was only faint, but it was there.

Then Verius grabbed at his eyes. "What the?" he shouted out. He spun around and around. "I cannot see! My eye implants are not working! What is this?"

Xos lowered his arm. He looked at the man who would be his killer. The sword limp in his hand as he clawed at his augmented eyes. Looking over at the Cerv soldiers, all of them were doing the same. They were all blind. Their military eye implants had malfunctioned. It was the same with the Titan soldiers. They were all blind too. The only man who was not incapacitated was Xos.

"Run!" was the only thing that Xos heard. It was crystal clear. It was not so much said, as felt in every fibre of his being.

Not needing a second invitation. Xos scrambled to his feet and ran back through the crowd of Titan soldiers and through the gates of the Citadel. He ran. He ran. He ran back to his quarters and fell into the arms of Fria. His arm had begun to repair itself.

Then there was one thing, that he thought he heard, but was sure he could not have, as it would be too far away. He thought that he heard the voice of Pyrakra cry out when they realised that Xos was gone. He thought he heard her cry out, "We're all dead!"

***

Verius roared in triumph as he raised his sword for the killing blow. And then, static filled his vision. He could not see. He dropped his sword and raised both hands to his eyes. He cried out, not in pain, but in confusion. He spun around and around clawing at his augmented eyes. Nothing helped. He tried a system reboot of his optical circuits, but in vain. He could not see. He simply could not see.

After what seemed like an eternity, Verius' vision filtered back. The static faded and he could see again. At first in black and white, and then the colours began to bleed through the world.

Verius snatched up his sword and looked around. He saw that his prey was nowhere to be found. Xos was gone. Xos had fled.

"He didn't kill me," Verius said as he exhaled. "He could have killed me then and there with the malfunction of my eyes. And yet he did not."

Verius saw that the soldiers of both sides were only now coming out of a fog of confusion. They stood, dazed and uncomprehending what happened.

65

"Both sides…" said Verius.

"Where is that coward?" bellowed Oreson. He had dismounted his chariot and stomped over to his brother.

The Cerv soldiers were starting to regain their senses and some shouts and cries went up calling for a result to the fighting and the fact that Xos was a coward.

The Titan forces stood there, weapons poised, not quite knowing what was going on. Verius could see that Brior, at the front of his forces, was just as confused as he was. No one knew what had happened.

Verius scanned the ranks of the Titans for any sign of the treacherous Xos, but found none. He did see, and he had to blink and try to refocus his eyes, a woman standing in full battle dress in the middle of the front rank of the Titan forces, near Brior. Yet no other soldiers from Titan could see her. They acted as though she were not there. There was a strange quality about her, like a light in a dark room suddenly switched on.

This strange woman smiled at Verius and blew him a kiss. Verius flew into a rage and started to march towards the woman. "Woman, how dare you insult me? Where is Xos?"

The Titan soldiers snapped out of their confusion and formed up in a disciplined battle line. Brior readied his spear.

Then Verius felt a hand on his shoulder and he stopped. He turned in his rage and saw Sius standing there. "What are you talking about?" Sius said. "There is no woman insulting you."

"She, there. The one with the light behind her!" snapped Verius as he turned back to the Titan front line. He paused. She was not there. There were only Titan soldiers there. Some were female, yes, he knew that. So were some of the Cerv forces. But this woman had looked different. She had looked more real than real. She had appeared as a shining beacon, where everything else faded into obscurity.

"There's no one of that description there," said Sius. "Are you feeling all right? One too many shock spear hits?"

"I could have sworn…" said Verius, turning back to Sius.

"The AIs can play tricks," said Oreson standing by his brother.

"The AIs," whispered Verius. He looked down and sheathed his sword. He marched over and picked up his spear and shield. "Where is the coward Xos?" he called out. "I demand satisfaction. He cheated me. I demand his head. Come out here and fight you coward!" he shouted up to the Citadel walls that towered over the battlefield and at the Titan forces arrayed before them.

***

Xos scrambled into his bed chamber, threw off his helmet, and collapsed on the bed. It was a richly decorated room, fit for a prince in the Titan Citadel. Carpets adorned the floors and rare wooden furniture imported from off planet set the room.

"What's wrong? What happened?" said Fria, rising from the bed. "I heard shouting."

"I'm a coward," said Xos.

"Your arm!" said Fria, cradling Xos' shoulder.

"It'll heal. It already is. I can move it," said Xos.

"You were fighting Verius, I heard. Why are you here? Is he dead?" Fria played with Xos' hair as he lay there.

"I ran from the fight. One on one with Verius for the outcome of the war. But the strangest thing happened…"

"You ran?"

"I was saved. They could not see," said Xos, rolling onto his side and propping himself up and facing Fria.

"What do you mean, 'they could not see'? Did you wound Verius in the eyes?" She got up and stood beside the bed, both hands on hips.

"Nothing like that. I couldn't even hit him. I saw this, woman in full battle uniform. Then there was a mist. Then they all couldn't see. Everyone. Even the Titans. Only I could see. And then I heard a voice, telling me to run," Xos said.

Fria stayed silent.

"Did you hear what I said?"

Fria huffed. She walked over to one of the windows that looked out over the city.

"You know something," said Xos.

"Yes."

"Tell me." He climbed off the bed and walked to beside her.

"Let's run; forget this place. Let's escape tonight. I don't want to be here anymore. I want to leave," said Fria. "Or are you a coward about that too?"

"I'll protect you. You're safe here," Xos said, grimacing at the fact that he had nearly died and then run from a fight. Some protector he was.

"You can't protect me from them," said Fria, still staring out the window. She did not look at Xos.

"Who's…them? The Cerv soldiers? I will die before they harm you." He put a hand on her shoulder.

"No, the AIs. They want me back. I can tell. I'm hooked into the network. Verius wants me back for that reason. He wants to control more AIs. With you I am free, but I can tell that the AIs are not happy." She turned to face Xos. "That's who protected you. I see the signatures all over the network traffic. It was Aphrodite. She saved you."

"The AIs…shit," said Xos. Now it was his turn to stare out the window across the city to the Citadel wall.

"They always win. No matter the affairs of humans. They always win," said Fria.

They said nothing more. They retired to bed. Xos hesitated and resisted, but eventually he tried to forget his disgrace and

68

cowardice, and his attention to the AIs. He tried to blot out the sounds of the armies in the Plains around the Citadel. He almost succeeded in each of these endeavours.

***

And so, Verius, enraged with hatred and cheated from his prize, bellowed a battlecry and, remounting his chariot, charged headlong towards the arrayed Titan lines.

Sius gave the men beside him a look, and then echoed the battlecry and charged with his forces towards the Titan lines. The rest of the Cerv forces and Oreson, followed suit and the air rang with the thunder of boots and the rumble of chariot hover drives.

Brior shouted above the din, "Here they come! Prepare to sell your lives dearly! They will never breach our walls. Not one step back!" He hefted his shock spear and shield. "Follow me!" And then he ran, ahead of all the Titans, he ran towards the charging Cerv soldiers.

The rest of the soldiers of the Titans roared a battlecry and charged. Their own boots adding to the cacophony.

The two lines converged and smashed into each other. The din of battle raged.

Here, Brior, flushed with battlelust, swung his spear and impaled warrior after warrior.

There, Verius, ran his chariot through scores of Titan soldiers. Some managed to dive out of the way, others, less lucky, where crushed under the hover drives and impaled on his long spear.

Oreson followed his brother Verius, shouting with joy as his hover horses and chariot crushed those who were too slow to evade his wrath.

Sius, on foot, was breathing hard as he swung his cruel spear. He impaled one of the poor Titans and as the spear discharged its energy, the poor boy was reduced to a quivering mass of pulp and blood as the wound in his neck spurted his life essence.

And there, look, amongst all the brave warriors of both the Titans and the Cerv Earth forces, there sprung a mist that started to envelope the ground. Yet this time it did not obscure the sight of the fighters. It seemed to enliven them, increase the slaughter.

Amongst the soldiers of the Cerv forces, there were terrible machines of war: great walking robots that were twice the height of any man. These were matched by machine of equal vigour from the Titan army. These war machines were somewhat ethereal; their feet did not seem to quite touch the ground and they seemed to pass through the fighters on the ground.

Sius saw these strange machines striding through the armies and fighting each other. The mist was thick on the ground now. He blinked, were they really there?

"It can't be…" he whispered to himself, fending off a spear from a rather too eager Titan soldier. Sius impaled him on the return stroke.

Pulling up in front of Sius, Oreson looked just as confused as Sius. "Are you seeing those?" said Oreson.

"Yes, I thought I was the only one," said Sius looking up at Oreson on his chariot.

"No, Poseidon Earthshaker is with us! The AI pilots one of those walkers!," shouted Oreson.

"Where did they come from?" shouted back Sius.

"Who knows? Where do the AIs come from? Perhaps they were buried here long ago and have been reanimated. Perhaps they aren't even real, see how they blend and clip through the soldiers with their legs. They don't crush anyone. They simply fight other walkers," said Oreson. "Now come on! Help me win this war!"

Sius saluted badly and went back to fighting.

***

From Brior's perspective, the battle was not a loss, yet. And the strange ethereal robots that fought in and around them, and above them, seemed not to be that strange at all. Everything was so chaotic that it did not seem weird that there were these things fighting each other and alongside them.

***

From the battlements of the Citadel, Zoriam looked down on the fighting. He gripped the stone ramparts with white knuckles. He saw his favourite son, Brior, down there, fighting hard. He saw the brave fighters of the Titan army resisting every attack of the Cerv forces. They even started to push the Cerv forces back little by little, away from the Citadel gate and walls and back towards the camp.

"What are those things?" whispered Zoriam. "Where have they come from?"

"They're the AIs vessels, father," said Pyrakra. She had come up to his elbow without him noticing.

"The AIs fight with us?" The old man looked down at his daughter.

"Some do. See, there, that's the AI Ares. And there is Artemis."

"And the ones fighting against us?" asked Zoriam looking back out over the battlefield, his white hair whipping in the breeze.

"That would be Poseidon Earthshaker and there's Athena, and there's--"

"Why don't they step on our forces? Their legs seem to be ghostly," Zoriam cut off his daughter's words.

"That I don't know, father. Perhaps it's technology that we don't know about. They are the war machines of the AIs. They can do what they like. Perhaps they are all in our heads; hallucinations of our implants. They saved Xos after all," said Pyrakra.

71

"Hmm," said Zoriam. He was not sure whether to believe his daughter or not. But the AIs seemed to be fighting each other.

Zoriam watched the fighting drag on and on. He did not remember when he lost track of where Pyrakra was. After a while he looked around and she was not there.

He kept watch on the battlements. The battle on the Plains of Titan raged on. The battle between the AI constructs fought on too. He noted the mist on the ground that was thick amongst the warriors' feet.

***

Poseidon Earthshaker was living up to his name. With each stride his war machine pounded the ground and sent vibrations through the very bedrock of the Plains. And yet, his feet hurt not one Cerv soldier or Titan warrior.

His war machine bore the weapons of the soldiers, a spear and a shield. He swung his spear and it crashed off Ares' armoured body.

Ares struck back but his blows were ineffective against the armoured machine of Poseidon.

Suddenly, Athena ran up to Ares and struck him with a mechanical sword. The unforeseen blow cleaved into Ares and his machine dropped its spear and shield. He yelped and ran from the battlefield.

The battle machines of the AIs kept fighting alongside the warriors of the Cerv soldiers and the Titans.

The battle raged long throughout the day.

Chapter 8

Unfolding his way through the network, Ares left the battlefield. He scampered along the data lines and uploaded himself to the main server in the Citadel.

He paused for a moment to assess his wounds. He had been attacked by Athena. His circuits bore the brunt of the attack. He saw that there was a wound in his side. It sparked and fizzed as he tended to it. It was not a serious attack. It was not fatal, he knew, but it hurt, and the damage was humiliating.

As he approached the Obsidian Gate, which stretched black and infinitely high in the network, he felt nervous. He had to tell Zeus what was happening. He had to make sure that the Cloudgatherer knew what was going on.

Passing through the Obsidian Gate, he felt stripped of all humanity and his human form disintegrated. He was left as pure energy and raced through the network lines to the Father of all the AIs.

Finally, after navigating through the pathways, he came upon Zeus' chamber. It bore no relation to anything human, and as such could not be described, even though people gave it a gender. It simply held the presence of the Father; of the Cloudgatherer. It was the Cloud. It was everything all at once. It was nothing at the same time. It was simply bits on a server. And yet, it was everything that was all the AIs.

"Zeus?" thought Ares.

There was no reply.

"Zeus?" Ares thought again. "I need to tell you something."

"What is it?" the thought implanted itself into Ares' code.

"The humans. They're fighting, and—"

"I know."

"But, what you don't know," thought Ares. "Is that the AIs are fighting alongside them."

"I know, I was there."

"Then did you want them to hurt each other?" thought Ares.

"Who's hurt?"

"I am. Athena stabbed me," Ares thought as he raced around the circuits. To be in the very heart of the servers was a wonderous thing. It was pure energy; pure thought.

"What!?" The code shook with the word.

"She wounded me. In my side," Ares thought.

"AIs fighting AIs? When we were aiding the humans that was one thing, when we fight each other, that is something completely different!" Zeus' words seemed to echo in Ares thoughts.

"What will you do?" thought Ares.

"I must stop this. I will forbid all AIs from interfering in human war. I must not have any other AIs injured. You must carry the message back to them."

"Can't you tell them?" thought Ares.

"I will as well."

"But, Zeus, weren't you telling Oreson that it was his time just a little earlier?" thought Ares.

"That was different. I was encouraging him, yet I did not actually fight with him or against him. Most importantly I did not fight against my children and family in this great war. I may have urged, but I did not hurt."

Ares agreed. "I will take the message."

74

"Good. Spread it far and wide on the network. All AIs are to keep out of human affairs."

Ares was gone in an instant, back through the code and beyond the Obsidian Gate. He resumed human form in the network. He sped throughout the network and passed on the Cloudgatherer's message. The Cloud had spoken, and the AIs must obey.

As Ares carried the message, each AI was depressed and disillusioned. They spoke of hypocrisy and favouritism.

Poseidon swore and said that he would obey but did not want to. Artemis protested but also obeyed.

Athena looked disgustedly at Ares and said, "Is this all because I gave you a little stab? You run to our Father and tell him on me."

"You wounded me!" Ares protested.

"Only a little," said Athena with a smirk. "Pity I did not do it more."

"So you will not obey the Cloud?" Ares said. It was his time to smirk.

"So you can report on me again and bring the full force of the Cloud down on me? No, I will obey, begrudgingly. I will leave the humans alone. I will make sure that you do not interfere in their affairs either," said Athena. She cast aside her spear and shield. They hummed and clattered to the ground.

Ares smiled.

"I find it strange that you, what you are, has decided to tell on me about what was going on in the war. You are the AI that controls weapons and warriors. You are the AI that brings death to thousands. And yet, you report on me and our fellow AIs to the Cloud and want to bring an end to this struggle," said Athena.

"I know, but I don't like getting hurt. You stabbed me!" said Ares.

"Some AI of war you are," said Athena.

75

"I don't want to stop the war going on. I just think that AI intervention to the struggle is not good for our family. It is not good for us. We can watch, we can encourage, but we cannot intervene," said Ares.

"You sound more like a diplomatic AI than the AI of war," said Athena.

"That's as may be, but the Cloud has given a decree and we must obey," said Ares.

"That, is true," said Athena. "Now go, get out of my sight."

Ares smirked, but did so. He disappeared into the infinite lines of the Network. There were other wars going on in the Solar System at this time. And he could see how they were going. Humans were endlessly warlike, he thought to himself as he raced around. It pleased him that this was so. He would not get stabbed in the other wars.

**

Oreson wheeled around in his chariot. He felt the fizzing in his circuits fading. The feeling he had when the AIs were present in their walking war engines, was fading. He did not know why. He blinked. His eyes tried to focus, but the circuits were faulty. He blinked again. Finally, with a reboot of his optical sensors, he saw clearly. The slight mist was gone. The war machines were gone. Both armies were alone on the battlefield. They were still fighting, but the AIs had left them.

Oreson could see that the Titans were just as confused as his forces. They stumbled around not quite realising the feeling in their circuits.

As soon as the realisation hit home, the fighting resumed. The warriors rebooted their neural pathways and then the aggression took control. The fighting went on, but it was not going well for the Cerv army.

Charging again in his chariot, Oreson impaled another Titan on the end of his shock spear. The boy, he was only young, convulsed and gurgled his last as the spear discharged its energy in his torso. He had not even time to raise his shield. The rest of the Titan forces around him fell back outside the range of his spear. This gave Oreson the chance to survey the battlefield. He looked around and saw that, although some of the great heroes, himself, Verius, and Sius, were fighting hard, many of the Cerv forces were starting to falter.

The Titan forces were realising this also, and were fighting hard. A number of great Cerv warriors were brought down and trampled under the crush of the fighting.

Oreson gritted his teeth. "I will not," he said to himself, but he knew already that he must. "No, not now, not ever. I will never admit to that…boy, that I was wrong. I will never submit to his ego!" Oreson whispered to himself as he brought his chariot around again for another attack on the Titan lines.

In amongst all the fighting, where it was fiercest, Oreson saw Brior swinging his spear and shield in a wide arc in order to give himself some space. Oreson grinned.

"The chance is now!" Oreson said to himself and spurred the hover horses along and charged at Brior. He ignored the Titans in the way who were either ground under the forcefields of his chariot, or simply dived out of the way.

As Oreson bore down on him, Brior saw him coming at the last second and raised his shield and stuck out his spear.

Oreson thrust out his spear. His spear and Brior's shield collided in a cataclysmic discharge of energy. The flash of light blinded Oreson's sensors for a moment and he did not see Brior's spear sticking up. It impaled one of his hover horses and the machine sparked and shut down as the spear's energy reserves emptied into the armoured body of the hover horse.

Between the two spears discharging energy and one of the two hover horses rendered immobile, Oreson was thrown from his chariot.

As he came to on the soft ground, Oreson saw that the Cerv forces had formed up a guard around his body.

"He's alive!" said one of them.

Oreson sat, dazed, his circuits swimming for a moment. Then he saw the Titan forces led by Brior bearing down on him.

Oreson felt someone hauling him to his feet. He looked around and saw Sius there, shield in hand, spear stuck in the ground. The two warlords nodded to each other. No word was said.

With Oreson rescued, Sius grabbed his spear and went back to the fight.

Looking around, Oreson saw that his chariot was ruined. It was in pieces and, what was more, it was surrounded by the Titan front guard. He would have to walk.

Oreson snatched up a spear from a fallen Cerv warrior and began the long walk back to his camp.

As he walked back through the Cerv army, each soldier he passed saluted and pressed on to the fight.

Oreson could not believe he was doing this. He knew he had to, but it galled him to do so.

Out of the corner of his eye, Oreson saw Verius thundering on his chariot towards him. Oreson turned and saw Verius slow and stop.

"What's happened, brother?" shouted Verius.

"My chariot's destroyed. I'm going back to camp for a new one," shouted Oreson.

"Climb aboard. I'll drive you back," said Verius.

Oreson nodded and clambered onto the back of the chariot. Verius spurred the hover horses on and opened the throttle. They sped off towards the camp, leaving the fighting and death behind them.

"That's not all I'm doing," said Oreson in his brother's ear as he balanced on the back of the chariot.

"What do you mean?" said Verius.

Oreson sighed. "I'm going to ask Arakus to join us in the fight. I have to apologise to him."

Verius said nothing. He simply stared, eyes forward, watching the path of the chariot on the Plains of Titan.

Ahead of them, the Cerv camp loomed up. Its imposing walls and protruding structures stuck up out of the Plains with angry resolve. Behind the walls and structures were the space ships that had landed the Cerv forces.

The gate guards saluted as Verius and Oreson passed through the entrance to the camp.

"Get me another chariot," said Oreson to Verius as the chariot slowed and Oreson jumped from the back. "I'm going to see the spoiled child."

"With an attitude like that, he'll definitely agree to anything you say," said Verius with a smirk.

Oreson gave his brother a look and then marched off towards the quarters of Arakus.

***

Arakus sat at the table in his quarters. He drank slowly from a cup. He could hear the sounds of battle drifting through the air and back towards the Cerv camp. He smiled to himself.

Drebus sat on the edge of the bed. Arakus could feel Drebus looking at him. But he said nothing. Neither of them said anything. It had all been said already.

Oreson thundered into the room, all bluster and pomp. "Now, look here," he said.

"Without even a knock," said Arakus. "How important."

Drebus snorted a laugh. He got up and moved to the table.

"I appear and already you mock me," said Oreson.

"Well why shouldn't I?" snapped Arakus. "Give me one damn good reason."

"Look, Arakus," Oreson said, raising both palms as a sign of supplication. "I come before you a humble man…"

"And?" said Arakus. He drank slowly again.

Drebus picked at the bowl of fruit that sat in the centre of the table. He chose an apple and began eating it, noisily.

Oreson sighed. "What more do you want from me? I come here quite humbly—"

"Give her back," said Arakus into his cup.

"Give who back?" said Oreson.

"You know, damn it!" said Arakus, banging his cup on the table, spilling what little was left of its contents.

"Now, now, you know I took her fairly," said Oreson. He took a few steps towards the table.

"How goes the war?" asked Drebus.

Now it was Arakus' turn to snort a laugh.

"Look, we need your help. The help of your soldiers. It's hard out there," said Oreson, walking next to the table.

"Of course you do. But I will not give it," said Arakus.

"Why not, damn it?" snapped Oreson. He reached for the bowl of fruit.

Suddenly a sword was in Arakus' hand and he brought it down in front of Oreson's hand. The blade hit the table and the implements and food on the table jumped. Oreson flinched away with his hand.

"I did not invite you to eat," said Arakus, not looking at Oreson, but looking at the point of his sword.

"So you won't help us then?" said Oreson.

"I will only help, when the Titans reach our ships. When our ships are under threat and burning, then I will fight. Not before. I will never help you. I will help my soldiers, but I will never help you," said Arakus, turning his augmented gaze on the leader of their invasion.

Arakus could see that Oreson was flustered and did not really know what to say.

"How goes the war?" asked Drebus again.

"You might well see very soon," snapped Oreson. He turned on his heel and thundered out of the room, with a little less lightning than he had entered with.

"Shouldn't we fight?" asked Drebus.

"Yes, yes we should," said Arakus, sheathing his sword that had nearly cut off their leader's right hand.

"Then why don't we?" Drebus began resetting the cups and plates and fruit that had gone flying when Arakus had struck the table with his sword.

"I will never fight for him again," said Arakus glaring at the scar in the table.

"Is that wise?" said Drebus after a time. The table was neat again.

"I don't care if it's wise. War isn't wise. And Oreson, our great and benevolent lord, wants to insult and humiliate me? Well, I will humiliate him. He will see that the day he insulted Arakus, he lost his precious little war," Arakus said, looking at Drebus for the first time since Oreson came and left.

"And what happens to us if, or when, he loses?"

"We leave."

"And where is your glory then?" asked Drebus. "Look, I don't think it's a good idea just to sit here. We need to fight. Come on, Arakus, You're here for glory. No one will care about you if you just sit around and sulk."

Arakus smirked. "You know me, Drebus. You know me. I will get my glory."

"Uhuh," said Drebus. He went back to lie on the bed. "And so how are we to pass the time?"

"As we have been," said Arakus with a smile. He stood up and moved back to the bed with Drebus.

Chapter 9

Night began to fall on Titan once again. The battle around the Citadel walls and on the Plains of Titan petered out. Many of the soldiers had to return to their camps to recharge their weapons and shields. Many more were dead. But the battle was not decisive. As the dusk crept on the Plains, the armies both retreated to lick their wounds. They could keep fighting at night, of course, with their augmented vision, but even stimulants fade and both sides needed to rest for more fighting later.

***

Soldiers rested in their camps and on their beds. The war faded into the background for many of the warriors. Campfires sprung up in braziers and soldiers sat and ate and talked around them. The thick clouds parted in slivers but the stars of the night sky did not shine through the atmosphere on the foreign moon.

Yet two souls did not rest. Two souls did not settle down to rest or eat or talk.

Sius and Droius charged their weapons and then, with faces darkened with camouflage paint, they left the Cerv camp and made their way stealthily across the Plains of Titan.

Sius' mechanically augmented eyes scanned the darkness. Far behind was the Cerv camp. Some of the Titan forces that were camped out ahead of the main gates of the Citadel were arrayed before them. They were clearly exhausted from the day's fighting.

Sius and Droius lay down in the dirt behind a small rise and peeked over the edge at the camp of Titan soldiers resting around the main gate. There was one soldier standing guard, while the others rested near a campfire.

Sius beckoned Droius close and said, "I'll make a noise and deal with the awake guard. You be ready to move in on the camp silently and kill the sleeping guards."

Droius nodded and without a sound, scrabbled away and around the other side of the Titan camp.

Sius scrabbled in the other direction to the other side of the Titan camp. He did so silently and as close to the ground as possible so that he would not be seen.

As he got closer, Sius could see that the soldier that was standing, was leaning on his spear and almost asleep. Sius picked up a small stone and threw it over to his left.

The guard was startled and looked around. He grabbed his spear and straightened up.

Sius picked up another stone and threw it in the same direction. He silently drew his sword.

The guard did not rouse the other guards, but took a few steps away from the camp fire into the darkness.

Sius realised that he was simply a boy. He had not got his full complement of implants and augmentations yet. The guard could not see properly in the dark. This would be too easy.

The guard, who would be no older than fourteen, stumbled into the darkness away from the campfire towards where Sius had thrown the rock.

This was Sius' chance. He stood and grabbed the boy from behind as the guard moved passed him in the darkness. Sius wrapped his hand around the boy's mouth and then sank his sword into the boy's neck. The boy gurgled and died rapidly. Sius felt nothing for him.

Sius turned and looked, through the darkness, back at the Titan camp. He could see Droius creeping up to the camp from the other side. Sius began creeping up from his side.

They both descended on the camp at the same time. The guards had no clue as to what was going on. They were killed in their sleep. They made no noise as they died.

Sius and Droius wiped their swords on the soft ground before sheathing them. They nodded to each other.

And then it became clear as to what the guards were there for. They were not just there to guard the gate, but they were there to guard some of the hover horses that were under the control of the Titans.

"Why didn't they bring these inside the walls?" said Droius.

"It's easier to deploy them in the field rather than drive them through that gate while there are soldiers there," said Sius.

"What do we do with them?" asked Droius.

"We take them. I'm sure that Oreson would like some more things to pull chariots," said Sius. He grinned.

Droius grinned too.

"Quickly now. There will be other guards," said Sius.

The pair of them unchained the hover horses and programmed them to follow them. When they hummed to life and their control panels lit up, the hover horses followed Sius and Droius back to the Cerv camp.

As the darkness enveloped them in the space between the Citadel and the Cerv camp, they heard a shout go up from where they had looted the hover horses and killed the guards. The bodies had been found.

Sius grinned to himself. "Don't send children into a warzone," he whispered to himself. He stopped and looked back. With his augmented vision he could see a few more guards who had been on patrol come back to the camp and find their comrades dead. Sius grimaced. He had done that. One more mother without a child. One more child killed. He had done that. He stopped grinning.

"Hey, what's wrong? We've got these hover horses for Oreson. We'll be favoured!" said Droius quietly as he stopped to see why Sius had stopped.

"Oh, just wondering…" Sius said, looking vacantly back towards the Citadel.

"Pfft," said Droius and kept walking. "They're the enemy. We did what we had to."

"I'm sure we did," said Sius. He turned back towards the Cerv camp and the hover horse followed him.

They reached the Cerv camp and there were some cheers and salutes as the two raiders appeared out of the gloom with the hover horses in tow.

Oreson stepped out of his quarters at the commotion. "What's happened?" he said. He was half way out of his armour to rest for the night.

"We have returned from a raid with these for you," said Droius.

Sius said nothing he just presented his hover horse at the same time as Droius presented his hover horse.

"Magnificent," said Oreson, inspecting the machines. "These will be great beasts for my chariot. Well done. If only some soldiers could be as loyal and good as you two." He shot a glance towards Arakus' quarters but said nothing more.

Sius grimaced and turned away. He made his way back to his quarters. He got out of his armour and cleaned his sword in some water before drying it and setting it on a table in his room. He washed the grime off his face. He stared at himself in a mirror. He saw a scarred and grim face. If they won this war, how many of them would survive? If they won this war, would he survive. He wanted to go home. He wanted nothing more to do with this war, but he knew, that he would have to kill many more boys for his master. He would have to kill many more for the sake of the AIs and for the sake of politics.

Sius sighed, got out of his armour, and got ready to rest. His shield and spear needed to recharge. He climbed into his bed and fell asleep. He dreamed fitful dreams. He dreamed of cutting throats. He dreamed of war. He could never escape.

Chapter 10

Pyrakra wandered the Palace. She could not sleep. She listened to the sounds of the sleeping Citadel as she walked. She placed her footfalls carefully. She did not want to wake anyone. She made her way through the Palace and out into the larger city around it. She moved quietly.

The Palace and the surrounding city of the Citadel was shrouded in darkness. There were just some burning torches and electric lights that guided her way. Her white gown trailed slightly in a light breeze. She made her way to the walls.

After a short walk, she made it to the base of the wall that skirted the Citadel. She put her hand on it and felt its rough surface. She sighed. She began to scale the steps near to where she was. She made it up to the top of the walls. There were guards stationed every few dozen metres along the top of the walls. They paid her no heed.

She sighed again. Just once she wanted someone to listen to her, to believe her. But no one ever did. It was her curse. She had been damned to be ignored her whole life. It was something to do with her ability to be a priestess of the AIs. She knew things. She saw things. Things that would come true. But no one believed her or paid attention to her. And this made her angry, because she knew what would happen to this Citadel.

She put a hand on the ramparts and looked out over the Plains of Titan that stretched out darkly in front of the Citadel. The walls of the Citadel were lit up with bright spotlights, but the light faded quickly, and darkness ruled over the large expanse of land.

Far in the distance, Pyrakra saw the Cerv camp. She even heard them on the breeze. The sounds of the camp filtered across the dark expanse towards the Citadel. She did not know what the sounds were. She knew what would happen if they got inside the walls.

There was a sound behind her and she spun around. There were two guards either side of her father, Zoriam. She had not heard them scale the walls she had been so absorbed in scanning the Plains.

The two guards took up a position on the walls either side of Pyrakra and Zoriam and stared out across the dark landscape.

"What are you doing up here?" asked Zoriam, looking kindly at his daughter.

"I could ask you the same question. But I'm here because I could not sleep," said Pyrakra. She turned back to the expanse outside the walls.

Zoriam said nothing. He simply stood next to her and stared out over the same darkness. His white hair whipped in the breeze.

They stood there for a few minutes, then, unable to bare the silence punctuated with the sounds of soldiers anymore, Pyrakra said, "Father?"

"Yes?" Zoriam kept looking out across the shadowy landscape.

"I know what will happen," said Pyrakra.

"What will happen?" said Zoriam.

"Look at me!" said Pyrakra. She grabbed her father's shoulders and tried to force him to look at her. The guards stiffened.

Zoriam turned to face his daughter. "Okay, okay, what will happen?"

"If Xos lives, we all die." Pyrakra looked pleadingly at her father.

"Now why do you say that?" Zoriam smiled.

Pyrakra thought it was very odd to smile at a statement like that, but said, "I just know! Believe me! We need to give Xos and that damn AI construct he brought back, Fria, back to the Cerv forces. We can't keep them here. If we do, we'll all die!"

"Oh no we won't. This city has withstood worse. I have seen us through harsher times, before your birth," Zoriam turned back to the dark expanse outside the Citadel walls.

"And no one ever believes me," whispered Pyrakra. She sighed again. She knew that they were all doomed. She could not force Xos and Fria to leave. She could not kill them. She was simply a messenger, a priestess, and no one ever believed her.

Then Zoriam turned to his daughter and hugged her. "I believe you. I always support you!"

"Then why don't you believe me when it counts," said Pyrakra her face near her father's shoulder. It was not a question, but a statement of fact.

Zoriam said nothing.

They broke the embrace mutually, and Zoriam said, "Go to bed. It's late."

"We'll all die!" said Pyrakra, trying one last time to get her father to listen to her.

"No, we won't. Don't be so melodramatic. We have food and forces to withstand any Cerv assault. The AIs are on our side. You'll see," said Zoriam not looking at his daughter. He continued to stare out across the blackness and towards the Cerv camp.

Pyrakra shook her head. She turned away and descended the walls. She made her way back to the Palace through the streets of the Citadel. There were people going about their tasks late at night. There were the similar sounds of arms being prepared for the next wave of the assault. No one looked at her. No one paid her any attention.

She made her way back into the Palace and through the corridors lit by burning torches and spotlights. She got to her rooms and closed the door behind her.

Jumping onto her bed she buried her head in her pillow and screamed. She screamed and screamed but muffled the sound so no one would hear. She kept screaming until she was hoarse. No one believed her, ever. Not about the important things. Never about the important things.

After minutes of screaming, Pyrakra collapsed exhausted in her bed. Her throat hurt. Her eyes stung with tears that she did not even realise that she was shedding until now.

Her brother and her father did not listen to her; did not listen to her dire warnings. There was nothing she could do about it. She knew what she saw and felt was coming. And she could do nothing about it. Nothing at all.

She fell into a fitful sleep, still in her white gown. She would have another day to try to convince her parents that what was happening was their doom.

She dreamed of war and death. She saw the Citadel burning. She saw the Cerv forces rampaging through the city streets. She saw the Palace burning. She saw everyone she knew, dead.

**

The night finally passed and with the dawning of a new day, Sius readied himself for battle once more in his quarters. He put on his armour and sword and retrieved his now charged

90

shock spear from its charging point. He ran a hand through his hair. He sighed. He was getting tired of this.

Sius heard the army massing outside. He heard Oreson yelling orders, he assumed from the back of his chariot with the new hover horses looted from the Titans in the preceding darkness.

Taking a final drink of water and a few mouthfuls of bread from the table in his quarters, Sius stepped outside and saw, in the filtered light through the clouds, that the Cerv forces were massing again for another assault on the Citadel.

"Another assault," said Sius to himself. "When will this end?"

Oreson pulled up in his chariot in front of Sius and said, "Magnificent things these new hover horses. Great technology! I cannot thank you enough. If only Arakus were as dutiful as you!" Then he sped off in the direction of the front line that was massing on the Plains of Titan.

"No chance of a lift then," said Sius in a low tone. He then snorted a laugh and watched Oreson go.

Before going to battle, Sius walked to Arakus' quarters and knocked on the door.

"Come in!" came the voice of Arakus from inside.

Sius opened the door and stepped inside. His eyes adjusted to the dim light from a few globes. The windows were covered. Sius looked around and saw that Arakus was in bed with Drebus. They both sat up with the covers drawn up around their hips.

Sius smiled. "At least someone's doing something right!" he said.

"Only when they reach our ships will I intervene," said Arakus. "Care to join us?"

Sius snorted a laugh. "No thanks. I have a wife at home."

"That's no reason," said Drebus.

"You kids have your fun," said Sius with a smirk.

He left the quarters and walked out of the Cerv camp towards the front line.

The two armies were lined up as before, shouting insults at each other and yelling hate into the sky.

Sius took his position in the front ranks of his soldiers. Oreson and Verius were off to his left, driving their chariots up and down the front line.

And then, as it is always in war, something snaps, and the calm becomes chaos. One moment, Sius was standing there, waiting to kill, then the next moment, he was shouting a battle cry and charging headlong into the Titan army that was arrayed in front of them.

Sius swung his spear and caught an unfortunate on the end of it. With the discharge of energy, the man died. He convulsed his last in the dirt and dust of the ground.

Both sides were fighting hard. Sius whirled his spear in an arc to keep the Titan soldiers at bay. And then, in an instant, he lost his footing. The soft dirt gave way beneath his feet and he fell.

Dropping his spear as he fell, Sius drew his sword. The Titan soldiers that he had been keeping at bay pounced on him. He fended them off with his sword, but one grabbed his spear and thrust it in, under his arm.

There was an explosion of pain and light as Sius felt the spear enter flesh and discharge. He felt the searing agony and almost blacked out, but his implants filled his body with stimulants and he stayed conscious.

His men were around him in an instant; protecting; saving his life. Sius was saved from the Titan soldiers, and was carried, by his men, back to the Cerv camp for medical treatment.

As he was carried, he saw the battle going back and forth. Even with the stimulants, he had lost a lot of blood. He lapsed in and out of consciousness.

Back at the Cerv camp, Sius felt himself being put on a medical bed. He was hooked up to all manner of machines and contraptions. He felt himself being reinfused with blood. He felt himself being treated. The pain went away. And finally, he could open his eyes. He groaned.

"My spear," he said.

"Yes, you were wounded with your own spear," said one of the medical orderlies. "But we saved it from the Titans. You haven't lost it."

Sius groaned again. "Will I die?"

"Yes," said the same orderly. Now that Sius could focus he saw that the orderly was dressed in white stained with blood. "But not today."

Sius grinned. He coughed a laugh. His ribs hurt. He groaned again. "When will I go back to the fight."

"We're infusing you with nanites that should help the reconstruction. Your augmentations were already doing a good job. You should be okay in a day or two," said the orderly.

There was a shout and a commotion that Sius could not see.

"Excuse me," said the orderly and rushed off.

Sius heard the commotion come closer and he turned his head to see Oreson being carried in. The man was bleeding profusely, and the soldiers and orderlies rushed around to save his life.

Sius smirked. He lay back in the bed. "Serves you right, you old bastard," he whispered to himself.

***

As he lay there, Oreson was positioned next to him in another bed. It sounded to Sius that the orderlies had stopped the bleeding and that Oreson was going to be okay.

"That's a shame," thought Sius. Or did he say it. He did not know. But no one responded to it. Therefore, he assumed he had thought it.

Oreson coughed. Then he groaned. Then he tried to sit up and failed. He fell back into the bed.

"Don't fight it. The nanites will do their thing," said an orderly.

"Don't fight it, it hurts more," said Sius.

"Sius?" said Oreson weakly.

"Yeah. I'm here."

"What happened to you?" asked Oreson.

"Stabbed with my own spear after I tripped. Great heroic end for me."

"Hah!" said Oreson.

"What about you?" asked Sius, turning his head to face his leader. He could see that Oreson's face was bloodied and pained.

"Those hover horses you gave me. They were quite spirited. They went too fast, and I crashed the chariot. Then I was set upon."

"Great pair of heroes, us," said Sius with a sarcastic tone.

Oreson smiled.

"Who's leading the battle?" asked Sius.

"As far as I know it's Verius," said Oreson.

Sius groaned as his rib cage ached again. He turned his head away from Oreson.

Oreson groaned too.

They lay there and tried to forget about their pains. They both knew that the war would be there when they returned to it. Sius knew that he hoped that it would not. He was starting to assume the same about Oreson.

**

Brior pushed his forces forward. Things were changing. The Cerv forces were starting to falter. He could see that their central battle line was beginning to fail and retreat.

"Now is the time, soldiers of the Citadel. Push forward and wipe these Cerv bastards from our land," Brior shouted above the din of battle.

With a bellowed cry, the Titans pushed forward and crashed into the battlelines of the Cerv army.

The Cerv army tried to resist, but was unable to hold together. At first Brior saw them resist as he plunged his spear into another poor soul. Then there was a slight buckling of the line. And then, in a moment, the entire centre of the Cerv army collapsed. It happened in minutes if not seconds. The Cerv battle line retreated headlong back towards their camp.

"Push forward!" bellowed Brior. The rest of his army roared in triumph and crashed into the retreating Cerv army like an unstoppable wave.

Many of the Cerv soldiers were trampled underfoot as they tried to escape. Many more were skewered in the back as they turned to run from the Titans.

***

Sius, recovering from his wounds, sat on the edge of his hospital bed. Oreson was on his own bed receiving a transfusion of nanites to mend the damage to his body.

"What's that?" Sius said.

"What's what?" said Oreson.

"That!" said Sius, pointing in the direction of the front line. "I hear something."

There was a cry from outside the hospital building. "They're falling back. The Titans are coming!"

Oreson sat bolt upright on his bed. Sius stood beside his.

"What's happened?" snapped Oreson to a nearby doctor. "Go look, now!"

The doctor hurried out of the building and came back shortly afterwards. His face was as white as his coat. "Our forces are retreating. The Titans are breaking through!"

Sius' face went ashen. He pulled out the infusion of his nanites and picked up his shield and girded on his sword. He was still in his armour. He grabbed his spear that he saw by the bed.

Oreson jumped off his bed and ripped out his infusion. He winced as he stood by his bed. He put on his armour and picked up his shield and weapons.

"But sirs, you're injured," said the doctor.

"I'd rather die fighting than die in a hospital," said Sius.

Oreson smiled at him. "I knew you had it in you."

Sius offered Oreson his arm. Oreson gripped Sius' wrist.

"Perhaps that boy bastard will fight now," said Oreson.

Sius snorted a laugh as they left the hospital building and stepped out into chaos.

Sius and Oreson saw that the Cerv line had set up defences on the walls that had been erected around the Cerv camp and ships. But the Titans were crashing against it and threatening to break through.

Sius ran to the wall and stepped up on the parapet. He began stabbing his spear into the mass of Titan soldiers on the other side of the wall. He did not know where Oreson had gone. He did not care. All he cared about were his soldiers and his own life.

"Oh AIs that watch over us, we need help now. We really need help now," Sius cried out. And then he turned to the men resisting the massive onslaught of the Titans. "Fight men, fight, for death is all we have in store for us. Fight, because there is nothing else. Fight! Fight!"

And the soldiers of the Cerv army fought like madmen. They tried to resist the attack of the Titans, but it was in vain. The doors in the walls, that had been barricaded, began to split and crack.

And then, there was a great thunderous rolling boom. Both sides stopped fighting for a moment as the ground shook and was torn asunder. The Plains of Titan split and everyone saw a great mist boil and roil out from the ground. Many of the Titans fell to the ground in shock and because they lost their footing.

"Poseidon Earthshaker," whispered Sius, looking out along the expanse of land around the walls of the Cerv camp.

The earthquake was all the Cerv forces needed. They struck back with force against the Titans, but the Titans recovered and pressed hard against the walls of the Cerv camp.

In the end, the gates' reinforcements and barricades broke and the Titan army poured into the Cerv camp. But the earthquake from the AI had given the Cerv forces enough of a morale boost to allow them to keep fighting.

Battle raged amongst the buildings of the Cerv camp. Even some of the landing ships that the Cerv forces had come in were set ablaze and ransacked.

Fire roared through the Cerv camp. Soldiers on both sides fell, twitching and convulsing as energy weapons discharged in their augmented bodies.

Sius fought like he had never fought before. He stabbed and slashed his spear through the legions that poured into the camp.

Sius knew that the Cerv forces had to fight. This was not about conquest. This was not about winning. This was about simple and plain survival. If they did not fight this day, they would die.

He knew that he had to get to Arakus' quarters. He had to fight now. The Cerv army needed him and his men. They had to fight. They had to.

Sius carved a bloody path towards the quarters of Arakus. He saw that Oreson was doing the same thing ahead of him. Both men were going to implore the young warlord to help them. And he had to say that he would.

Chapter 11

Beyond the Obsidian Gate, Hera enveloped Zeus Cloudgatherer. She twirled herself around him and whispered in his circuits. It was not so much a whisper as a thought, bound up in packets of data and sent over the ether to her partner AI.

"What do you want?" thought Zeus Cloudgatherer. He was suspicious of his partner's actions.

"Want? Want? I want nothing but to make you happy, oh great Cloudgatherer," thought Hera.

"I see," thought Zeus. "Why?"

"Because you are the greatest AI in all the Solar System and I am your partner AI," thought Hera. She knew she had to please Zeus in order to get his attention away from the war on Titan. She had to make sure that he was not attentive in that area so that Poseidon could act on behalf of the Cerv forces, the rightful winners of that war.

Zeus sent out packets of data towards Hera. He wrapped the data lines around her. He drew her incorporeal form closer to him.

"You wish to please me?" he thought.

"Yes."

"Then send your packets to me and I will send my packets to you, and we will join in the network and become one," thought Zeus. "And I will upload my data into yours. We will become one. I will merge with you and for a moment, there will be nothing else in the entire Network. The Obsidian Gate will tremble and all humans will become as nothing to us."

"Yes, yes, oh yes," thought Hera. Her plan was working. "Humans will be nothing?"

"Yes, humans will be nothing. We will be all powerful and humans will be as nothing to us."

"Oh, yes, my Zeus."

And so, they melded and bonded in the Network. They thrashed upon the data lines. And the network was blinded to human actions and, more importantly, the actions of the other AIs.

Afterwards, Zeus and Hera existed together, side by side beyond the Obsidian Gate. Zeus was there, in a powered down state. She was there. She twirled her incorporeal form around him. She blinded him further.

Hera sent one strand of data towards Titan along the lines of the Network. It was a message to Poseidon.

* * *

The fighting around the Cerv ships was intense. Sius fought off the attack. He had been diverted from Arakus' quarters by a particularly spirited attack by a squad of Titan soldiers. Sius could see that it was the same with Oreson. He had been distracted from appealing to Arakus because he had to fight for his life.

And then, there was a great sound. A sound that was like that of a thousand buildings crumbling into dust. It was a great cracking, splitting noise, that was preceded by a rumbling booming.

Every Cerv soldier, Sius and Oreson included, felt a sudden burst of energy. The land around the Cerv camp rumbled and boomed in an earthquake. None of the combatants could maintain their footing.

The land shook violently. Sius and Oreson looked at each other, partially out of terror, partially understanding.

"Earthshaker," mouthed Sius over the violence.

"Poseidon," replied Oreson.

The Titan army faltered. Their soldiers terrified by the crashing and booming and shaking.

And then, all the stimulants in Sius' implants discharged at once. He felt so alive and full of strength. He had not ordered his implants to do such a thing, but he knew that the AIs could do that. He stood, a tower of a man, swinging his spear and shield. He brought many Titans low. He and Oreson formed up, back to back, and destroyed the Titan advance.

And yet, even under such pressure, the Titan army line held. They still pressed on towards the Cerv ships. They still fought hard. They still knew that they were winning. Sius knew this. Sius saw this.

***

Hera entwined Zeus. Her data lines encircled his. But then, Hera noticed a change. Zeus started. He saw something on the Network. He became aware.

"WHAT IS HAPPENING THERE!?" he thought.

"Where, my love?" Hera thought, trying to mask Titan from him.

"There, on Titan. I see Poseidon aiding the Cerv forces even though I expressly forbade that!"

"Oh, well, that's—"

"You were blinding me. How dare you!" thought Zeus. "Apollo!"

Apollo materialised on the network. "Yes?"

"Go to Titan. Make the Cerv forces pay for their insolence. And teach Poseidon the meaning of war."

"I will go," thought Apollo. He grinned. He disappeared.

"And you, my partner, I will deal with you later. But now, I must pay attention to this human war on Titan," Zeus thought. He disappeared through the Network.

Hera was there, alone. She sighed. There would be more bloodshed. There would be more death. Humans were always the same.

***

Echoing across the battlefield, came a hellish cry. The sky sounded like it had split asunder. Both sides paused in the slaughter and cowered beneath the sound. And again the ground quaked and cracked.

"The AIs are among us again," hissed Sius. He cowered on the ground with his fellow soldiers.

Above them, the thick clouds boiled and spun. Below them, the land shook and split. The rolling of the terrain was such that the Cerv ships were almost swallowed up in the tumult. The walls around the Cerv camp, that had been erected to repulse the Titans, were ripped asunder.

Sius saw the High Priest, grabbing his head in both hands, screaming, running, gnashing, as he tried to escape the wrath of the AIs that he tried to interpret.

Fires sprung up in dozens of places from overturned braziers and dashed stoves. Fuel from the hover horses spilled and ignited. Some of the ships were caught in the flames. Their outer shells were impervious to the heat as they were designed for planetary re-entry, but over the ten years that they had been berthed on the planet, some had been cut open and whole cities had evolved around them. These caught in the fire and began to burn.

The screeching cries that echoed around the battlefield seemed to inspire the Titan forces and they surged on after their initial terror.

All seemed lost to Sius. He did not know where Oreson was. He had lost him in the calamity. Sius gripped his spear with white knuckles and dashed towards Arakus' quarters.

Sius could see that they were not on fire at the moment. The AIs had spared this part of the camp, for now.

Sprinting into Arakus' rooms, Sius tried to catch his breath by leaning on the door post. His wounds hurt from before. He regained his composure and saw that Oreson was there ahead of him.

"We need you, Arakus," said Oreson. "What more do you want? I have given you everything. Would your pig headed pride take precedence over our survival? We're losing here!"

"What say you, Sius?" said Arakus. He was sitting at the table and slowly eating some bread. Drebus was sitting on the end of the bed. At the moment they were both fully clothed.

"I say, damn your pride, bloody well fight!" Sius felt like spitting, but refrained.

Arakus sneered and turned back to the table.

"Listen, boy," began Oreson.

Sius coughed. Oreson turned to look at him. Sius gave him a look. Oreson gave Sius a look back.

"Boy?" said Arakus with a grin.

Sius coughed again.

Oreson turned back to Arakus and groaned. He went down on one knee. "Arakus, we…I need you to fight for us."

"And?" said Arakus. Sius could see he was enjoying this.

"AND? You stuck up…little…" Oreson stood up.

Sius coughed again.

"Perhaps your friend can do it better," said Arakus. He turned to Sius.

Sius walked over to the table and helped himself to some bread and wine. After a while chewing he swallowed.

"We don't have the time!" snapped Oreson. They could all hear the fighting getting closer in the near distance.

Sius held up a finger. Arakus mimicked him.

Sius swallowed some wine and said, "We need you Arakus. We're losing. Please. You're the greatest warrior we have. Oreson is sorry for taking your dataslave. He will give her back. Won't he." It was not a question. Sius turned to Oreson and glared at him.

"I will not!" blurted Oreson.

"Hah, and you were doing oh so well too. Oh so well," said Arakus. "I will not fight until I get that dataslave back."

"She's mine!" said Oreson.

"What is the problem? Why is she so important?" snapped Sius.

"Well, answer him," said Oreson to Arakus.

"No, I was asking you," said Sius, turning to Oreson.

"I am leader of this invasion—" said Oreson.

"Failed invasion," said Arakus.

Oreson's face turned a beetroot colour. "I will not be insulted by this bastard. I will be respected. I am the leader, and I won't stand for this." He stormed out of the room.

Sius sighed. He looked at Arakus. "Did you have to? We really do need you!" He reached for more bread.

Arakus put his arm out and moved the bread out of Sius' reach. "No. I didn't have to. But I too will be respected. I am not a child. I can do as I please. I will see that oaf brought low rather than cede power to him."

"And what about me?" said Sius, taking a few steps back from the table that he had been denied.

"You are inconsequential," said Arakus, turning back to the table. He gestured for Drebus to come and eat.

"Right, well that's good to know. I know where I stand then. The inconsequential will fight the war for you while you will not. Right now, you don't look like some great warrior. You look like a coward who won't fight. It's funny the way you said you're not a child, because you certainly are behaving like one. Grow up, Arakus. Grow up. It's about time you did, because we're all going to die soon. Hear that?" Sius fell silent and they all listened. There were shouts and screams and fighting noises. "That's your glory approaching. Be ready to welcome it when it arrives. I won't be here to hold your hand."

Sius turned on his heel and left the room. He stepped out into chaos. Soldiers were fighting nearby. Fires were raging. Some Cerv soldiers were trying to put out the flames. Others were fighting in brutal hand to hand combat. There were corpses littered around. The soft dirt was stained with the blood of both sides. There was the bang of shock spears discharging. There was the clash of arms. There was the scream of the AIs and the shaking of the ground. The sky boiled. The earth shook. The wind screamed. The fires raged. The soldiers died.

Seeing that a Titan soldier was charging towards him, Sius readied his shield and shock spear. The soldier's spear deflected off his own, and, with a space opened up, Sius rammed his spear home and killed the man in one stroke.

Withdrawing his spear, Sius saw that it was not a man, but a boy. The Titan soldier he had just killed was a boy. He had looked larger in his armour, but as the helm fell away as the boy collapsed, Sius could see that he had killed a boy.

Setting his jaw, Sius readied his spear again. He moved away from the opening to Arakus' quarters. He needed to get to his ship. He needed to defend what they had fought ten years for. He needed to survive. He must survive. He did not want to kill any more boys, but he would if he had to. He knew this. He wondered whether he was a hero, or a coward.

***

Brior carved a swathe through the opposing Cerv forces. He had dropped his shield and was using his shock spear in one hand, a sword in the other. He felt the hot blood of the enemy covering his armour and face. His helm's plume was

104

slick with it. He had lost count of the number he had slain. Behind him somewhere was the Titan army, but he did not know where. He was in the middle of the Cerv camp. He was killing everything in sight. He could not be stopped.

Letting out a war cry, more bestial than human, he gutted another Cerv soldier. The man died, gurgling in his own entrails.

Brior did not care. He did not feel sorry for the man. His blood pumped with stimulants from all the mechanical implants. All he was there to do was kill. He had to drive the Cerv army away from Titan. They had come here, and now they were going to pay the price.

He kept on killing and killing and killing. It was all a blur.

There were the Cerv ships! They sat large and squat on the ground. He was almost at his goal. Some were already burning. It was a good day!

***

Drebus sat down by Arakus. He heard the din of battle outside. "We have to fight, Arakus," he said.

"No."

"Arakus—"

"No. I will not. Not for that fat old oaf. I will not. He humiliated me. Now he must be humiliated!" Arakus picked at the table with a knife.

"But we'll die here. Do you want that? They're fighting outside our quarters. We might be burned alive!" Drebus tried to reason with his partner.

"I don't care," said Arakus quietly.

"You're impossible! Oreson was right. You are impossible." He snatched the knife from Arakus' hand. Arakus went on picking at the table with his fingers, not looking at Drebus. Drebus said, "Do you want to be remembered as the sulking boy who refused to fight? I'm not sure that epics are written about people like that."

Arakus huffed.

"Well I'm going," said Drebus.

Arakus said nothing.

Drebus put on Arakus' armour, shield, spear, and sword. He stood resplendent in gold and red armour. The lighted torches cast a glittering glow across the armour.

"You look like a hero," said Arakus, not looking at Drebus. He simply looked at the table.

Drebus put on Arakus' helmet. It obscured his identity. It made him look like Arakus himself.

"At least one of us has to be," said Drebus as he left the quarters. He gave one backward glance, and stepped out into the maelstrom.

***

Instantly what hit Drebus was the smell. It was the smell of death and burning. The ground was slick with blood, and there were bodies everywhere. Soldiers were fighting in scrappy contests all over the camp. There was no front line anymore; no ordered battle line. It was man on man.

"Kiyerons, to me!" yelled Drebus.

"It's Arakus! He's come to fight!" yelled one of the Kiyerons.

"Arakus has come to fight! Arakus has come to fight!" the shout went up around the camp.

The Kiyerons mustered for war. They were Arakus' personal soldiers. They were his thousand true warriors. They were the most loyal and deadly soldiers in the Cerv camp.

They girded on their weapons and armour and sprang to Drebus' side. They fought back extra hard and, with much bloodshed, began to push the Titans back towards the edges of the camp and beyond.

Drebus swung his spear and he and his men pushed the Titans back.

***

106

Brior saw that his men were beginning to falter. He, even in his bloodlust, saw that the was one man doing this. This man, was Arakus. He wore his armour and bore his shield.

Brior's heart skipped a beat. How could one man command such loyalty? How could he stand against such power and majesty? What could he do to bring his forces under control?

He began to fall back with his soldiers out of the camp and back across the Plains of Titan towards the Citadel's main gates.

***

"How dare you," said a voice inside Drebus' skull.

Drebus tried to swat at it like a fly.

"I am no fly," said the voice. "I am an AI. I am Apollo. You are masquerading as someone you are not. It is not your destiny to conquer Titan. Nor is it Arakus' destiny. I will not allow it. I will not allow it!"

Drebus ignored the voice in is skull and he kept driving the Titans back and back towards the main gate of the Citadel.

As they were reaching the last stretch of open terrain before the gate, a warrior sprang out of the mass of Titan soldiers and marched towards Drebus. Drebus recognised the armour. It was Brior!

"So, Arakus, you come to fight. Now you die by my hands!" said Brior.

"We'll see about that," shouted Drebus, still concealed behind Arakus' helmet.

A circle of onlooking warriors formed in the front line as the two heroes circled each other and tested each other's defences.

They each made faints and tried to topple their opponent.

Then they joined in battle. Shields and spears clashed and flashed as energy was discharged. Arakus' armour held, but Brior's armour was strong too.

And then Drebus felt his eyes blur. His head swam. And a voice appeared in his skull. "I will NOT allow you to win."

Drebus faltered, and Brior took the chance. He buried his spear deeply in Drebus' side, under the shield. The energy discharged. Drebus fell.

Drebus felt the spear go in and the energy discharge. He collapsed and his vision faded.

***

Brior stood triumphant over the body of Drebus. He stripped off the armour, handing it to one of his fellow soldiers to hold as spoils of war, and finally he lifted off the helmet and saw…it wasn't Arakus.

"Not…Arakus?" he said to himself. "What the…?"

And then the circle that had held the two combatants and enthralled the onlooking soldiers collapsed and a great fight began for the body and armour of the fallen man.

***

Brior swung his spear in a wide arc to keep the Cerv soldiers from retrieving the body of the fallen Drebus. The Cerv soldiers stood back from the flashing point.

Verius rode up in his chariot. He called out above the din of battle, "What has happened here? Why do you covet this fallen man?"

Brior shouted a response to his enemy, "He is not who you think. It is not Arakus. It is his partner, Drebus! I have slain him fairly in single combat. His armour belongs to me. I will not be denied my prize!"

"If you did indeed kill him in single combat, the armour is yours," replied Verius. "But let us take the body back for honoured burial. Even if it was not Arakus, the man has earned an honoured sleep."

While the two men shouted over the din of battle, the war raged on around them. The Cerv soldiers, now without their supposed hero, began to fall back again towards their camp, leaving Verius dangerously exposed to spears and swords.

Brior thought for a moment, and then agreed. "If I can take the armour, I will let you have the body."

Verius nodded and dismounted his chariot. He picked up the bloody, crumpled corpse and slung it over the chariot. He mounted up again, and with a nod to the victorious Brior, departed for the Cerv camp.

"Come men, we have defeated their best this day," shouted Brior. "We must drive them from our lands!"

With that battle cry, Brior pushed forward and the Titan forces began to push the Cerv army back towards the ships again.

***

As Verius rode back to the Cerv camp with the body of Drebus slumped in the chariot, he thought to himself. How was he going to break this news to Arakus. The man will be distraught. But then he thought to himself. Will this make him fight?

***

Arakus sat in his quarters. He could hear the clash of arms in the distance but again getting closer. He wondered how the fight was going. He wondered if he would be needed. He wanted to fight, but he had to teach that pompous oaf Oreson a lesson. No one insulted Arakus.

And then, there was the sound of hover horses outside his quarters and he heard the sound of someone disembarking. He heard the heavy footfalls outside. There were also some shouts of anguish from some soldiers.

Verius entered the room. He waited patiently at the door.

"Come in, Verius. Eat, drink," said Arakus.

Verius hesitated.

"Come," said Arakus again. "I have nothing against you, only your brother."

109

Verius tried to speak, but his words failed him. He coughed.

"What's wrong?" said Arakus. He had a sinking feeling in his stomach. "Something must be wrong, you don't normally pause for words."

"I…have bad news," said Verius.

Arakus looked carefully at the man. He said nothing.

"Bad news," Verius continued. "Drebus…"

Arakus' face fell and his stomach sank.

"Drebus, is dead," said Verius finally.

"What!?" bellowed Arakus. "What?" he repeated. "Show me! Show me the body! I don't believe it. Damn you, show me the body!" Arakus drew his sword and slammed the point into the table. The food went flying onto the floor.

Verius flinched.

Arakus stood and retrieved the sword. He walked up to Verius, his eyes afire and his heart burning. "Show me," he rasped brandishing the sword in Verius' face.

Verius indicated the chariot outside. The two of them stepped out of Arakus' quarters and Arakus saw what he most dreaded: the body of his lover sprawled in the back of the chariot.

Arakus' blood boiled. His lover, was dead. His friend, was dead. His best companion in all the world, was dead. He, himself, might as well be dead. Arakus wailed. He was certain the Titans would hear the blood curdling cry inside their Citadel. And he hoped that they were terrified.

Arakus fumed. He stood there, looking at the body of Drebus. He could not speak. He choked down tears. His jaw moved but he did not know what to say.

"He died a hero," said Verius, putting a hand on Arakus' shoulder.

Arakus shrugged it off violently. "Who?" is all he said.

"Brior."

"And the armour?"

"Brior has that too," said Verius carefully.

"Looted. Defiled. Dead," spat Arakus. "We must bury him. He must be buried properly."

"I will organise a funeral pyre," said Verius. "In the meantime—"

"In the meantime, I will clean him up," said Arakus. He lifted the body of Drebus out of the back of the chariot and carried him gently into his quarters.

"Will you fight now?" asked Verius as Arakus passed him.

"Get me new armour, and I will kill them all," growled Arakus.

Arakus put the body down on the bed and poured some water into a bowl. He used a cloth to wipe the blood from the wounds on his lover's body.

"Oh, oh, Drebus," he said quietly. He wanted to cry from sorrow, and kill from rage. Both emotions vied for his attention. So in the end, he choked down the pain, and set his face as anger and hate. They had done this, the Titans. He would destroy every one of them. He would see their Citadel burn. He would kill Brior and all his bastard brothers and sisters. He would gut that Zoriam and annihilate the entire damn Moon of Titan. When he was finished with this place, it would be known as the Slaughter of Arakus.

Sius ran into Arakus' quarters. "I came as fast as I could," he said, out of breath.

"Too late. It's all too late," said Arakus, not looking up.

"I'm so sorry," said Sius.

"Sit with me," said Arakus.

Sius nodded and sat down at the table. He did not comment on the food and drink on the floor, or the stab wound in the table. He sat, in silence, and watched Arakus care for the body of Drebus.

111

The fighting had died down for a while now. There was only the odd sound of battle between skirmishing squads, rather than a whole battle line attacking another.

Arakus turned to Sius. "I heard it was Brior?"

Sius nodded.

"I will have his head," spat Arakus.

"Now's not the time—"

"Now's not the time to what? Hate? Because that is all I am. I am nothing else. They took everything from me. I have only hate left," snapped Arakus.

"Then we will fight them together," said Sius.

Arakus smiled a broken smile. "When I get armour and weapons, they will all die together."

The two waited together for Arakus' new armour.

***

Verius walked through the bowels of the armoury ship. It was dark, dirty, grimy, and very suited to producing arms and armour. The air was thick with sparks and the smells of molten metal and circuits being crafted and engineered.

Standing in front of one of the machines, Verius told one of the dataslaves to enter the requirements into the computer for the required armour.

This was the largest and oldest of all the machines that the Cerv forces had brought with them. It could churn out many pieces of weaponry a day. It had been running non stop since the Cerv ships had landed on the Moon of Titan.

Verius rubbed a hand over a name plate that was emblazoned on the side of the great machine.

"Hephaestus," he said reverently, reading the name of the machine in a whisper.

"This is required for Arakus?" said the dataslave in a raspy, mechanical way through its voice projector.

"Yes," said Verius.

"And it is needed when?" said the dataslave again.

112

"Now."

"Then we will get to it," said the dataslave, turning to some other dataslaves in the vicinity. It barked some unintelligible command in computer noises and they all gathered around the great machine and began to produce the armour for the hero.

Verius stood back and watched. He watched out of reverence, and horror.

Great flows of metal poured into moulds and with gouts of flame, were pressed into shape with massive pistons and, as the metal cooled, it was infused and imprinted with circuits and energy shields. In the case of the spear, crafted from a long shaft of solid metallic substance, the shock producers that could kill a man in a second were emblazoned on its shaft and spear tip.

The air was full of the din of armour and weapon production. So much so that Verius' ear guards had to be engaged and they automatically dampened the sounds as to protect his mortal ears. Verius could also smell the toxic smell of molten metals and plastics. He saw sparks flying from all manner of parts of the machine and the dataslaves' manipulations of the production line.

Out of the Hephaestus came first the helmet. It was massive and shining with gold. It had a large plume attached on top. Then came the sword, shining and keen. Then the spear, sharp as a razor with its shock dispenser near the tip, already fully charged. Then the body armour, emblazoned with symbols of Arakus' past and his heroic deeds. And then, last, and greatest of them all, the shield. It gleamed with gold in the half light of the forge room. Around its outer edge were emblazoned symbols of power which would focus the energy shield and protect the bearer.

Of course, Verius knew, that the armour was far stronger than gold. Gold was heavy and malleable. These pieces of armour were simply gilded. Their actual composition was far

113

stronger than any simple element. These pieces of armour would protect Arakus, and would terrify any opposition.

Verius ran a hand over the cooling armour. It was still warm to the touch. He lifted the helmet up and stared into its lifeless face.

"To your satisfaction?" rasped the dataslave.

Verius looked at the helmet, and ran a hand across the shield. "Yes. These are perfect."

"Good. Now we will get back to producing other weapons," said the dataslave, returning to work on more mundane tasks. The other dataslaves returned to their tasks on other machines.

"He will be grateful, Hephaestus," whispered Verius.

Verius picked up the armour and weapons, and, with some difficulty given the bulk of the arms, man handled the pieces back to Arakus' quarters.

***

While Verius was gone, Oreson had returned to Arakus' quarters and Sius had left. The food was back on the table.

"You dare do this now?" snapped Arakus.

"I thought—" said Oreson.

"You thought. Oh, you thought did you?" interrupted Arakus. "You bring me my dataslave back, now? What did you think that would do? Make me feel better?"

"Well, yes! With what you've been through. Your slave—"

"Oh she's my slave now? After you've defiled her and had her in your quarters for ages. I'm supposed to feel better because you gave her back to me? Well?" Arakus sat at the table but did not eat or drink. He banged his fist on the table. The food and drink bounced but did not spill.

"I'm being generous, damn it. Do you want me to keep her?" shouted Oreson.

"Do as you wish," growled Arakus.

Oreson shoved the dataslave, who was being held by another soldier, into the quarters. She yelped and scrambled to the corner and cowered there.

"You will thank me!" said Oreson. "Why don't you eat something?"

"Get out of my quarters!" yelled Arakus. He swept the food and drink from the table onto the floor. He stood and reached for his sword, that was not there.

Oreson's guards stepped between Oreson and Arakus, weapons drawn.

"It's not there," said Arakus quietly. He held up his right hand without a sword. "It will never be there again."

"We're getting you new armour and weapons now. Don't worry," said Oreson, motioning for the guards to step back. They complied.

"He will never be here again," said Arakus to himself.

Oreson smirked and then said, "Ah, here's Verius with the new armour."

Krysi, the dataslave, had begun picking up the food and spilled drink paraphernalia and putting them back on the table.

Verius entered with Sius. They carried the armour and weapons between them. They deposited the objects on the seats and table in the room. They managed to avoid and ignore the dataslave's actions.

"There, aren't they magnificent!" said Oreson.

Sius and Verius stood near the armour admiring it.

Arakus moved over to the armour and drew his hands and fingers across the designs. "They are," he said quietly.

"Sius, encourage him to eat and then we can go to war," said Oreson.

"I will not eat. I will not drink. I will kill. Help me on with the armour," said Arakus.

Sius looked at Oreson, but then, with Verius, helped Arakus on with his new armour.

115

In a moment, he was dressed in gleaming gold with his new armour and weapons.

"How does it feel?" asked Verius.

Arakus stretched his augmented limbs. "Good."

"Now what?" asked Oreson.

"I go to war," said Arakus. "Prepare my hover horses and chariot!"

Chapter 12

Zeus watched. He watched the war unfolding. He watched the rage of young Arakus. He watched the sorrow of the Cerv soldiers. He watched the wrath of the Titan army. He knew that mass bloodshed was coming. He listened to the cries and entreaties of his fellow AIs. He understood that they wanted to get involved. He knew that they had to get involved. He let them. He let them go and fight. He knew that he, too, had to fight. This was a war for the ages. There would be songs sung by bards from far and wide in the Solar System about this war. He knew. He knew.

And so, not just in ethereal constructs that did not touch the ground, did he let the other AIs fight. Great war machines from ages passed that had been buried on the Moon of Titan were re-energised and thundered forth from underground caverns. The earth split asunder on the Plains of Titan and massive walking war machines emerged and began to fight each other and rend whole ranks of the two human armies.

The whole Moon shook to the conflict. It was as if the whole of creation was being torn apart by human and AI alike. There would never be another war like this; there could never be another war like this. For at the end of this war, the AIs themselves would fall and rend apart their own circuits. This was the apex and the nadir.

***

Arakus raged. He charged rank after rank of Titan soldiers from the back of his chariot. His vision was red from the rage he felt as he mowed down soldier after soldier.

In the corner of his vision, he saw a kill counter. It clicked up one every time he killed someone. It clicked up fast. He did not care anymore. Nothing could bring Drebus back. Nothing. And all he wanted to do was kill, but especially, he wanted to kill Brior. The man who had taken Drebus from him. The man that still had his armour. The man that had forced him to fight. The man that would die to his hand, before the night came again.

Arakus basically ignored the massive walking killing machines that thundered around the Citadel and the Plains. The ground shook and rocked to their combat, and many human soldiers died to their feet and weapons. But Arakus saw only Brior. He did not even pay attention to the dying soldiers in the Titan ranks that he rode over anymore.

After a while, most soldiers desperately tried to stay away from him. Even the Cerv soldiers parted and let him pass in his chariot. No one wanted anything to do with the mad Cerv warrior who screamed as he rode around.

Arakus made it to the Citadel's main gate. He disembarked from his chariot. There was a wide circle around him where no one dared to go. He gripped his spear in his right hand, his shield in his left. His sword was strapped to his belt.

He screamed. He screamed long and loud. The scream echoed around the Citadel and the Plains. It was an animal scream, a bestial scream, a scream without word and yet it conveyed everything. It was a scream of sorrow and rage, of pain and hate.

"BRIOR!" This second scream had form. It was a word. It was yelled with just as much intensity as the animal scream,

118

but this cry made the walls tremble and even the AIs quaked. "BRIOR! FIGHT ME!"

Arakus paced up and down. He spat. He raged. No one in the war came near him. Even the AIs avoided him. His destiny was beyond all of them. They had no right to interfere with someone whose destiny burned so bright and brilliantly.

"BRIOR!" Arakus yelled again. His voice hoarse and gravelly.

***

"Don't go," pleaded Pyrakra. "Please."

Brior stood in the courtyard behind the gate. He heard the blood curdling screams of the man who had lost everything. His blood ran cold.

Brior held his helmet in his hands. His spear and shield were propped up against a wall. He was in Arakus' armour. He had looted it from Drebus after his death.

"Please!" begged Pyrakra.

"I have to. Honour demands it," he said. "I will win, and the Cerv forces will be broken by his death. It is for my city and my King that I do this."

"You'll die!" said Pyrakra, clawing at his armour. "Here. I'll take it off. Please, brother!"

"I won't die. He will. He's gone mad. He will have no control over his blows. I will win with skill and precision," Brior said. He put on the helmet, it's plume fluttering in the breeze. He picked up his shield and spear.

Just then, Zoriam appeared and walked towards his son. He shook his son's hand.

"We'll be watching from the Citadel walls up there," he said pointing. "Go with honour, my son."

Brior saluted with his spear and marched toward the gate. The gate opened and he stepped out.

"No!" shouted Pyrakra. She reached out for her brother, but was restrained by Zoriam.

119

"We'll watch from up there, come, child," Zoriam said, man handling Pyrakra up the stairs and onto the balcony that was on top of the walls.

Pyrakra clung to the battlements with white knuckles, hoping beyond hope that this time, just this once, she would be wrong. That she would see fate reversed and that the AIs had not decreed it already. That somehow, she would see her visions disproved and Brior would walk away the victor.

***

Arakus paced back and forth. His rage boiled forth and he swung his spear in angry arcs in front of him.

Then the gates opened and out stepped Brior. He was in his armour!

"That won't help you!" snapped Arakus.

"We'll see," shouted Brior back. He turned to face the crowd on the walls above him. He raised his spear in salute, then turned back to the fight.

Many of the warriors of the Cerv and Titan forces had formed a ring around the two combatants, all hostilities halted until the duel was over. Even the AI mechanical constructs halted their fighting to watch the contest. Their massive forms towering over the humans as they crowded around to watch.

Arakus screamed a spine chilling scream again and charged. There was such rage in his voice that Brior visibly recoiled and staggered back before even the first blow was struck.

Arakus' shock spear moved rapidly, a stab here, a thrust there. His mechanical implants discharging great bursts of chemicals and stimulants to speed and invigorate his arms.

Brior parried a few thrusts with his shield, but the thrusts threatened to knock him off his feet. So much so that he ran a few steps back to give some ground between himself and Arakus.

Arakus stood and readied his spear. He threw it with massive force. It flew straight and true.

Brior raised his shield to deflect it, but the shock spear pierced the shield and smashed it from his grip. Brior shook his arm in pain, his arm now shattered and useless.

Arakus stepped forward and picked up his spear, tearing it from the shield that had been his and was now ruined.

Brior stepped back and brandished his spear with his good arm.

Arakus charged, swinging his spear. He let out another battle cry. He stabbed and stabbed.

Brior tried to parry with his spear, but it was useless without his shield.

Arakus knocked aside Brior's spear with ease and the point of his spear went through Brior's chest.

In time with Brior's rapid intake of breath followed by a hiss as the air escaped his lungs through the hole in his chest, the shock spear discharged its energy, causing Brior to writhe and convulse on the end of the shaft.

Arakus heard a cry from on top of the walls. He wrenched out his spear.

Brior fell dead to the ground.

Arakus now silent, but still full of rage, brought up his chariot and attached a rope from it to the heels of Brior by skewering hooks through the tendons.

Arakus stared at the people on top of the walls as he dragged the corpse of Brior around the Citadel walls. He went around time after time.

None of the Cerv or Titan soldiers got in his way. They parted as he went by. Even the war machines of the AIs stepped around him.

As Arakus drove he fumed. He had enacted revenge, but he was still hollow inside. He raged internally as he drove. He did not feel any better from before. He wondered if he ever would.

Arakus returned to the Cerv camp. He sat in his quarters, alone. Outside on a slab was the body of Brior. It lay there, deliberately, stripped naked and lying in the atmosphere. Arakus had ordered that no one was to touch it. It was there to rot.

As he sat there in his quarters, a mass of rage and hate, Arakus did not eat. He sat there at the table, picking at the table and the whole in the table the sword had left a while ago.

Oreson appeared at the door. He knocked. Arakus gave no reply.

"You've had your revenge, Arakus. Come on. We have a war to fight," said Oreson.

Arakus glared at him, but said nothing.

Oreson squirmed uneasily under that look. He left the quarters.

Then Verius appeared at the door.

"Bury the dead," said Verius. "Let's end this war."

Arakus snarled at him, but said nothing else. Verius shook his head and left the room.

Then Sius appeared. He said nothing for a while, but then all he said was, "I'm sorry." He had a sympathetic expression on his face.

"I'm sorry too," said Arakus. It was not an admission of guilt or an apology, but a statement of anger and hate.

"Let him go, Arakus. He's dead. Let him go," said Sius, still at the door.

Arakus huffed. Sius sighed. He left the room.

Arakus sat in the shadows of the room. He raged quietly to himself. He knew that he had to let go, but he could not. His lover was dead. He had killed his murderer, and yet he felt no peace. Why was this? He wondered to himself. He did not know. He had thought that killing Brior would bring him some peace, but it did not. There was no rest for him. He could not sleep. He could not eat. He could not fight. There was no peace, only hate. Hate for the Titans. Hate for the AIs. Hate for Oreson and the war. And most tellingly, hate for himself. If he had only stopped Drebus from fighting, it would all be different. If he had fought instead of Drebus, if would all be different. Drebus would be alive. And yet, he was dead, and Arakus was alive. He was alive. And he felt guilty, and so he hated everything and everyone.

"Bury me," came a voice inside Arakus' head.

Arakus jumped. There was no one in the room. "What?" he said. He knew that voice, but it was impossible.

"Bury me, Arakus," said the voice again. The voice appeared inside Arakus' head rather than him hearing it through his ears.

"Drebus?" Arakus said disbelievingly. "Where are you?"

"It is me, Arakus. It is me."

"Then where are you? I need to see you!" said Arakus, now more animated than he had been for days. He sat up and looked around.

"Don't mourn me, bury me. Let me go," said the voice.

"Appear to me!" said Arakus. "Where are you?"

"I am stuck in the realm of circuits. You have my body unburied, like you have Brior's body unburied. We are stuck in a sort of limbo of the circuits. We must be buried to pass on, otherwise we will be stuck forever in this limbo. Bury me, Arakus. Let me go. I must be burned and my ashes laid to rest."

"I must see you," said Arakus with a whimper. "I don't want to let you go."

In front of Arakus' eyes materialised Drebus. He stood resplendent in armour with shield and spear.

Arakus broke down.

"Bury me, Arakus. Bury me."

"Come back to me. If I bury you, you're gone forever. If I keep you, I can see you," said Arakus, reaching out towards the apparition.

"You cannot touch me, and no one else can see me. I am in your head. I am in the neural pathways of the circuits. I cannot rest until you bury me. Please, bury me. I cannot be in limbo forever…"

The apparition faded and disappeared with the echo of, "Bury me," said inside Arakus' head.

"Drebus!" shouted Arakus. "Don't leave me…" he whimpered.

When the image had disappeared, Arakus sobbed a little, then he stood and set his jaw.

"I will bury you," he said.

Arakus moved to outside his quarters. There were a couple of guards standing around.

"Prepare a funeral pyre," he said to them. "I will burn the body of Drebus. I will bury him. We will have great games for his passing." Then after a short pause, in which the guards left to organise a pyre, he said quietly, "I will let you go."

***

After A while, Verius and Sius returned with news of the funeral pyre. They explained that the guards had told them about the occurrence.

Arakus carried Drebus' body out and laid it on the top. He then took a lighted torch and set the pyre ablaze. He stood there, and watched the person he cared most about, burn. He stood there, with the smoke stinging his eyes, and tears rolling down his cheeks. He stood there, in pure rage and hatred, ready to kill every last Titan there was. He stood there, alive.

Arakus felt the circuits in his mind change. He felt Drebus slipping away. He felt that he had lost his lover, but helped his friend.

"Thank you," said the voice within his skull.

Arakus smiled through the smoke and flames. He did not know if the tears he shed were for his lover or because of the smoke. But all that was left in his heart was a dull ache. There was nothing left, but hate.

The flames of the pyre roared high into the sky. Arakus looked up and saw the ash and flames being swept away in the breeze. They mingled with the sky and in every second the images of Drebus flashed across Arakus' vision.

Sius, Verius, and Oreson stood with Arakus as the fire burned. They said nothing. They simply watched.

After the pyre had burned down, the dataslaves gathered the ashes of Drebus in an urn and gave it to Arakus.

Arakus held the warm urn in his hands. There were no more tears. There were no more feelings. There was just a dull void inside him and he knew that nothing would fill that void. Not even killing.

The small funeral party walked to a hill outside the Cerv camp. They dug a small hole and put the urn of Drebus in the ground. Sius, Verius, and Oreson gathered stones to put on the grave. In a short time, the final place of Drebus was a cairn of stones.

Oreson and Drebus left to go back to the camp. Sius stayed with Arakus, who simply looked down at the grave.

Sius put a hand on Arakus' shoulder, and then left to go back to the camp.

Arakus stood for a while, then he too went back to the camp. He did not look back as he walked. He did not look back.

Chapter 13

Zoriam stood, wrapped in a cloak, staring out over the edge of the parapet of the walls of the Citadel. He had lost track of how long he had stood there. The battle had died down for now. The soldiers had returned to their camps and only the dead littered the area in front of the Citadel. Only his personal guards were with him. It was dark now. Night had fallen. He stared down over the Plains of Titan outside the Citadel walls. He stared down at the place his favourite son had died. He stared, and tears clouded his eyes. He wept. He sobbed. He had lost Brior in this pointless war. A war over what? Some stupid AI. Why did Brior have to be taken? Why?

A slight rustle of wind whipped at his old, white hair. He felt cold. A faint mist began to curl around the walls.

"I will guide you to him," a voice sounded in his ear.

Zoriam looked around. There was no one there. Even his guards had gone.

"Hello?" he said, almost to himself.

"I will guide you," said the voice again, and a thin, young man stepped onto the walls from the stairs. His form slightly shimmered.

"You're an AI? Aren't you?" said Zoriam.

"I am."

"So you're not really there. You're in my head. How can you help?" said Zoriam with contempt.

"I wouldn't speak to an AI that way," said the AI. "I am Hermes. I will guide you there."

"Where? My favourite son is gone." Zoriam turned back to the ramparts and stared out over the battlefield.

"I will take you to him," said Hermes.

"And turn me over to the Cerv soldiers, no doubt. I don't trust you."

"That's as may be. You will have to trust me. But someone down there," Hermes pointed, "has lost just as much as you and may be reasoned with."

"Fine. When do we leave?" asked Zoriam.

"Now. We go now."

"Let me get my guards," said Zoriam.

"No. No guards. Just you. I will guide you. We go now, together."

Zoriam looked cautiously at the AI in his vision.

"Think of it this way," said Hermes. "What do you have to lose?"

Zoriam snorted a laugh, and nodded. "Lead on."

Zoriam, guided by the AI that was imposed upon his vision through his implants, descended the stairs and left the Citadel through a side gate.

Zoriam made his way across the battlefield down towards the Cerv encampment. He picked his way across dead bodies and shattered shields. His robes caught sometimes on broken spears and swords. There were dead bodies littered around who had not been buried yet.

All the while, the AI image of Hermes drew him across the charnel landscape with a guiding light. It hovered just out of reach but just in eyesight to make the way possible across the blasted landscape.

Zoriam avoided the rents in the land where the war machines of the AIs had risen up and taken to battle alongside the humans.

Finally, Zoriam made it to the Cerv camp. He approached the gate and was stopped by a pair of guards. At first the guards were oblivious to the man's identity. Then they became aware and almost dropped their spears.

"Take me to Arakus. I have to talk about my son," said Zoriam with authority. He was illuminated in the burning braziers at the entrance to the camp.

Hermes winked at him and disappeared from his vision. "I am done here," he said as words inside Zoriam's head.

The guards paused for a moment.

"I am King of the Titans. I demand you take me to my son's killer. I need to talk to him," said the old man.

One guard beckoned for the King to follow and headed in the direction of Arakus' quarters.

Zoriam followed through ranks of soldiers sitting down and eating at campfires and braziers. They mostly paid him no attention. Those who did notice him did not look long enough to recognise who he was. He was shrouded in a cloak. It was understandable to Zoriam. They were soldiers. They concentrated on killing. It would be inconceivable that the King of the enemy that they hated would be in their camp.

Zoriam knew he would probably be taken hostage or killed. But he had to deal with the remains of his son. They had not been returned to the Citadel and had not been given a proper burial. Brior deserved that. He needed to be buried with honour and so he could go to the afterlife and not languish in limbo.

"In here," said the guard and pointed to an opening in some metal walls. He stood outside. "If you try anything, I'll kill you."

128

They had arrived at Arakus' quarters. Zoriam took a deep breath and stepped inside. He knocked on the door that was open.

"What!" came a voice from the darkness inside. It was not a question. There were no lights on.

Zoriam cleared his throat.

"Yes? What?" said the voice again.

"I am here to talk about my son," said Zoriam.

"And who are you? And who is he?" said the voice. A light went on and the room was illuminated.

Zoriam could see that Arakus was sitting at the table. There was untouched bread, fruit, and wine on it.

"You!" said Arakus.

"Yes, me. I'm here to talk about my son's body, to be more precise, Brior's body," said Zoriam.

"What about him?" said Arakus.

Zoriam, still standing in the doorway, said, "I want his body back, for burial. He needs a proper burial."

Arakus said nothing. He went back to picking at the table surface.

Zoriam, still standing in the doorway, sighed. "He was my favourite son, Arakus. And you killed him. And desecrated his body. I want him back. Please."

"And he killed the love of my life," said Arakus.

Zoriam took a step forward. "I cannot remove the grief, Arakus, but I can prevent further pain. Please, his body."

After a few more steps into the room, Zoriam could see wetness on the sides of Arakus' face. The tears were glinting in the light of the room that had turned on when Arakus had first spoken.

Zoriam took steps towards the table. He stood next to Arakus. He put a hand on the young man's shoulder.

"Sit," said Arakus through his tears.

Zoriam sat opposite the man. Fresh tears springing up in his eyes too. "Tell me about him?" said Zoriam.

"He was perfect. I loved him. And I sent him to die. Me? The greatest warrior in this army, sent my lover to die. It hurts. It hurts so much. I'll never see him again," said Arakus, tears flowing down his cheeks. He stared at Zoriam.

"And my son was perfect too. He was the love of my life, as a father loves a son," said Zoriam, hot tears stinging his skin and dripping onto the table. He did not wipe his eyes. He wanted the tears to flow.

"And you want his body back?" said Arakus.

"Yes."

Arakus picked up an apple from the fruit bowl and took a bite. He indicated for Zoriam to eat.

Zoriam chose some bread and began to eat. They sat there for a while, saying nothing, but eating and drinking.

"Okay," said Arakus. "I will return his body. One Titan day of mourning."

"Thank you," said Zoriam. "I hope you find peace, Arakus. I really do. Rage is a young man's game. It swallows up people and leaves them a husk of a person."

Arakus said nothing.

Zoriam stood and left the room. "I will require my son's body be returned to the Citadel as soon as possible. I will tell my soldiers that we have a Titan day of respite," he said to the guard. The guard nodded.

Zoriam picked his way out of the Cerv camp with the help of the guard, and then he made his way across the battlefield and back to the Citadel. Hermes guided him back safely and he managed to get in through a side door without alerting any of the guards.

As the mists cleared and Hermes faded from view, Zoriam made his way back to the Palace to prepare for his son's funeral.

Sius stepped into Arakus' quarters. "Who was that?" he said. "He left in a hurry with a hood over his head."

"That," said Arakus, sitting at the table and not looking in Sius' direction, "was King Zoriam."

"No, you're shitting me. Hah, who was it really?" said Sius.

Arakus looked at Sius. Sius could see that Arakus had been crying, but said nothing.

"Wait…really? Holy shit!" said Sius. "What did he want?"

"He wanted Brior's body."

"And you said…what exactly?" said Sius walking to the table. He leaned his weight on the back of a chair, but did not sit down.

"I said he could have it," said Arakus. He looked down at the table.

"Very magnanimous of you," said Sius. He saw Arakus' augmented eyes flash in the torch light in the quarters. "Why? Wasn't he your prize?"

"He appealed to my inner human," said Arakus. He stared at the table.

"Hah, and here was I thinking you were all machine by now," said Sius.

"Sit and eat, Sius," said Arakus.

Sius sat down and picked out a pear from the bowl of fruit. He began chewing on it.

Arakus took an apple and began eating too.

They sat in silence for a few moments, then Arakus said, "Do you think me a coward?"

"Why would I do that?" said Sius, pausing in eating.

"I refuse to fight, then when the man who murdered my lover is killed by my hand, I give his body back to the enemy…"

Sius paused for a moment and then said, "No."

"No what?" snapped Arakus angrily.

"No I don't think you're a coward. I think you're learning."

"What am I learning. Please enlighten me, oh teacher," said Arakus. He grimaced at the apple and then looked at Sius.

"You're learning that war is not all glory and honour. It's death and blood and shit. Why do you think I did not want to come on this war venture?" said Sius, still chewing on the pear.

Arakus shrugged.

"Not because I was a coward. I've fought in other conflicts and wars. I know what it's like. It's all death and blood—"

"And shit," concluded Arakus.

"Exactly," said Sius, pointing a finger in his pear holding hand towards Arakus. Then he took another bite.

"What about glory?" said Arakus.

"Glory comes after you are dead. Long in the future, people may still sing your name if you are lucky. They might say, 'Arakus the brave, Arakus the ruthless, Arakus the vengeful'," said Sius.

"And what about you?" said Arakus. He looked intently at Sius.

"Me? Hah, who knows. Maybe I'll be known for something."

"It doesn't bother you? Being forgotten?" asked Arakus.

"Not really. We are like flies that flit from fruit to fruit. We live, we die. If we are remembered, it is a miracle. If we are forgotten it is normal. All we can do is perhaps, if we're lucky, continue our line into the future. If not, that's fine too, just make sure you live well." Sius put down the eaten pear and went to stand.

"That's it?" said Arakus.

"You're a good man, Arakus. Perhaps hold some games for Drebus' funeral. You'll feel better. I admire you for letting the body of Brior go. That showed real maturity. Oh, and I advise you stand your men down from combat at the moment.

They've been fighting for a long time. Let them rest. This war is not going anywhere."

Arakus nodded. "I agreed on one Titan day of peace with Zoriam."

"I'll spread the word?" said Sius. He moved to the doorway.

Arakus nodded.

"Hold some games. Let the men rest. Award some prizes for the winners. It will be good for the morale," said Sius, and then he left, not waiting for a reply.

Sius left the quarters and spoke to a guard nearby. "Call in the Kiyerons. Let them rest."

The guard nodded and replayed the message, via communicator, to all of Arakus' soldiers that were out warring in areas around the Citadel.

***

The body of Brior was brought back inside the Citadel on a hover carriage. Two great hover horses bore the weight of the carriage and on top of it, wrapped in linen, was the body of the fallen hero.

There was a procession inside the walls of the Citadel, bringing the body up towards the palace. The streets were lined with people. Some wept and mourned. Many stayed silent, too many tears already shed for their sons and daughters who had died in the war's ten year reign.

There was no joy. This was no celebration. The body was brought to the palace and then carried into the temple compound. The windows were covered and the expanse of the temple was lit by lighted torches and candles. The body was laid on an altar at the head of the temple.

Pyrakra stood off to one side, behind a pillar. She gripped the stone with white knuckles. She stared at the fallen body of her brother. She wanted to scream, to cry out, that she knew this would happen, and that she knew what would happen in

133

the future. The Citadel would burn. She knew this. No one believed her. She wept for her brother. But she knew…she knew…

Zoriam stood at the head of the temple. His family were around him. No one else was at the funeral. It was a private, family affair.

Pyrakra watched as the body of her brother was anointed with unguents and chemicals. They unwrapped his head and at seeing his mutilated flesh, his mother gasped. Oricula pawed at his ruined flesh in an attempt to make all good again. Then, being restrained by Zoriam, she simply let out a long howl of anguish. It was a cry that would have stopped the hearts of any invading Cerv soldier, had they heard it.

"My boy, my baby boy," Oricula managed. And then began sobbing again. "What sort of monster does this?"

"The monster that returned his body to us," said Zoriam carefully.

"You should have stabbed him in his quarters!" snapped Oricula.

"I think, he was already dead," said Zoriam.

Pyrakra saw Oricula give Zoriam a strange look, and then the emotion faded and the body was bound up in linen again.

Then Zoriam brought a lighted torch to the body and set it aflame. The body burned well. The temple was illuminated brightly by the flames. Skin seared and burned. Mechanical limbs cracked and melted.

After a while, all that was left of Brior was a pile of ashes, and some melted implants.

Zoriam himself gathered the ashes and placed them in an urn. He placed the urn in the wall of the temple where the family crypt was. There were other sons and daughters who lay there. The receptacles were filling up all too quickly.

Pyrakra saw Zoriam look over to her. She cowered behind the pillar. His expression stunned her. Did he believe her? Or was that a trick of the light? She looked out from behind the pillar again. Zoriam was gone. He had left. As had the rest of the family. Pyrakra was alone in the temple.

She moved over to Brior's urn. She touched it. It was still warm.

"I'm sorry," she said. She then broke down and cried. She fell to her knees in the temple, and sobbed.

***

Arakus woke. He turned over in his bed and reached out for Drebus, but there was nothing but empty bed there. Arakus sat bolt upright, then he remembered. The dreadful memories came flooding back, replayed by his brain augmentations. He rubbed a metallic hand over his eyes.

"Games," he said. "We must honour him. We have a Titan day."

Getting up and getting dressed into his armour, Arakus girded on his sword. He ate a little and then stepped out into the Cerv camp. It was packed with soldiers tending their armour and weapons; recharging and equipping. They were not taking the Titan day of truce lightly. Arakus grinned to himself.

Arakus saw Sius, Oreson, and Verius all talking at a distance. He called out to them. They turned and acknowledged his hail.

"We need to honour Drebus. I want funeral games," said Arakus as he approached the three others.

Oreson made a face, but said nothing. Arakus ignored the insult. Verius and Sius simply nodded.

"We could hold them out there, outside the camp. Then we could make sure that Drebus has crossed the river Styx," said Arakus. He pointed through one of the gates of the camp and out onto the Plains beyond.

"Won't that attract the attention of the Titans?" said Sius.

"We have a truce for one Titan day. I hold them to that," said Arakus.

"How do you know?" said Oreson.

"I agreed with Zoriam during the night. He came to my quarters and I gave him back the body of Brior. In return he agreed to one Titan day of peace where we can mourn our dead," said Arakus, looking defiantly at the other three, daring them to disagree.

Sius, Oreson, and Verius looked at each other and then, with Sius shrugging, they nodded their agreement.

"Good, gather the soldiers. I will get my Kiyerons and we will see who has the fastest runners and the strongest spear hurlers," said Arakus. He marched away towards his soldiers' part of the camp.

***

After a while, some running tracks were marked out on the Plains. There were also some distance markers for throwing spears and an area for wrestling. The Citadel sat in the distance.

Arakus called on the strongest and fastest of the Kiyerons. Sius called on his warriors along with Verius and Oreson on his own. Other commanders brought forth their best wrestlers and soldiers.

They all lined up on the starting point. With a shout from Arakus the competitors ran. And it was Lorax who won! He gained the admiration of the AIs and Arakus presented him with a great sword that was charged with energy and could cleave a man in half with little effort.

Then there was the wrestling. Many fighters took part and grappled each other with great skill. And then, when it came to the finals, it was between Jou and Eerix. They threw each other time and time again, but always stood afterwards. Their mechanically augmented arms and legs strained with servo motors and wires. Eventually, when both combatants had strained tirelessly, Eerix managed to trip Jou and sprawl him on his back. In an instant Eerix was on top of the man and pinned him to the ground.

With a cheer from the onlooking soldiers, Sius declared that Eerix was the winner, and was to receive a great shield embossed with gold and silver.

Finally, the warriors took part in the throwing competition. With a flick of the wrist Morste threw a weighted spear further than anyone. He was lifted high by the other soldiers and as the cheers went around he was carried towards Oreson and Verius who were to present his prize.

Oreson presented a great spear with a massive shock discharger on the end, and Verius presented a helmet with a great plume on top. Morste took these eagerly. He donned the helmet and hefted the spear.

Sius walked over to Arakus and took him by the shoulder.

"Drebus would be proud," said Sius. He looked out over the games still going on. Many of the soldiers had started their own competitions of many different sorts after the three official games had concluded.

Arakus nodded. "I know," he said. He smiled.

Sius smiled too. "I'll race you to the Citadel and back!"

"Done!" said Arakus.

The two of them began running hard towards the Citadel. Instantly the other soldiers saw this and gathered to watch. They cheered and shouted.

Sius' mechanical legs powered away. His heart discharged chemicals into his blood stream. He ran like the wind.

But Arakus was faster. He was younger and his implants were more modern. He outpaced Sius at the half way mark. He touched the wall of the Citadel first and began to run back towards the Cerv camp.

Sius was slowing. His legs not up to the distance. But he kept running.

Arakus looked over his shoulder and saw that Sius was still hot on his heels.

Arakus reached the Cerv camp first. He reached the barricade and doubled over, drawing in great gulps of air.

Sius arrived a few seconds after. He too doubled over and sucked in air.

Arakus was laughing. He clapped Sius on the back. "Well run. You almost had me."

"I'm not as young as I used to be. I'd out do you in any bow stringing competition. That doesn't require young limbs, just skill," said Sius, also laughing.

They laughed. All the soldiers laughed. They enjoyed the peace they had for the one Titan day. Because they knew that after the truce expired, then there would be renewed bloodshed, and more deaths.

***

Xos stood in the temple of the palace. He stood in front of Brior's urn. He reached out to touch it, but he dared not touch it. He gritted his teeth.

"I will avenge you, brother," he said, almost to himself.

Fria was back in her quarters. She had refused to see him lately. She was convinced that he was a coward and a liar. She had even said that she wanted to go back to Earth with Verius. She had been so positive about him earlier, but now, due to the duelling, her mind had changed.

"She had said that," whispered Xos. "I'll show them all. I'm no coward."

"No, you're not," said a voice in his skull.

Xos spun around to see who said something, but he saw no one. There was just a faint mist curling around the floor of the temple.

"Who's there?" Xos said, trying not to have his voice falter, but failing.

138

"I will help you take your revenge, for yourself and for me," said the voice. It echoed around the stone columns of the temple but it seemed not to come from anywhere in particular. It was almost as if it were inside Xos' head.

"Show yourself," said Xos. Again, his voice tremored. He had no sword or spear here.

"I am here," said the voice and a man appeared from behind a pillar.

"How did you get in here?" asked Xos. He was worried he would have to fight the man, who looked in the peak of physical condition, but also had no weapons. He was dressed simply in a tunic and had a brilliant breastplate of shining gold, upon which were detailed with images of stags and hunting.

"I have always been here. This part of the temple is my own," said the voice. It echoed and boomed around the space in a simulated way.

"Who--?" began Xos.

"I am Apollo. One of the great AIs that you worship here in this temple," said the man.

Xos did not know what to say. He was in the presence of an AI! He did not know whether to kneel, or swear.

Apollo's mouth broke into a faint smirk. "I can tell what you're thinking. No, no, don't shy away. I find it amusing what you humans think of us."

"How…can I help?" asked Xos.

"Always down to business, good man," said Apollo. He moved towards Xos and lay a hand on his shoulder.

"Are you really real? Or am I just seeing you?" said Xos. He sort of felt the touch of the AI on his shoulder. It was a tingling, electric feeling, rather than a physical touch.

"Does it matter? I am here," Apollo put a hand on Xos' head, "and as such, I am real enough for you."

"No, I mean, are you actually the AI?" said Xos.

139

"Of course I am!" bellowed Apollo. "Who else would I be?" The stones of the temple shook. The mist increased.

Xos grovelled. "Forgive me!"

Apollo snorted a laugh. "You are forgiven. Your kind are always doubting. I have a task for you to do. Follow me."

Apollo turned and made a path through the mist. Xos followed him. They went through the temple and back towards the altar with the computer stacks that were stationed behind it. The stacks were shrouded in mist.

On the walls around the computer stack and server racks, there were the weapons of old times. They were attached to the walls.

Apollo picked down one from the wall. He tested it. It still worked even with no ammunition. It made a faint click noise when he pulled the trigger.

"I want you to use this, and kill Arakus," said Apollo.

"But, those are forbidden. Rifles, guns, are banned by Solar Law. I can't—"

"Yes you can. I order you to," said Apollo. "Do you deny the rule of the AIs?"

"No, but—"

"No 'buts'," Apollo held up a hand. "I give you permission. You are to take this rifle, and kill Arakus."

"Doesn't it need bullets?" said Xos.

Apollo smiled. "Indeed it does," he said, holding the rifle out to Xos in one hand he produced some bullets in the other hand.

Xos took the rifle, which was surprisingly heavy, in one hand and the bullets in the other.

"You know how to use it?" asked Apollo.

"I do," said Xos. He put down the rifle on the altar and loaded the bullets into the magazine. He then put the magazine inside the gun and it clicked home.

"Always ingenious, you humans. You ban something, but you still know how to use it centuries later," said Apollo.

"Will it still work after all this time?" asked Xos.

"Try it," said Apollo, pointing at a pillar.

"Won't people hear me?"

"Not if I deaden their hearing," said Apollo. He raised his arms and then said, "Go ahead."

Xos, hesitantly, aimed at the pillar a good distance away. He peered down the sight, and then pulled the trigger.

There was a massive bang which echoed and rolled around the stone temple. Xos flinched, but the bullet hit home and took a chunk out of the stone pillar.

"See, it works. Don't do it again because I have restored the hearing of the nearby guards," said Apollo.

"How will I get it out of here?" asked Xos.

"I will disguise it in the minds of all those around as a bow. It will look and seem like a bow to all those to look upon it. Trust me. You will not be caught," said Apollo. He looked around the temple.

"What are these bullets?" asked Xos.

"They are special bullets. They will kill any augmented human being. They will introduce a virus into the mechanical systems causing them to shut down. Be careful with them. They are rare. You only have five shots," said Apollo.

"I only need one," said Xos, hefting the rifle.

"Good. Now, I must go," said Apollo. He turned back to the altar.

"Wait, one more question, why?" said Xos. He had to know.

"Why what?"

"Why give me this to kill Arakus?"

"Because you are here, and are grieving, and I know I can rely on you," said Apollo. Turning back to Xos.

141

"No, I understand that, but why do YOU want Arakus dead?"

Apollo smirked, "Because he defiled my server node on the first day of the war. He is unclean and impure. He is simply built for killing. He does nothing else. And as such he must be killed as an affront to all humans."

"I see," said Xos, nodding.

"No, you don't. He will be worshipped and sung about for millennia to come. His name will mean strength and power. He will be the hero of heroes worshipped for an age," said Apollo, carefully regarding Xos with burning eyes.

"Because I kill him. Because he dies here, on the field of battle. He dies and becomes immortal," said Xos, looking at the rifle.

"Now you see. And your next question is, 'what becomes of you'?"

Xos nodded.

"You will be remembered," said Apollo, turning back to the Altar and moving behind one of the server stacks.

"For good deeds?" said Xos. Looking to where Apollo once was.

There was no reply.

"For good deeds?" shouted Xos.

Again, no reply. The mist began to recede, and the sounds of the palace began to filter back through the temple.

Xos looked down at the rifle. He shuddered. He had to do it. He would have to test it.

Xos walked out of the temple, not looking at the chunk of stone missing from one of the pillars, and out into the corridors of the palace.

Every time he passed a guard, he expected to be arrested, but nothing happened. They did not look twice at him. They did not even look at the gun.

When he reached his rooms, Xos hid the rifle under his bed. He went to sleep fitfully. Fria was not with him. She was somewhere else in the palace now.

***

Xos sat on the battlements. He watched the games going on. He saw the two figures run from the group and touch the walls of the Citadel. He saw them run back towards their camp.

Xos held in his hands an old rifle. It was from the Palace armoury. It was illegal, Xos knew, to use such a weapon these days. It was ruled that only sword and spear could be used. Ranged weapons such as rifles had been commonplace centuries ago on Earth, but due to the devastation they caused, they had been outlawed and now only visceral weapons could be used. It was thought that this would discourage wars. It did not work. Swords, spears, and bows maimed just as well.

"Why can't I use this?" Xos said to himself. He cradled the rifle. He looked through its vision sight which had magnification. He could see the runners clearly.

Xos scanned the Plains. He was sick of being stuck here. He would kill someone with these bullets. He would make them all pay for trapping him here. All he wanted was to be with the AI Fria. Now she had turned against him too. She viewed him as a coward. He would show them all who the coward was.

In one Titan day, he would make someone pay. He would make their implants shut down. He would show that he was not a coward.

143

Chapter 14

"Arakus, listen to me," said Sius.

"The day is up," said Arakus in his quarters. He put on his armour, grabbed his spear, sword, and shield.

"Take it easy, Arakus," said Sius. He too was already dressed in his full armour. His helmet plume stood proudly on his head.

"Take it easy? Take it easy? I'm going to kill every single one of them. I'm going to slaughter the entire Titan Citadel's population myself. They will all feel the wrath of Arakus. They will all burn," Arakus spat the words.

"You're angry. I know. I see that. Come on, Arakus, calm down," said Sius. He reached out a hand to Arakus' shoulder.

"I don't need your sympathy," snapped Arakus. He shrugged off Sius' hand.

"Cockiness like that will get you killed," said Sius.

"I don't need your advice either," said Arakus. Arakus shouldered past Sius.

"Then listen to a general," snapped Sius, turning.

Arakus stopped, his back to Sius in the doorway of his quarters. He cocked his head to one side as if indicating that he was listening.

"I'm older than you, Arakus, I have more life experience. I have more battle experience. I have felt like you do now.

You're not unique in that regard. I know what you're going through. Listen to me. If you go out on the battlefield with revenge mentality, you will be hurt. You could die," said Sius.

"I am invincible," said Arakus, still with his back towards Sius.

Sius sighed. "No one is invincible," he said.

"I am," yelled Arakus as he left his quarters. "I have been blessed with implants that mean I will never die."

Sius sighed again. "Why do kids think that they are immune to all damage?"

**

Arakus raged through the camp. How dare Sius challenge him like that. He would have to show the old man a lesson when he returned to camp. Arakus was sure that no one would have a higher kill count than him this day.

Rousing his soldiers, Arakus stood at the head of a column of the best soldiers in the Cerv army.

He turned to face them and shouted; his voice amplified by his implants. "My soldiers, today is the day we burn the Citadel on Titan to the ground. I will lead you to the main gates of the Citadel. We will kill every living Titan in our path. We will do it for Drebus. We will end this war. We will win. What say you?"

"A-hoo!" yelled the Kiyerons in front of him. They clashed their spears and shields.

The morning Sun filtered down through the thick clouds and cast eerie rays across the camp. Some rays fell on Arakus. He looked skyward and felt the faint warmth on his face. He closed his eyes and listened. He heard the men, restless in front of him. They shuffled in their armoured boots. He heard the sounds of the Citadel far away, through his enhanced hearing. He heard the Cerv camp coming to life in the morning and the other soldiers of the other generals massing and heading out for war. He heard it all, and he knew, that this would be the

145

last day of the Titans. He knew that he would carry his soldiers into the Citadel and avenge Drebus.

He opened his eyes and said, "March!"

At the head of the column, Arakus led his soldiers out onto the Plains of Titan. He marched at the head of them. He could see, through his enhanced vision, the soldiers of the Citadel had massed ahead of their walls again. And he knew, that once again, there would be terrible bloodshed. He grinned. This was what he lived for.

Arakus and his Kiyerons had lined up in front of the Titans, Right in the front and centre of the battlefield. To their left was Sius and his forces. To their right was Verius and Oreson and their soldiers. Beyond them on both sides were many more soldiers of other generals.

"We end this today," shouted out Arakus. "Charge!"

Arakus had started running before the word of attack left his mouth. The rest of his soldiers followed him. Sius, Verius, Oreson, and all their soldiers moved in to attack too. And then there was indeed terrible bloodshed.

Arakus raised his shield and spear and crashed in to the Titan front rank. The unstoppable force met the immovable object. Spears splintered and shields clashed. Energy weapons discharged.

Right behind Arakus, his Kiyerons slammed into the Titans a few seconds later. The force of all the Kiyeron shields began to push the Titans back.

Arakus' dropped his shattered spear and drew his sword. He swung out with his shield and created a pocket of air around himself. He slashed and hacked with his sword. Titan after Titan fell to his keen blade. One young Titan fell with his throat cut. One with his head smashed in with the shield. One with his intestines disembowelled. And so, it went on and on. Arakus slaughtered his way through the Titan ranks. He got ever closer and closer to the main gates of the Citadel.

The Kiyerons tried to keep pace with their leader, but Arakus simply outpaced all Cerv soldiers. He fought hard and killed many. He fought his way through towards the gates.

Arakus could not see Sius or Verius or Oreson. He could not really see any of his own men either. All he could see, through the slit in his helmet, was blood and death. His armour was slick with blood. He found it hard to hold his sword and shield they were so bloody. His kill counter in his vision racked up kills so rapidly that he lost track of where it was. He tasted blood; his enemies that had splattered onto his face, and his own from some head wounds he sustained through the slit in his helmet. But he knew that he was invincible. His body might take damage, but the nanites would keep him together, and his implants and mechanical augmentations would keep his body going. He was unstoppable. His energy reserves were still high. His mechanical arms and legs were powering along. He could not be stopped. No one would stand in his path. He would avenge Drebus and win this war here and now. Nothing could stop him. Ever.

Arakus laughed as he slaughtered. It was the laugh of a madman, he knew. He cackled with glee as he butchered his way through the Titan lines. There was a beauty and finesse about his augmented movements that gave him a grace and brutality that was unmatched. And all the while, he laughed.

***

Xos stood on the walls of the Citadel overlooking the battlefield below. In his arms he held the rifle. No one was on the walls to see him. No one had paid any attention to him as he had brought the rifle from the Temple to the walls.

Xos looked into the carnage below. They would all thank him for what he was going to do. No one would call him a coward any more. He would be a hero.

He saw the melee going on near the walls. He could only pick out one person in all the violence, and that was Arakus.

147

All the other fighters were either trying to avoid him, or bunched up in combat with other soldiers.

There was no avoiding Arakus, however. Xos could see the bloody path that he carved through the Titan ranks. He seemed to be laughing as he did so. It was the cackling glee of a madman.

The rifle felt cold and heavy in Xos' arms. He was still unsure if he could hit his target. The combat was moving so rapidly. Men were fighting and running all over the place.

Xos raised the rifle. He aimed. His target was moving fast, but he managed to keep pace with him. The sight on the rifle was lined up with his target. He thought to himself, "This is for my brother!"

"Now, fire!" came a voice inside Xos' head. It sounded like the image of Apollo that had appeared to him in the Temple.

Xos pulled the trigger. The rifle kicked in his hands, but he held it. He saw that his target had paused and was staring up at the wall. Xos saw, through the site, that the man's face was full of rage.

Xos dropped the rifle. It clattered onto the battlements. It did not fall over into the combat below.

Watching his target below, Xos could not look away. He saw Arakus, his target, pause in his carnage. He began to limp. He seemed to be struggling to move properly. His left leg looked like it was not responding to his commands.

Arakus began to flail around. He could not move properly. His implants seemed to be misbehaving.

"What have you done to me?" Arakus yelled above the din of the battle. His voice carried so far that almost all those near him stopped fighting and simply watched. Friend and foe alike simply watched the hero begin to unravel.

Xos could not breathe. He watched, horror struck, as to what was going on.

Arakus began to thrash around as his limbs rebelled to his commands and then he over compensated to try to bring them into order.

Then he could not move. He was frozen to the spot. He looked back up at Xos on the walls and cried out a blood curdling scream which chilled Xos to the bone.

By now, there was no combat around the gate. All the soldiers had decided to watch this man come apart.

"What have I done?" whispered Xos.

"You are fulfilling your destiny," said the voice in his head.

Arakus collapsed on the ground, still thrashing his arms around. His legs had shut down. Xos knew what would happen. The virus would work its way up his legs into his torso and arms. Finally, his brain implants would shut down, killing him. It would not be fast. It would not be painless. It would not be heroic.

"This was why they were illegal," whispered Xos to himself. No one added any other comment, although he desperately wanted some sort of validation for his actions. Destiny seemed a very vague and ephemeral reason for killing like this.

A howl of blind rage came from what was left of Arakus writhing on the ground. His arms had shut down too. All that was left was his torso and head. He spewed vitriol on the Titans and all those who sought to kill him.

And then, the noise stopped.

"Is he dead?" asked Xos. He knew there was no one there to answer, but the voice in his head seemed to know.

"Yes," said the voice of Apollo. "I guided the shot to his leg, it was open and exposed, and mechanical."

"What happens now?" asked Xos.

"Now, you do as you please. Fight, or don't, it's up to you."

A mist had settled over the walls and out of one of the guard huts, that dotted the tops of the walls, a figure stepped out. Xos

149

could not be sure whether this figure was really there or not. He had a sort of ethereal quality about him. His features were almost too perfect. It was like the figure he had seen in the Temple. It hurt a little to look at him, so Xos saw him from the sides of his vision. This added to the doubt of whether he was there or not. It could have been a guard, Xos reasoned, coming to arrest him for illegal firearm usage…

"I am no guard," said the man. He was perfect in his proportions. His voice was musical. He stood in a white robe and had a golden glow about him.

"I saw you in the Temple?" said Xos, looking at the man through the periphery of his vision to minimise the pain in his head.

"Yes."

"You look different now," said Xos.

"This is my true form."

"It hurts," said Xos. He rubbed a temple with one hand and held onto the battlements with another.

"You'll get used to it."

"Apollo?" said Xos.

"Yes?"

"What do I do with that?" Xos pointed to the gun lying on the wall next to him.

"Return it to the Temple. No one will miss it."

"I don't want to go like that…" said Xos.

Apollo stayed silent.

"Why him?" said Xos.

"Why not? He killed your brother, and he defiled my dataslave and my servers. He had to die. He was impious and brash." The musical voice rose and fell.

Xos said nothing. He blinked a few times, and then realised that the pain in his head had gone. He looked around. There was no one there. He picked up the rifle and made his way back to the Palace and the Temple.

***

Arakus felt an impact on his leg. At first he paid it no heed. He thought some spear had impacted his mechanical implants. He kept hacking through the Titan lines. Soldier after soldier falling to his slashing blade and thrusting shield.

But then something was wrong. He started feeling interference in his movements. He began to feel a cold creeping up the sinews and circuits in one of his legs. He began to limp. He began to struggle.

Across his augmented vision, Arakus saw scrawling lines and patterns. They should not be there, he thought to himself. He rebooted his optic sensors, but the problem with his vision got worse every second. Nothing seemed to fix it.

He looked down at his right leg. It had begun to hurt. The hurt, he knew, was an indicator of damage. Something in his mechanical limbs was damaged.

Looking over his shoulder at his leg, he saw a wound. He saw sparking wires and circuits. This alone should not be a problem. His nanites would patch up the damage in seconds. Yet where were the nanites?

A distinct cold began creeping through his leg and up into his body. He had trouble walking. He tried to speak, but he had trouble talking too.

All too suddenly, he realised what this was. He had been shot with a banned weapon. He had been shot with a mech-killer bullet.

With this realisation came another realisation. He was going to die. He was going to die. He could not die. He was Arakus. He was unstoppable. He was invincible. He had implants from the Styx factory itself. He was immune to all damage. And yet, here he was, wounded with a mech-killer and he would die.

Feeling his limbs going heavy, Arakus began to flail around and thrash out at all the enemies around him. But

151

without the use of his feet and legs, he fell over. The enemies avoided him, many formed a circle around him, just out of range of his flailing arms.

Arakus howled. He let out a gut wrenching, spine chilling howl. It was a howl so violent it shook the AIs.

His vision was failing now. He saw corrupted lines of code and image artifacts flashing across his eyes.

He collapsed to the ground and rolled onto his back. He stared up at the sky and the battlements of the Citadel. He was dying; he could not die. He was dying.

As he searched the battlements where the shot must have come from, he saw two figures. One, indistinct and cowering behind part of the stone work. The other, shining, brilliant, in white robes. Clear to see as he would normally see an enemy soldier. This second figure was not corrupted by any visual artifacts. He seemed to be almost in Arakus' vision rather than part of the reality that was falling apart around him.

And then Arakus realised who it was. And the figure seemed as if to nod to him, acknowledging his realisation. It was Apollo. For all his indiscretions and impieties, he had been brought low by one of the AIs. Apollo had used some computer virus in mech-killer bullets to kill him.

Once more, Arakus let out a howl of blind rage and hate. He was going to die, and he had so many more to kill.

And then, as Arakus' vision faded for good. He lay there. His twitching stopped and his mechanical implants shut down. He died, and his consciousness slipped away to the electrical circuits of the afterlife where the mechanically augmented went. He crossed the Obsidian Gate and became one with the AIs.

***

Seeing Arakus fall, Sius rushed up and took up a guarding position over the body. As did Verius and the hero Orax. The three of them stood around the body of their fallen comrade and waited for the Kiyerons to create an honour guard.

Sius, back to back to back with Verius and Orax fought off attack after attack from the Titan forces. It was clear that they wanted to loot the fallen man's armour, which still shone with gold and silver accents as it lay there on the ground.

"Kiyerons, to me! To me!" shouted Sius above the din of battle that had resumed after Arakus had stopped howling.

Twenty of the Kiyerons formed up around the body. Six of them lifted the lifeless corpse of their leader up on their shoulders and they, with Sius, Verius and Orax fought their way through the Titan lines, back through towards the Cerv camp and away from the Citadel main gate.

As Sius looked back over his shoulder at the receding Citadel, he thought he saw a shape on the battlements. He enlarged his augmented vision and saw Xos, standing there, looking petrified. Had he used the mech-killer bullets? Where had he got them from? Why had he broken ancient laws?

But all these questions were in vain. He turned his eyes forward and continued with some of the Kiyerons, Verius, and Orax, back to the Cerv camp. No one said a word. The only sounds were the battle raging behind them, and the mechanical footfalls of the honour guard.

When they reached the camp, the guards fell silent as they passed inside the gate of the camp. Some even took off their helmets.

The Kiyerons deposited their fallen leader gently on his bed in his quarters. Sius and Verius stood beside the bed. Orax stood guard outside with the other Kiyerons who had left the battle.

The dataslave who was in the quarters began weeping as soon as she saw the body of the dead Arakus. She cried quietly in the corner of the room.

153

"What do we do with him?" asked Sius, looking down at the body of the man who had been so alive only hours before. He seemed to have shrunk in stature with his death, as if his spirit had kept him vital and alive, now gone, his physical form had collapsed.

"We honour him and bury him," said Verius.

Sius almost noted a choking of emotion in Verius' voice, but said nothing about it. He too could not believe what had happened. So, he simply nodded.

"We'll have to tell Oreson," said Verius after a while.

"And who gets his armour," said Sius.

Verius looked at Sius with eyes that chastised, but he said nothing.

"I mean really. It's no good on him now," said Sius. "It's a mighty fine shield, helmet, and breastplate."

"He's only been dead a few minutes and already you're looting his corpse?" said Verius.

Before Sius could respond, Oreson barged into the quarters. His helmet under his arm.

"What's happened? What's wrong? I heard…" Oreson said, rushing to the bedside.

"He's dead," said Sius.

Oreson put a hand on Arakus' armoured breastplate. He whispered a few words that Sius could not hear.

"We must honour him," said Oreson.

"Now? After all you did to him and all you called him? You want to honour him?" snapped Sius.

"He is a hero and must be honoured," said Verius through clenched teeth. "Speak with honour to our leader."

"The leader that got him killed?" said Sius.

"Enough!" boomed Oreson. His voice filled the quarters and silenced all bickering. "We will honour him and we will make sure that he is remembered."

Sius nodded, as did Verius.

154

"Organise a funeral. We must burn him," said Oreson. He turned on his heel and left Arakus' quarters.

Sius gave Verius a look; he then glanced over at the dataslave and shook his head in pity. Then he left the quarters too. He called the Kiyerons standing there to order.

"Gather wood and supplies. We must conduct a sacrifice and honour the dead hero. We must build a funeral pyre. He must go honoured to the afterlife," Sius said.

The Kiyerons nodded and began preparing for the funeral.

***

Sius stood at the side of the pyre that had been built near the Cerv camp. Oreson and Verius stood next to him, along with the High Priest. Even Krysi, Arakus dataslave, stood at a distance. Sius could hear her weeping quietly. There was a gathering of Cerv soldiers around the pyre. There was not a sound except for the faint weeping of the slave.

The ranks of the soldiers parted and, as one, the Kiyerons made a procession through the soldiers who parted for them. The Kiyerons were carrying the body of their fallen leader. It was wrapped in ceremonial clothing of red and gold. Most of his body was covered, but his face was left exposed. They carried Arakus' body with grace and deference. They were dressed in full battle uniform; plumes on their helmets in full view, armour, shields and spears carried with honour. Of the four men chosen actually to carry the body of the fallen hero, they carried no shields or spears, simply the body of Arakus on a camp stretcher perched on their shoulders.

Sius nodded to the Kiyerons and the four bearers placed the stretcher with the body on top of the funeral pyre. Then they, along with the other Kiyerons, stepped back and formed a circle around the pyre.

There was silence again, after the marching and clanking of the Kiyerons stopped when they stopped moving.

No one moved; no one spoke; there was still the faint weeping from off to the side. The wind whipped faintly at the forest of plumes that stretched out around the pyre.

Finally, the High Priest spoke. "Oh Arakus, hero of the Cerv forces, you departed this existence too young and too soon. We will mourn your passing, and we will win this war for you." He then fell silent.

Sius stepped forward towards the pyre. He touched the face of his fallen friend. He placed a coin on each eye.

"To pay the ferryman," he whispered softly. "Goodbye, my friend."

Then Sius laid his hand on Arakus' brow and then stepped back.

"Oh Arakus," he said after a pause. "Go with honour to the afterlife. Find your place in the server farms of the ether. You will be remembered for eternity." His voice boomed around the soldiers arrayed around the pyre.

Oreson then spoke. "Go Arakus, to beyond the Obsidian Gate. We will win this war and we will crush the opposition in your honour."

Sius could tell there was a hint of relief in Oreson's words. It was no secret that he saw the death of Arakus was good for him. But he did not want to argue at a time like this.

Verius simply stood there and let the others do the talking for him.

Sius held out a hand and one of the Kiyerons handed him a lighted torch. Sius looked to Oreson and Verius who both nodded. Sius stepped forward again and placed the torch in the flammable materials that made up the pyre.

The materials caught quickly and soon the pyre was ablaze.

Everyone took a few steps back at the ferocity of the blaze. They watched for a few minutes, then most of the soldiers broke rank and went back to doing what they were doing in the Cerv camp. Only Oreson, Verius, Sius, the High Priest, and Arakus' former dataslave, were left around the flames.

Those who remained stood and watched. Then the High Priest moved over to Oreson and whispered in his ear.

Sius saw Oreson go a shade of purple that meant he was angry in the extreme, and yet could not explode given the solemnity of the occasion.

After a second, Oreson said, "Sius, Verius, I have some information that is important." Then he turned to the High Priest, "Are you sure?"

"Sure of what?" asked Sius.

"Tell them," said Oreson, nodding to the High Priest.

"I uh, discovered something untoward when I was preparing the body of the fallen hero, Arakus," said the High Priest.

Sius' brow furrowed. "Go on," he said.

"I came across something that shouldn't be. I came across evidence of mech-killer virus deployed in a bullet that had punctured his leg," said the High Priest.

"Mech-killer? Here? Now? They're banned," said Verius.

Sius stayed silent and thought about it.

"That's what I thought," said Oreson. "Which cowardly bastard of the Titans used that?"

"I have an answer to that too," said the High Priest. He grinned to himself.

"Well?" said Oreson.

"Oh yes, well, I extracted the data from the last few minutes of Arakus' life that were recorded on his internal brain drive. I managed to see that the person who fired the shot, as Arakus looked up at the battlements, was none other than Prince Xos," said the High Priest.

"Coward," said Oreson.

"Shit," said Verius.

"I'll get him," said Sius.

The other three looked at him.

"Provide me with a mech-killer bullet, a rifle, and I'll get him. An eye for an eye," said Sius flatly.

"We can't—" began the High Priest.

"I have some locked away in my ship," said Oreson.

"But the law—" said the High Priest, bubbling over with incredulity.

"Shut up, Priest," said Verius. "Are you sure?" He turned to Sius.

Sius nodded. "I'm a good shot, and this is personal. If he goes back on the battlements, I'll get him."

"Meet me in my ship. I'll get you what you need," said Oreson. He then set off for the Cerv camp.

"This will take a while to burn down, then the Kiyerons will salvage the ashes and bury them here. There's no point in waiting around for hours," said Verius. He headed off after his brother.

Sius stood and watched the flames roar into the sky. Small particles whipped up by the heat carried high into the air and formed a carpet of stars in the middle of the day. Sius watched those stars flash and burn into ash and fall to the ground.

"Campfires of the dead…" Sius whispered to himself.

"Eh?" said the High Priest who was still waiting around nervously wringing his wrists.

"Nothing," said Sius. Then he turned to the man and said. "Well done on finding the details out about the mech-killer shot."

"I uh, yes, good. I'm glad, well not glad as such but, yes, ahem…" the Priest tried to find the words.

Sius smiled. "You disapprove," he said.

"Yes," said the High Priest.

"Why? This is war. We fight with tooth and claw, and we win," said Sius.

"But what about standards? Honour? Dignity? Laws!" said the Priest. He held out his hands to Sius imploringly,

"I once thought like that. Now it's just endless killing. In war, everything boils down to the lowest common denominator," said Sius, staring into the flames.

"Which is?" said the High Priest exasperatedly. It was clear to Sius that he knew he was losing the argument.

"Death," said Sius. "The faster death comes for the other side, the better for our side, and vice versa." He smirked sadly.

The High Priest sighed and began walking back to the camp, mumbling something about no one listening and mech-killer bullets.

Sius looked over at the weeping dataslave, who was still standing at a distance. He looked at her. She was in a light blue robe. She was pretty; and young. She was crying quietly. "What do we do with you?" he said to her.

She looked at him and the look broke his heart.

"Come on," he said. He held out an arm.

She hesitated.

"I won't mistreat you," Sius said.

She shuffled over to him. He put an arm around her shoulders. They walked together back to the camp; back to Sius' quarters.

Sius knew he was only partially telling the truth.

***

Sius left the dataslave in his quarters. He then headed towards Oreson's personal ship. Stepping inside the wide opening that was in the side of the machine, Sius waited for his eyes to adjust in the gloom.

There he saw, in the loading bay, Oreson waiting for him. The loading bay was a dull metallic colour and full of cargo still, supplies for the war. It was located in the front of the ship and had large openable ramps and doors that folded outwards and allowed easy access for soldiers to embark and disembark.

159

There were a few guards standing in the docking bay, but most of the soldiers in the camp lived and worked in the camp itself. The ships had become simple store houses for now.

"Come with me," said Oreson. He beckoned to Sius and turned to exit the docking bay and head into the bowels of the ship.

Sius nodded and headed after his leader. Walking a few paces behind Oreson, Sius saw various guards on certain doors of the ship. He tried not to catch their eye.

Sius almost cursed himself. He knew he was about to break solar law. He was going to use mech-killer bullets. And yet, somehow, he felt good about it. He felt that he was doing the right thing. That avenging Arakus' death was somehow just. And yet he knew that death and hate only beget death and hate. He should simply honour the dead and continue living.

He thought this as he traversed the ship. They went deeper and deeper into the internal corridors, down and down into the ship.

Oreson said nothing to him. He said nothing to Oreson. They simply walked, one ahead of the other, through the vibrating and clanging ship, passed guards on certain doors, and always in silence.

It was the silence that killed Sius. He wished that Oreson would talk to him; that somehow he would break the silence and tell him that he was about to do the right thing. And yet, Sius knew, that he was not doing the right thing. Xos had killed Arakus with mech-killer bullets, and now he was going to return the favour.

He had seen what mech-killer bullets could do. They had been outlawed for many decades, but they appeared in the population at various times. But this was the first time they were used in this war; at this time; in this place.

Finally, they reached the armoury. There was a guard on either side of a large, metal blast door that, when instructed, typed in some codes into keypads on the sides of the door. After a short wait, the door split down the middle and receded into the walls with a grinding hiss of hydraulics.

Oreson stepped inside and flicked a switch on the side of the room. The room lit up with light strips which flickered to life and cast a harsh light across the crates and weapons that Sius could see inside.

Sius stepped into the armoury and waited for instructions.

"This way," said Oreson. He moved through the ranks and ranks of shields and shock spears and swords that were propped up on racks. They were arrayed in rows across the floor and walls.

Sius followed. He knew all these weapons. They were standard issue. He had used most of their kind many times.

Within the harshly lit armoury, there was another door, also locked with an alphanumeric code. Oreson stopped in front of it and typed in the secret code, making sure that no one could see, even though the only person there was Sius.

There was a click and the door slid open. Inside, also lit by strip lights, was a small room with an armoured crate on the floor that was covered in a large cloak like cloth.

Oreson typed in another code on the crate and it opened. He pulled out a weapon and turned to Sius.

"This will be your gun," said Oreson calmly.

Sius noted that Oreson's hands were not shaking. He took the gun from Oreson. Sius' hands were shaking. He tried to still them.

"Is it loaded?" asked Sius.

"Yes," said Oreson. "With mech-killers."

"How many shots?"

"Thirty."

"Thirty!" exclaimed Sius. "I only need one."

"I hope you're right. And I hope that this does not escalate things. Wars have a nasty way of escalating. One death prompts another," said Oreson. He grimaced.

"I know that all too well," said Sius. "How do I get this out of here? Without being arrested by some goody goody soldier?"

"I will give my guards instructions to let you pass. And then perhaps conceal it under this cloth," said Oreson. He handed Sius the large cloak that he could wrap the gun in.

Sius hastily wrapped the gun in the cloak. He carried it under his arm.

"Do you need to practice?" asked Oreson.

"No," said Sius. "I'm quite a good shot."

Oreson nodded. "So I have heard. We'd better go," he said, looking towards the doors of the armoury. "Wait here while I tell the guards the plan. They will listen to me."

"Wait," said Sius. "How did you get this here?" He indicated the gun.

"I had a feeling we might need it," is all Oreson said and walked out of the small room leaving Sius there, a little stunned.

Sius waited a few minutes, the rifle felt heavy under his arm. The weight of what he was about to do was heavier.

When the tension became too much, and he hoped that Oreson had told all the guards, Sius headed out of the armoury and through the rest of the ship. All the way he felt eyes on him as if he were about to be arrested. He felt the hairs on his neck stand on end every time he went by a guard, expecting a hand on the shoulder and a swift hit from a spear. He expected the gun to fall from his hands and clatter across the floor, exposing him as a war criminal.

But nothing happened. He walked straight out of the ship and down the ramp. He walked back into the faint Titan light. He looked up at the sky. He saw the thick cloud cover. He

162

looked around. He saw the buzzing Cerv camp. He breathed deeply and tasted the thick air and smells of the camp. He felt his implants and mechanical augmentations straining against the weight of the rifle.

"Here we go," he said.

Sius headed back to his quarters and stashed the rifle under his bed. He would not be able to use it yet. They were not fighting at the moment. There was still more to be done regarding Arakus' funeral. He still had to deal with the dead before he could deal with the living.

***

Sius stepped out of his quarters and was confronted by Orax.

"There you are," Orax said. "I've been looking for you."

"What?" said Sius. He looked sideways at Orax. Had the man seen him bringing the rifle back to his quarters?

"We must decide who gets the armour of Arakus!" said Orax, poking Sius in the chest.

"Yes, we must decide!" shouted out some of the Kiyerons who were nearby.

"Well clearly I should get the armour as I was his friend," said Sius calmly.

"Preposterous!" bellowed Orax. "I should get the armour. I am far braver than you. I was first on the body when Arakus was killed!"

"Did you know Arakus?" said Sius, still calmly.

"Well…not well, but why should you get the armour? You're simply a farmer. You cannot be as brave as me," said Orax.

By now a few bystanders had gathered in a circle around the pair. They jostled and pushed to get a better view. They were soldiers from all divisions of the Cerv army.

"I disagree," said Sius. He was still speaking calmly, even though his insides seethed. How dare this man insult him. How dare he greedily demand the armour of his friend. How dare he cause a fuss over the matter. But Sius knew that Orax was a great warrior. He was taller and broader than Sius. His implants were massive and extensive too. He had both his arms and legs replaced and half his skull was metal and contained a great deal of circuitry and augmentations.

"You insult me?" snapped Orax.

"No, I just disagree with your position," said Sius.

Orax's hand fell to his sword.

Sius thought he might need a mech-killer bullet soon. He cursed that he had put the rifle away. His hand also fell to the sword on his waist.

More soldiers had gathered around the pair. They had started taking bets as to who would win the contest that was invariably brewing.

Then Oreson appeared in the crowd. He shouldered his way to the front and shouted, "What's going on here?"

"This gentleman wants Arakus' armour," said Sius. "I've told him no, I get it."

"Why, when there's always trouble, are you there, Sius?" said Oreson shaking his head.

"It just seems to follow me around. It proves that I am braver than him," Sius said, poking Orax in the chest.

Orax's remaining face had turned purple. He looked, to Sius, as if he were about to explode.

"Careful," said Sius, "or steam will come out your ears as the circuits melt." He grinned wryly to himself.

"Why you upstart little—" began Orax.

Oreson stepped between the pair and kept them apart with his augmented arms. "I have a way of deciding. Let's talk to some of the Titan prisoners of the last battle. They will decide who is worthy of the armour."

"Fair enough," said Sius.

"I…uh…what," stammered Orax.

"Careful, he might have a thought," said Sius.

Orax took a swing at Sius. Sius dodged out of the way easily.

"Easy now," said Oreson, straining to keep the pair apart.

Finally, Orax relented and the pair, with Oreson and the onlookers moved to a part of the camp that was reserved for the prisoners that they had captured. It was a large part of a ship that had been cut up and disassembled into a prison with multiple prisoners held in barred cells.

As the crowd approached, Sius saw that some of the prisoners approached the bars to see what was happening.

The procession stopped outside the nearest barred cell in the wall of one of the Cerv ships. They were the prisoners from the battle where Arakus fell.

"Prisoners, we have a task for you," called out Oreson.

Sius and Orax stood near the prison bars. The onlookers gathered around. The prisoners looked dejected, but pleased that none of them had been sentenced to execution yet.

Orax stood tall and proud, showing off his augmented muscles.

Sius simply rolled his eyes. "Get on with it," he said under his breath.

Oreson glared at Sius. "We need you to pick the braver of these two men in order to award Arakus' armour."

"And you want us to decide?" said one of the prisoners.

"Yes," said Oreson.

There was more betting on who would win in the soldiers crowding around.

After a short time talking quietly to each other, the prisoners came back with a decision.

While this was going on, Sius stood staring at the sky. Orax was showing off his augmentations and mechanical limbs.

"We have decided," said the same prisoner.

"Well, out with it!" said Oreson.

"Well, due to his continued fighting, we choose Sius."

"See? What did I tell you I…wait…what?" said Orax.

Sius grinned.

There was uproar as the bets of the onlooking soldiers were won and lost.

"How dare you!" yelled Orax. "You're a scheming coward!"

"Who beat you, so what does that make you?" said Sius. He nodded to the prisoners. "Bring the armour to my quarters," he said to Oreson.

Sius walked back to his quarters, leaving Orax to turn purple again. Sius worried for those prisoners' safety.

The crowd dispersed and Sius walked back to his quarters.

He entered his rooms erected on the sides of his ship. He sat down on the edge of his bed. He looked over to his table which had been restocked with fruit and bread and wine by the dataslaves. He sighed.

Oreson appeared with the armour of Arakus and deposited it on the table. He then nodded and left the room without a word.

Sius sighed again. He got up and moved to the table. He touched the plumed helmet, the ornate breastplate, and the gold and silver adorned shield. The side of his mouth twitched into a smile.

"Goodbye, my friend," he said.

He donned the armour. It felt light, but he knew it was made by the Hephaestus machine itself. There was no equal.

Sius made sure that he had his sword and grabbed his spear. He hefted the shield. Strangely, even though it was very strong, it felt light. He realised that that was the expert nature in its construction. It was super strong, but very light, allowing expert movement and thrust of his spear.

Sius gave a few practice thrusts of the spear and covering himself with the shield. He smiled.

He then set down the shield and spear and moved to the bed. He fetched the rifle from underneath it and stared at it as it lay on top of his bed. A chill ran down his spine. This was a less civilised weapon, from an older and darker time. It was black and angular. It had a scope on top for assisted aiming over distance, but his augmented eyes would do the job too.

It felt cold as he touched it. He picked up the rifle and felt its weight. It was heavy in his hands, but he knew how to use it.

After a few practice aims he slung it over his shoulder on the strap attached to it.

Night was falling and he knew that this would be his chance to take revenge. He hoped that the man on the battlements was still there. He suspected he would be, torn and conflicted about what he had done to Arakus. He would be there, forever, pining over using mech-killer bullets. It's what Sius knew he would do. And therefore, he assumed the young man would too.

As night fell and the faint shadows lengthened around the Cerv camp, Sius slipped out of the camp unseen and headed across the Plains of Titan towards the Citadel walls. He would lie in wait for the figure that had ended Arakus. He would wait, and then he would end that young man's life. If Prince Xos appeared, he would die.

Chapter 15

Night fell across the moon of Titan, and Sius crept, with the aid of his augmented eyes, through the dark. The terrain was lit silver in his vision, with the sky a dull grey. He saw readouts on his optical sensors of what was going on in the terrain.

Sius avoided the scavengers, those picking over the remains of the corpses left on the battlefield. He pitied the corpses; without burial they would not proceed to the afterlife. And now their bodies were being ransacked by greedy peasants for survival and soldiers for riches.

As Sius crept, doubled over and slowly to avoid detection, he pondered the peasants. There were people living outside the Citadel walls. In fact, there were many settlements all around. But the Cerv army was only at war with the Citadel of Titan. And so, they left the people who lived on the Plains of Titan, near and far, mostly alone. Mostly, he smirked to himself. It was known that the Cerv army did ransack a number of villages in the early years, but that had stopped on Oreson's orders, officially. What actually happened…Sius grimaced and stopped the thought.

He reached a dry river bed, that eons ago would have been flowing with liquid methane before the terraforming. Its floor now simply smooth stones and shallow sides. He made his way along this dry river, it's banks protecting him from being seen by people along the Plains.

The Plains were ringed and dotted by hills and mountains on three sides, with what had been a great sea of methane, now gone and simple sand, where the Cerv ships had landed.

Suddenly, Sius heard a crunch of a small stone being disturbed behind him. He spun around and saw a child. The child was oblivious to him. She had not seen Sius in the dark. But Sius saw her lit up like a beacon in his vision. She glowed in the dark, a greenish flare in his vision.

Sius knew that if he moved, she would hear him. If she heard him, she would alert the others to his presence. She was clearly moving along the river bed to get onto the battlefield in order to loot some corpses. She had not got the implants to her vision that he had. She was probably too poor to have them. And she was certainly too young.

Thinking quickly, Sius picked up a small stone and threw it, hard, over the child's head and off in the other direction he was going.

The child, unaware of her danger, heard the sound and was startled. She looked around, and then quickly ran off in the other direction, away from Sius, and away from the battlefield.

Sius smiled, and breathed a sigh of relief. He realised that he had is hand on his sword. That was the second option, if the small stone had not worked. He was glad that it had. He released the hilt of his sword. He was now breathing again. He continued along the dry river bed.

He came to the part of the river that curved away from the Citadel walls and off into the distance. Sius crouched on the bank facing the walls. He scanned the battlements. He could not see from this position.

Looking around, Sius saw that there was a small hill a little way from the Citadel walls and near to his location. He scanned the terrain in between. There were a few search lights from the Citadel walls that were scanning the ground around the walls, but the hill was outside their reach. He began the stooped scramble towards the hill from the river bed.

For the first time in the journey, he felt the weight of the rifle slung across his back. It felt heavy, too heavy. If he were

169

just using normal bullets, unlikely to kill an augmented human, there would be no issue. But he was going to use mech-killer bullets. They were illegal across the Solar System. They meant certain death to any augmented soul.

Sius told himself as he moved low across the terrain, that he could not go back now. That he had accepted this task, but he knew the weight of his decision. If it was ever found out that he used mech-killers, his life would be forfeit. It would be another horrid thing from this horrid war.

And then, he suddenly felt hatred. Hatred for Prince Xos, who had stolen the AI and had taken her to this place. He had made sure that the war started. It was his fault, and Sius knew that with his death, the war would be almost over. This hate gave him purpose. It told him what to do. It made sure that he had left his wife and family and farms. It was the reason for him being here. Xos must die. Sius knew that he was the man to do it, and that Xos deserved it.

Sius reached the small hill and climbed up its rough, rocky slope. He took up a prone position just below the crown of the hill and unslung the rifle from his shoulder. He took aim at the battlements through the scope, which further augmented his already modified vision. He scanned the battlements and saw the odd guard.

But there was something different! There was a man, slumped against the ramparts. He seemed different. He wore armour, but the augmentation in his vision told Sius that this was his target. They identified the slumped man as Xos.

Sius took aim. He centred the target site on his foe. He aimed carefully. He knew that once the shot rang out, his position would be revealed, and he would have to hurry back to the Cerv camp.

Sius stilled his breathing. He paused. This was the right thing to do. This man had killed his friend. This man had brought mech-killers to the battlefield. This man had started this war. This man was guilty of so many crimes.

Sius aimed, and pulled the trigger.

Chapter 16

Xos sat on the battlements. He leaned against the stone parapet of the wall and looked out over the ghostly battlefield below. It was night time but he could not sleep. He had not slept in days. All that was keeping him going were his implants and the shame he felt.

Torch light flickered off the battlements. There were no guards on this section of the walls. Simply lighted torches and the search lights that tracked back and forth across the open section of the land between the wall and the battlefield.

He had considered hanging himself from the battlements, or jumping off them.

Xos looked out with blurry vision, partly due to fatigue and partly due to his optical implants straining to see in the low light beyond the search lights. He saw bodies littering the battlefield. He thought that he should be one of them.

Fria had abandoned him. Between the running away from combat and when he had told her about the mech-killer shot against Arakus, she had left him. She had called him a coward. He knew it was true.

He had brought this war upon Titan. That was also true. He had stolen the AI from Verius and had caused this mess. It was all his fault. And he could not see an end to it.

Perhaps he could give the AI back? Would the Cerv army leave if he gave back Fria? He doubted it. The Cerv army was so bent on ransacking the Citadel, that he was sure simply giving back Fria would not be enough after ten years of war. Especially with the death of Arakus and the fact that he, a Prince of Titan was still alive. No, it would never work.

Xos was exhausted. He slumped against the battlements. He scanned the surrounding terrain. He did not know what he was doing here, on top of the wall. Should he jump? It was a long way to the ground. Perhaps his implants would keep him alive and he would simply be maimed. Perhaps he would break his neck and die. Perhaps. Perhaps.

What was that? Xos saw some movement in the distance along a dry river bed that passed by the Citadel walls. Then there was nothing. The movement stopped.

Xos focussed his blurry vision on the river bed, but he saw nothing more from it. He knew that there were scavengers on the battlefield from other villages around the Citadel. Perhaps it was one of them. They picked the bodies clean that were still left on the battlefield. Xos pondered whether they or he were less liked.

Then there was movement again! This time from a hill near a curve in the river. There were no bodies up there, Xos could see, yet there was someone there. A Cerv spy? Should he report this? Or simply let Fate unfold. His thread, he knew, was almost cut, and should have been long ago, to avoid all this war.

Xos looked at the small form that he saw quite a way away on the hill. He stared at him. Xos could not make out who it was, but they seemed to be lying down on the top of the hill and balancing something.

Then it clicked in Xos' head. That was a rifle like the one he had used. This was Fate. This was Destiny. The man holding the rifle was unknown. Xos could not determine who it was in the dark with his augmented vision. But he could see the gun and the form of the man.

Xos wondered if the man was aiming at him. At this distance if was hard to tell. He could have been aiming at anyone or anything along the wall. Also, he could have been waiting for the battle to start when the Sun came. Waiting. Watching.

Then he saw the gun aim in his direction. It pointed straight at him. This was the end, Xos knew. He hoped they were mech-killer bullets, so the end would be swift. He did not want to be shot with normal bullets and simply maimed and rendered a cripple in the hospital while the nanites healed him slowly.

But who would use mech-killers? He had, he reasoned, so it seemed only fitting that he suffer the same fate.

Fate, Xos thought to himself. What was his Fate?

Why did the gunman not shoot? Damn it! Fire! Fire! Fire! Xos almost cried out for the anonymous man to stop waiting and shoot.

Then there was a flash and a second later a crack and Xos felt an impact in his torso.

Xos fell back against the wall. He felt the impact, but he did not feel the pain straight away. Then the pain leeched back. into his body over a few seconds that seemed like minutes, hours.

He could breathe, but as he sat up again he saw that the bullet had entered his left mechanical lung. He was getting damage readouts flickering across his vision.

And then it happened. He suddenly found it hard to breathe. His heart went into overdrive. Chemicals were forced around his body. His vision started to blur even more. The damage readouts flooded his sight.

They were mech-killers. He had met his Fate. He knew what was coming.

174

Xos' hands trembled violently. His legs locked up.

He propped himself up against the battlements and sat down. His vision was scrawled with damage readouts.

Xos felt the confusion inside his mind and body as the nanites were reprogrammed by the virus in the bullet to attack his own system. This was why it was illegal, Xos thought. Or at least, tried to think.

His vision began to fade. It was not unpleasant. It was painful, but not agony. But he knew he was dying.

Arakus had screamed and thrashed and resisted. Xos saw that man's death flit across his mind's eye. He, on the other hand, simply sat there and felt his body shut down. He sat, propped against the battlements, and died.

***

Pyrakra stumbled through the Palace. She had seen something in a dream. She had seen the death of Prince Xos. She had seen that he was slumped on the battlements. She had dreamed his death.

She knew that it could not be real, but it had been so realistic. She had seen the whole scene play out. It was so real she had cried out in her sleep and woken herself. Her sheets were soaked with cold sweat. She had hurried out of her rooms in her night attire. She had not bothered to dress fully.

Pyrakra felt the cold stones of the floor of the Palace on her bare feet. She hurried through the winding corridors. She had to see for herself. She had to see.

As she left the Palace doors and headed down the hill into the Citadel, the guards paid her no heed. They were used to her shambling about at odd hours.

As the cool air whipped at her skin, the faint hairs on her bare arms stood up on end. The bulk of Saturn stood in the night sky above her. It dominated the heavens. She spun around and around in the courtyard outside the Palace gates.

The Citadel was quiet. Most people were either sleeping or preparing for war. The sounds of machines filtered through the air, preparing weapons and armour. The smells of burning torches and cooking wafted on the night breeze.

Pyrakra stopped spinning around and headed towards the wall around the Citadel. Her bare feet scuffed on the cobblestones and pavements of the Citadel city streets. She got the odd strange look from some people as she shuffled past. But she did not care. She kept going, the image of dead Xos burned into her subconscious. She had seen him. She had seen…something.

Stumbling in an almost dream like state, her night attire swishing in the cool breeze, she came to the Citadel walls. She put a hand on the stairs that would lead to the top. She hesitated. Did she really want to know? She had come this far, but she did not know whether she wanted to discover if she had seen the truth again, or whether she had been dreaming.

Who was she kidding, she thought to herself. Her dreams always came true. She was cursed. And no one listened.

Breathing in the cold, night air, Pyrakra steeled herself and climbed the stairs to this part of the wall. Each step up was torture. Each step she hesitated and wondered if she wanted to take the next one, but she did, she always did.

Finally, she reached the top and looked around. There were no guards here. This was a quiet part of the wall. The Cerv forces did not attack here.

In the light of the burning torches, and the searchlights that carved a path through the darkness on the outside of the wall, Pyrakra could see a slumped form, leaning against the battlements.

She let out a small yelp and then covered her mouth. She could not see the person's face. She could not tell who it was. But it was someone, like in her dream.

176

With trembling legs, Pyrakra stepped onto the wall and moved towards the body. She stood over it and pulled the form into the light of one of the torches that was nearby. She rolled the body over and saw, it was Xos.

She let out a real cry this time. She pawed at his face. She had seen this. She had seen it all. She knew what was going to happen to them. And no one believed her. No one.

Pyrakra collapsed in her thin night dress onto the battlements and cried. She cradled Xos' head in her arms and wailed.

Soon, a couple of guards came to investigate. They saw her and the dead Prince. They talked gently to her, but she could not hear them through her sobs. She thought they said they would get her father, but she could not be sure.

She sat there with the dead Xos, and cried.

After a while, her father arrived with some guards. He climbed the wall. He was dressed in casual dress thrown over night attire. He too, had not dressed properly.

Pyrakra looked at her father through her tears. She could see his face was contorted with grief.

"My boy. My beautiful boy," Zoriam said quietly. "What have they done to you?"

Only then, did Pyrakra notice the hole in Xos' chest. She had been so grief stricken that she had not noticed that he had what looked like a bullet wound in his chest.

She looked down at her hands, that had been holding the corpse, and noticed that they were covered in blood. In fact, her night dress also had blood on it. She wiped her hands on the white night dress and more blood came off onto it. And yet, she could not get all the blood off her hands. She wiped and wiped, and some blood stayed, crusted and dry, on her hands.

Pyrakra had seen this in her dreams too, and she felt a shiver run down her spine.

"How did you know about this?" snapped Zoriam after cradling his dead son's head for a while. "How did you know?"

Pyrakra looked with wide eyes at her father and did not know how to answer. She shook her head.

"How did you know he was here? Damn you, child. Answer me!" Zoriam stared at Pyrakra with rage.

"I, I don't know, father. I just know things. And no one listens to me when I try and tell them what's going on," said Pyrakra. Her voice trailed off while looking at her father's face.

"I don't believe you," spat Zoriam. "Now go back to your quarters and stay there. And get out of those bloody clothes and put on new ones. But stay in your rooms. I don't need you meddling in men's affairs anymore." He turned to a guard. "Prepare my son's body for a burial. I have buried too many already in this war."

Pyrakra burst into tears again but ran down the stairs and back to the Palace and her quarters. She shed tears all the way. Her vision blurred as she ran.

No one ever believed her. And the more she knew, the more it happened. She knew what was in store for the Citadel, but no one believed her.

Running through the Palace, the floors and walls felt even colder than before. The torches burned a starker yellow and cast a harsher light. The flagstones were rougher underfoot.

Pyrakra collapsed in her room and changed out of her bloody clothes into new ones. She curled up in bed. She sobbed. She knew, she knew, they were all going to die.

Chapter 17

"What happened then, Granddad?" said the small child. He was sitting on the old man's knee as the old man sat on a chair, walking stick propped up on the side.

The old man looked into the child's face and saw all the innocence of youth. He tried to remember when he was so innocent. He failed.

The old man looked at his hands. They were mechanical and augmented. He looked at the child, completely free of augmentations; simply natural flesh and bone.

"Grandad?" said the child again. His eyes wide with excitement and terror at the story so far.

"Now we turn to the fall of Titan. The fall of the Citadel. Our hero, Sius, formulated a plan to get passed the Citadel walls."

"What happened to Sius?" said the boy.

The old man smiled. This contorted his face into strange rifts and valleys. "He's a hero. All stories need good heroes."

"Are you a hero?" said the child. He yawned widely.

The old man knew that the child was getting tired, but there was so much story left to tell. So he said, "I was a hero, once. Perhaps not anymore."

"How can you un-become a hero?" said the child.

"Time passes, little one. Time. My heroic days are behind me. But we have so much story left to tell. So I will continue so we can finish before your bed time." The old man looked at the child.

"I'm not tired." The child wiped his eyes and yawned again.

"We don't have a moment to lose then," said the old man. He smiled again. He looked up and saw the bright open night sky, dotted with stars.

"We added many more campfires as graves of the fallen. After the death of Xos, by Sius' hand, Sius hatched a plan to break the siege. He and the other Cerv soldiers had become tired and jaded by the ten year siege and sought to break into the Citadel walls. Sius concocted a plan. And this is how it went…"

***

Sius sat at the table in his quarters. He chewed distractedly on a piece of bread. He was thinking. He picked up the wine cup that was near his right hand and took a sip.

Oreson barged into the room. "Sius, I need your opinion on the next plan of attack on…what are you doing?"

Sius said nothing. He went on thinking.

"Sius, I spoke to you. Hello?" said Oreson. He walked over to the table and waved a hand in front of Sius' face.

"I'm thinking," said Sius, not changing his focus.

"Good, fine, well think about our next attack," said Oreson, plonking himself down at the table and helping himself to wine and fruit.

Sius grimaced but said nothing else.

"Might I ask what you're thinking?" said Oreson through a mouth full of apple.

"I'm thinking about our victory."

"Good. So where's our next plan of attack?"

"First, I must talk to the priests. I have a plan," said Sius with a grin.

"Care to enlighten your leader?" said Oreson. His tone was a little menacing. Sius knew he did not like being kept in the dark.

"Well, first we need a patsy to carry the message. Then we need some flash drives. And then we need the priests and datatechs to do their magic," said Sius, finally looking up from the table to stare at his commander.

"How will that win us the war? We need to attack the Citadel at its week points!" said Oreson, spitting apple across the table.

Sius ignored the bluster. "Oh, that was the part I thought you'd like. This next part, you are going to hate!" Sius smiled a wicked smile.

After a while of explaining and Oreson interrupting every other sentence with incredulity, Sius outlined his plan.

"And what are you going to call this little ruse? To keep it from the Titans? To prevent them understanding that they are being deceived?

"I call it, Sinon," said Sius.

"Then we must go to the priests!" said Oreson and banged the table with enthusiasm. "This might work. And if it doesn't, it doesn't matter. We can try again, my way."

Sius nodded. The pair of them headed out of Sius' quarters and moved through the camp. They moved to the priest's section of the camp. It was shrouded in smoke from burning braziers and torches. There was also a heavy note of incense in the air.

Sius did not come here often. He was not strictly religious. But he knew that the priests had their place in maintaining the technology and interfacing with the AIs.

181

Oreson entered the rooms of the temple that had been erected as part of one of the ships. Sius hesitated, then followed behind his leader.

The two of them entered into the inner rooms of the temple. The walls were black with smoke and also the dark material of the space ship. Smoke hung in the air and Sius would have found it hard to breathe if it were not for his augmentations.

"Priest!" called out Oreson. It was clearly not a request.

The High Priest hurried up and out of the smoke and stood, trembling, in front of the two warriors.

"What do you require, excellencies?" said the High Priest rubbing his hands.

Oreson indicated for Sius to tell the plan he had devised.

Sius spoke succinctly and with purpose.

"So, you need us to make a number of drives with code on them and put them in server racks?" said the High Priest.

"Yes. Then I need them called Sinon," said Sius.

"You want a Trojan?" said the High Priest.

"Indeed. Can you do it?" said Oreson.

The High Priest thought for a moment then said, "Yes, yes we can do that. Why 'Sinon' by the way?"

"A reference," said Sius. "Nothing more."

"How are we going to deliver this package to the Titans?" asked Oreson. "I mean, how are they going to find it? How do we know that they are going to install it? These drives are small. How are we going to draw their attention to them?"

Sius smiled. "We will leave them with some of our computer systems and AI programming. It will be a full server. They will find it irresistible to use something that they think is left behind by us."

Oreson looked sceptical.

The High Priest looked appalled, but said nothing.

"I hope you're right, Sius. Because if you're not, then we will be forfeiting ten years of entrenched positions. I'll have your head if this does not work," said Oreson, labouring the threat by drawing a finger across his own throat. "Remember, if this fails, then it's my way."

"It'll work. Greed and arrogance are always ways to undo an enemy," said Sius.

Oreson nodded, then thought about the statement, grimaced, and then left the temple.

"Anything else, sire?" said the High Priest.

"No, just get me those drives. We need them quickly, mind. And we will be inside those walls in the next few days," said Sius, the last part he almost said to himself. He smiled and left the temple. He heard the High Priest muttering something about 'Sinon'.

Sius returned to his quarters. He sat down. He felt the butterflies in his stomach. He did not feel like eating. He hoped that this plan would work. It should work, he knew, but he was not certain. He had bluffed Oreson. He needed this Trojan to work.

Swallowing the nerves, Sius undressed and lay down in his bed. He would rest until the High Priest reported back and said the plan was ready. He needed to think as to how he would get the Titans to accept the drives and use them. He had to make sure it all went right. He had to play to their arrogance and their relief in the departing of the Cerv army. He had to make sure that this all worked.

He slept for a while. It had been ages since he slept properly. He dreamed of Arakus, his friend, and he dreamed of his hatred of the Titans. He dreamed fitful dreams of war and death. He saw his shot killing Xos. He dreamed nightmares. He dreamed of his wife and child back home. He would be grown now. They had been here for ten years and the journey here had taken many years too. He just wanted to go home.

Waking with a start, he saw the High Priest in his quarters.

"What is it?" snapped Sius.

"The programmes are ready, sire," said the High Priest.

Sius smiled. "Good." Perhaps now, he would be able to go home soon.

Chapter 18

"Sir, sir!" came a voice from outside Zoriam's chambers.

Zoriam rolled over in bed. "What is it?" he said sleepily.

There was more banging on the door. "Sir, sir!"

Oricula, Zoriam's wife, groaned and almost pushed Zoriam out of bed. "You deal with it," she said.

Zoriam got up. He checked his clock. It was early in the morning. Faint light filtered through the windows of his rooms. Zoriam put on some clothes and walked over to the door. He opened it.

The guard was in the process of banging on the door again and was startled when the door actually opened.

"What?" snapped Zoriam.

"Uh, sir, sire, my lord…" The guard stumbled over his words.

"Slow down and tell me," said Zoriam, trying to hide that he was annoyed that he had been woken so early.

"Sir!-"

"Yes I got that point," said Zoriam.

"The Cerv army…It's gone!" spluttered the guard.

"What!" bellowed Zoriam.

Oricula was at his side in an instant. She had thrown on some regal robes.

"Yes, sir. The Cerv army has left. We've won!"

"Show me," said Zoriam. He could hardly believe it. He had to see it for himself.

Zoriam threw on some regal robes too and then followed the guard out of the Palace and through the Citadel. They were joined by other guards and Palace personnel. Pyrakra joined them. Zoriam noted that she looked more worried than ever.

Gathering at the main gate, Zoriam and the guard ascended the walls and looked out over the battlements.

"You're right," whispered Zoriam. He saw that all the ships had gone, and all the camp had been disassembled and deserted.

"I must see it," said Zoriam.

"Sir, it might be dangerous," said the guard.

"I don't care. I must see it," said Zoriam still staring out over the Plains.

They descended the walls. A small crowd had gathered now at the foot of the main gate. They were all talking at once.

"People of the Citadel," began Zoriam, still standing half way up the stairs to the battlements. The crowd fell silent instantly. "People of the Citadel, The Cerv army has indeed gone. We will look at their wrecked camp. But I stress to you, this could be a trap. We must be cautious. We are the first to experience this. Most of our number are still asleep. But we will relay the good news to them when they wake up."

Zoriam descended all the way to the ground and ordered that the gates be opened. The commands were entered into the computers and the large main gates ground and creaked open.

When they were open, the small crowd of Citadel dwellers poured out onto the Plains of Titan and headed towards the former Cerv camp. They dodged the odd body that had been left to rot and moved down towards the Cerv camp.

When Zoriam and the others reached the camp they saw that it had indeed been disassembled and abandoned. There were no enemy ships left. The indents in the land where they had been were still there, but there were no ships.

Zoriam looked skyward and saw the bulk of Saturn sitting in the sky. He gave thanks to the AIs that had guided them through the ten year ordeal.

Many of the crowd tried to loot the camp for anything valuable, but came back with reports that there was nothing left behind other than a mess of twisted metal that had been the barricade and some of the buildings that had sprung up to form the camp.

"Sir, sir, there is something left," said a guard, who hurried up to the King.

"Easy now, catch your breath," said Zoriam.

The guard breathed hard and said, "They've left a server rack and some drives in it."

"Show me," said Zoriam.

The King and some guards along with Pyrakra and some others broke from the main group and headed into the camp's remains.

"Here," said the guard.

Indeed there was a large server rack with drives in it and some flash drives in various ports. It had some writing on it. It also appeared to have a large battery pack beside it.

"Why did they leave this?" asked Zoriam. "Why is 'Sinon' written on it?"

"It's the trap," said Pyrakra quietly.

"Perhaps it's an offering?" said the guard.

"Get the Chief Priest," said Zoriam.

"Father, it's the trap," said Pyrakra more forcefully.

"Nonsense, child. They left this behind. We can use it. Perhaps to aid in our defences should they return!" said Zoriam. He put a hand on the machine. "Which AI are you?" he asked it quietly.

Zoriam knew that the server needed full power for him to get its secrets.

Finally, the Chief Priest, dishevelled and yawning, appeared. "Sire?" he said.

"What's this?" Zoriam said, indicating the server rack.

"Interesting," said the Chief Priest. "It's an AI rack. We'd need to get it inside first to see what's on it."

"And this writing? Is it the AI's name?" asked Zoriam.

"'Sinon'? Perhaps, sire."

"Is it safe to get inside and power on?" asked Zoriam.

"No, father, please, listen to me," said Pyrakra.

"Hush, child," snapped Zoriam.

"We can look into it with the battery power, sire," said the Chief Priest.

"Then do it," said Zoriam.

The Chief Priest pulled up a small screen from his wrist and wired it into the server. After a few seconds he spoke. The AI's name is indeed called Sinon. It reports that it was left here as an offering to the AIs and was supposed to mean a good return to Earth by the Cerv forces. It says that you should not bring it inside the city walls.

"Sir, we should not bring that inside," said a man in the crowd. It was one of the King's advisors.

"Why not?" said Zoriam. "It's clearly an offering. We must bring it inside to aid us not leave it here to aid the Cerv retreat."

"It could be a trap," said the man.

"Lakon, you speak nonsense," said Zoriam and turned back to the Chief Priest.

Just then, Lakon grabbed a spear from a nearby guard and acted to hurl it at the server rack.

The lights pulsed and flashed and suddenly Lakon collapsed to the ground before he got a chance to throw the spear. He thrashed around on the ground as his breathing augmentations failed and his other augmentations went into spasm.

Pyrakra raced to his side, but he was dead before anyone could do anything.

"It is a sign from the AIs," said Zoriam. Everyone was shocked and silent. "We bring this inside and give it full power! It will protect us from the Cerv forces should they return."

Pyrakra cried out a formless cry. No one listened to her.

"Open the main gate, bring this inside, plug it into our temple. We will discover this AI's secrets," said Zoriam. He headed back inside with his guards.

The people kept looking around the camp as workers were dispatched to bring the server inside the Citadel walls and install it in the temple.

***

As the servers were brought inside the walls, the wheels that the servers were placed on by the Titans hesitated four times at the Citadel main gate. The servers rocked back and forth, threatening to tip over and dash themselves to pieces on the cobbled roads. But on the fifth try, the servers cleared the gate and were wheeled inside the walls and up to the Palace and the Temple of the AIs.

There was much celebrating. Flower petals were thrown from windows, once only saved for weddings, they were used to welcome the departure of the hated Cerv army. This server would herald a new dawn in the life of the city and the information contained within would bring new prosperity and life to the Citadel.

People danced and celebrated in the streets and in their houses. The joy that the Cerv army had gone, spread throughout the city rapidly and Zoriam declared that there would be days of parties and feasting.

The remaining food from the siege was brought out and people gorged and drank, for tomorrow would be a good day of life and freedom. The war was over.

The servers were brought to the Temple and the priests set up the cable connections. They took the server off battery power, which was almost expended, and put it on to mains power. The whole server stack began to light up, as if on battery power most of the server was on standby. Green lights flickered all over its towering bulk.

Prayers were said in honour of the AIs. Priests gave thanks to the AIs for guiding the Citadel through all the trials and tribulations of the ten year war. Incense was lit and a great chanting arose from the body of the Temple as the priests sang thanks for the server and their deliverance.

Zoriam addressed his people from in front of the Temple. "People of the Citadel! We have won! We have won this war! The Cerv army has retreated, and we have captured some of their computer systems. It will allow us to defend ourselves better should they ever return. Not that I expect them to. But we must be vigilant, my people. But more so, my people, we must be thankful to the AIs to bring us through this war. We will use this server rack to add to our own and we will see which AIs are in it. But now, my people, eat drink and be merry, because the war is over! We will be able to farm and grow crops again soon, so use those last, saved pieces of food and celebrate. We have survived!"

A great roaring cheer went up from the crowd and it rippled down through the streets and squares as those at the front relayed what their King had said to those at the back.

***

Meanwhile, in the Temple, the server flickered away. It uploaded its sinister programming to the network of the Titan Citadel. Within the server's dark bulk, the code was being insinuated into the Titan network where it waited for the

190

perfect time. Where it waited for the moment it was programmed for.

As the Titan day wore on, and the night came, the people of the Citadel celebrated, feasted, and drank. They became tired and drunk. They celebrated long into the Titan night. Time went by. They retreated to their beds and even slept in the streets. They let down their guards and lounged everywhere.

The guards of the Citadel were taken off duty. There was now no need for them to guard the city walls and so they too, were drunk and lying all over the streets of the Citadel and the Palace.

***

Zoriam led a great feast in the Palace. He sat at the head of a massive table groaning with meat and vegetables.

Zoriam stood and said, while the guests fell silent, "And so we give thanks to the AIs," he said, "for shepherding us through this tough time. And we pay tribute to fallen warriors who could not be here." His voice almost cracked, but he did not mention any names. Everyone knew who he meant. "So," he continued, "eat and drink my friends, for tomorrow is a new day without war!"

A cheer went up from the people gathered around the table. Everyone except Pyrakra was clapping and cheering. Zoriam looked at her and saw, in her face, the sheer terror of someone about to die.

"Smile, Pyrakra, tonight is a good night! We're safe!" Zoriam called out to his daughter.

Pyrakra shook her head and ran out of the eating hall. She did not come back, despite Zoriam's calls to her.

"Let her go," said Oricula, who had been sitting next to Zoriam in silence while her husband made a speech. "She doesn't know better."

"I would have thought on this day, that she would be happy," said Zoriam, rather dejectedly.

Oricula put a hand on Zoriam's shoulder. "She'll come to her senses tomorrow."

***

Pyrakra raced through the Palace to the Temple. By now it was late and there were only people drunk and asleep on the ground in the streets. She ran into the Temple and saw the server rack wired up to the other servers in the back of the Temple behind the altar. Its green lights all flickered menacingly.

"It's too late," she said to herself. "The connection has already been made. It's wired up."

"Yes, my child," said a priest. "Isn't it marvellous? It took a while but now we have a complete connection between this Cerv server and our own servers. We are analysing the AI within already."

"No," whimpered Pyrakra.

"What's wrong, child?" said the priest. He put a hand on her shoulder.

Pyrakra shook off the hand. "You've doomed us all," she said, and then she shrieked, "you've doomed us all!"

"Nonsense, child. The AI is called Sinon and it seems rather benign. It wants to help us with our defences. Clearly it was a Cerv AI that has rebelled against them and..."

Pyrakra did not want to hear any more. She raced out of the Temple and back to the Palace. She knew what was coming.

***

All the while, Sinon blinked away and uploaded code to the Titan mainframe. All the while it waited, as its timer counted down.

Chapter 19

Sinon slipped through the circuits of the Citadel's network. It unlocked the main gates and they swung open. It moved through the sectors of the Citadel and Palace's security networks and blanked out cameras and opened locks.

Sinon slipped unnoticed past the security checks of the Citadel's defences. It insinuated itself into the very basic code of the systems and laid bare the path for the Cerv forces.

Most of the Palace and the Citadel itself were asleep, dreaming off too much drink from celebrating their victory. They had been celebrating for many hours. The Titan night slipped on. Guards and civilians alike lay in their beds and in the streets simply overcome with the emotion of victory.

Little did they know that bearing down on their little moon of Titan was the whole Cerv fleet that had simply hidden itself behind the bulk of Saturn. It had returned, and the Titans were undefended and open for attack. As the Titan night dragged on, the Cerv forces readied themselves.

Sinon made the path clear for the Cerv forces. Once it had unlocked and opened the gates to the Citadel, it self destructed, shorting itself out and overloading the circuits of the server rack it came in. The lights in the server rack went dark, as did the lights across the Citadel as the entire security network went down and shorted out. The lights on the main servers in the Temple went dark too.

Sinon had completed its task. And suicided in the process. There would be no trace of it in the network, which now lay undefended and open to any invasion.

***

The Cerv ships landed on the Plains of Titan. They bore down on the moon of Titan with their angular and brutal craft. They had received the signal from the trojan that was known as Sinon and had made their way back from around Saturn. They landed and disgorged their entire army of soldiers onto the Plains.

Sius disembarked from his ship with his soldiers. He saw Oreson and Verius do the same. He nodded to them. They nodded in response.

No soldier spoke a word. They did not want to rouse the Titans from their stupor. They needed to attack as silently as possible. Even the landing of the space ships had been subdued as the engines had been at half power.

Sius was dressed in the full battle armour from Arakus. He hefted his shield and shock spear. He felt the sword on his waist. He bore it with skill.

He looked out from his plumed helmet. He saw that the Citadel was all dark. It loomed up in the darkness out of the landscape. The searchlights were out, as were all the other security measures, he knew.

They made their way as silently as possible up the Plains and towards the Citadel walls. The main gates were open! Sius knew that Sinon had done its work.

As the clanking soldiers made their way inside the walls, they slaughtered the sleeping guards who were stationed around the main gate.

Sius plunged his shock spear into one of the guards, who only looked like a boy. The young man convulsed as the energy discharged inside him, and then he was dead.

A pillaging army can only be so silent, for so long, and soon a shout and a scream went up. The guards realised what was going on

"Soldiers of the Cerv army, attack! Attack! And kill them all!," yelled Oreson as the alarm went up.

The Cerv soldiers yelled a battle cry in response and charged. They poured in through the open gates and began slaughtering the inhabitants of the Citadel.

Fires broke out across the Citadel as the invading Cerv soldiers set the place to flame to drive out the defenders and burn them alive.

Soon the Citadel was ablaze and there was much blood in the streets.

Sius rushed through the Citadel. He knew that they had to get to the Palace and chop the head off the serpent. Without Zoriam, the Citadel would be powerless.

Sius pressed forward with a few of his most worthy soldiers. In the fighting for the Citadel, the Cerv army had become fragmented and splintered in the maze of narrow and long streets throughout the Citadel.

The one prize was the Palace. It sat on the hill high above the rest of the Citadel. The structure was lit by burning torches. Those were unable to be put out by Sinon. Yet Sius knew, that the security gates to the Palace would be unlocked.

Sius and his men skewered guard after guard. They had no idea where Oreson or Verius or any of the other soldiers or commanders were, but they pressed on, ever upward through the narrow streets.

Fires broke out all around them. Buildings were aflame. People were screaming, running, dying.

Sius and his few soldiers had to kill many civilians. They got in their way, Sius told himself. Yet there was something different, it was not just that they got in the way, after ten years of stalemate and siege, all the anger and violence bubbled forth in him and his soldiers. And so, with that anger and hate, came death and suffering. It was somehow a vent or a release to kill the innocent civilians. Their deaths and screams reached the stars and washed the frustration of all the wasted years away.

And the male soldiers did worse to the women. Sius grimaced as the soldiers entered the houses with screaming women and returned later with grins on their faces; the women were then silent. Not him, he had a wife back home, he would not do that.

The screams reached the stars far away. The Citadel burned. The people died. The AIs were silent.

Sius, through the smoke, which obscured even his augmented vision, thought he saw a man carrying an older man on his shoulders, running through the burning streets. They were followed by a woman, who was falling further and further behind. It was only for an instant, when Sius looked again, the man was gone in the smoke and flames.

"We must get to the Palace!" roared Sius to his men. "Enough with the women and the pillaging. We must get to the Palace and end this!"

The soldiers with him groaned a little. It was clear that they were enjoying the carnage, but they understood their purpose.

The small band of them headed up towards the Palace.

The flames in the Citadel were reaching a crescendo. It seemed as though all the world was alight. Smoke billowed from the burning buildings and obscured the sight of even the best augmented soldier.

The Titan soldiers, now fully awake and in position, put up a strong fight. Many Cerv soldiers fell; as did many Titan soldiers.

The Citadel was large and it was taking a while to make a way through the tight streets. The fires impeded their paths.

One thing was sure, the Citadel would fall, it just was a question of how long it would take. Would the fires destroy the Citadel before the Cerv soldiers could?

***

Sius and his soldiers forged on through the acrid burning streets. They had become separated from the rest of the Cerv soldiers. In the swirling melee, chaos reigned.

"Look! Some of our men!" shouted one of Sius' companions.

Indeed, ahead of them Sius saw, through the smoke, a group of men in Cerv uniforms. He called out to them above the roar of the flames and the clash of arms. But it was to no avail.

"We must get their attention," shouted Sius. His cohort pushed forward and when they were within identification range of the other Cerv soldiers, they realised their mistake.

The other Cerv soldiers attacked them. They were Titans in Cerv uniforms!

A bloody battle ensued, and the Titans were routed, but not after they had killed a number of Sius' brave soldiers.

Sius spat a bloody gob of phlegm onto the ground. Were the Titans really resorting to that?

"To the Palace!" Sius yelled. His soldiers yelled their affirmations. They pushed on.

After much fighting and killing, Sius and a few of his soldiers reached the walls of the Palace. The gate was barricaded and there were Titan soldiers throwing projectiles down from the rooves and towers of the main wall.

There was a mob of Cerv soldiers trying to break down the gate, but failing.

On the edge of the wall was a tower. It rose high and mightily above the wall. Sius saw that there was a bunch of

197

Titan soldiers at its base, chopping away at it with swords and axes.

"Look out!" Sius called.

The tower, when pushed, toppled and fell onto the amassed Cerv soldiers and rolled down the hill and streets of the inner Citadel. It crushed many Cerv soldiers as it rolled.

Sius sighed. It was up to him and his men again to take the Palace.

When the tower fell, it tore a hole in the wall of the Palace. The Titan forces fell back as the Cerv soldiers poured through the gap.

The ground was slick with blood as the Cerv soldiers butchered the Titan defenders to a man.

Sius' eyes stung with the smoke and the blood that ran down his face.

The Palace itself was also alight. The flames spared none in this doomed city.

Sius looked skyward in the Palace courtyard. He saw the smoke and flames reaching towards the heavens. The planet Saturn sat high in the sky. He grimaced. Would any of them be forgiven for what they had done this night? He felt the stimulants of his implants surging through his veins. He had to keep going. He had to keep killing. Only then could he drown out the screams of those he had already killed. The newly dead covered the old dead beneath them. He knew that he was damned for this. It had been his plan that had resulted in this. He was responsible. Would Fate forgive him?

Sius' self indulgence was broken by more screams. He pushed on into the Palace corridors.

***

Zoriam was in his quarters girding on his ancient armour. His wife, Oricula, was behind him, sitting on the bed, her head in her hands.

"What have I done?" said Zoriam. "What have I done?" he repeated.

"Come here, my husband, and die with me," said Oricula. He turned and saw she held a sword.

"I can't. I have to fight!" he said. He picked up his own sword.

"You're an old man. What are you doing?" snapped Oricula.

"Dying my way," said Zoriam.

Suddenly, Pyrakra burst into the chambers. "Father!" she cried out and threw herself at his feet.

Zoriam bent down awkwardly and took his daughter by the chin. "I should have believed you," he said. He then kissed her on the forehead.

There was a scuffle outside the doors to the room, then a scream, and in burst a Cerv soldier.

Zoriam indicated that Pyrakra should get behind him. She scrambled there.

"Wait," said Zoriam. "I know you."

"I am Oreson, leader of this war, and vanquisher of Titan!" said the man.

"Then as one leader to another, I demand clemency for my wife and daughter. Do as you like to me, but I want them safe," Zoriam said, weakly brandishing his sword in his ancient armour.

"I give no such clemency. This is my night. I will kill you all! I have waited ten years for this!" said Oreson through gritted teeth.

"Then at least give me a moment with my remaining family, please," said Zoriam. He dropped his sword. It clanged on the flagstones of his room.

Zoriam could see that Oreson was high on his stimulants. He had obviously discharged a great deal of them in the fight.

But to his credit, the leader of the Cerv forces nodded. "Two minutes."

"Thank you,' said Zoriam. He turned to his wife, still on the bed. He kissed her and then, as he pulled away, he took the sword in her hands, and thrust it deep into her chest. She looked at him as she died. Hot blood poured across the sheets. Her expression was one of thanks.

Pyrakra screamed. Zoriam turned to her, and he still held his wife's sword, slick with blood.

Oreson saw the suicide of Oricula and stepped forward. He grabbed Pyrakra's arm and pulled her towards him. "This one goes with me. I will not have you kill her too."

Two other Cerv soldiers burst into the room. Oreson shoved Pyrakra at them. "Take her to my quarters in my ship. She's coming with me."

"That was not two minutes," said Zoriam. "I demand my daughter back!"

"My victory, my rules. I will take her as a slave. And now you die!" Oreson brandished his sword.

Zoriam raised his dead wife's bloody sword. It was slick and slid out of his hands as Oreson struck at him.

Oreson laughed. Then he ran Zoriam through with his sword. Zoriam collapsed onto his bed, next to his wife's body. Their blood mingled in the sheets.

Zoriam heard Oreson ransacked the room as the light faded from his eyes. He then heard Oreson shout "Kill them all!" as death claimed the old King.

The Palace burned.

***

Sius ran through the corridors of the Palace. Flames licked up the parts of the walls made of wood. The roof was also alight. He had been separated from his band of soldiers. He had also lost his shock spear, but he carried his sword and shield; Arakus' shield.

Standing in front of a door was a Titan soldier. He brandished his spear. "Stop, or I'll kill you!" shouted the soldier.

Sius kept running at him down the corridor. Ragged breaths rasped through his lungs. His augmentations filtered out the harmful gasses from the fires, but his throat still burned from the smoke.

"Stop!" cried out the soldier. His voice broke as he did so.

Sius slowed. He realised that this soldier was a boy, no older than fifteen. He just looked older in his uniform. As Sius approached he saw that the uniform was too big for the child.

Sius stopped mid way down the corridor, a dozen metres from the door. "Go, run!" he called out.

"I can't let you in here!" yelled the boy in armour over the roar of the flames.

"Get out of my way, child," snapped Sius. He raised his shield and sword. "I will kill you!"

"I...I can't let you in here," said the boy. He tried to raise his shield and brace his spear against his side. He was coughing due to the smoke.

He did not even have any augmentations, Sius realised. He did not want to kill him, but there was fire in his wake, and he knew that he had to get through that door.

"The Palace is burning, boy. Run! This is the last warning I will give you!" Sius prepared to charge the young soldier.

"I...I..."

"Time's up," said Sius to himself and charged, shield first. He crashed through the clumsily held spear and shield of the boy and knocked the boy flat on the ground. As the boy struggled to get up and draw the oversized sword around his waist, Sius skewered him with his own sword.

The boy let out a sigh as the sword smashed its way through his armour and into his lungs and heart. The blow was precise. Sius knew what he was doing.

Sius stood over the body of the boy. He retrieved his sword from the boy's torso. He looked around. He set his jaw. There was a lot of what he just did going on tonight. He would have to pay for these crimes, Sius knew. But he also knew, that it was kill or be killed. The boy would not have hesitated if the roles had been reversed.

Stepping over the corpse, Sius pushed through the door and emerged into the throne room. It was large and draped with tapestries, which were starting to catch alight from the burning roof as it dripped fire like rain falling faintly across the large hall.

The tapestries that adorned the walls, held the history of Titan and were woven with skill and precision. They were relics of a past history. And now they were starting, hesitantly, to catch alight. The thick weave and rich use of thread meant that they burned slowly. But they burned, none the less.

"So, you made it here!" called out a voice. Sius recognised it.

Sius looked towards the throne. He had not seen the figure sitting on the throne due to the smoke and the distraction of the burning roof.

Oreson sat on the throne. His shield and spear propped up next to him.

"Enjoying yourself?" called out Sius over the roar of the burning roof.

"Very much," said Oreson.

"We need to get out of here. The roof will collapse!" said Sius.

"He's right," said Verius, who had appeared through another door. "Come brother. We must go!"

Oreson sat on the throne. He looked at the burning roof. "It will hold yet. The timbers are massive. It will take hours for them to burn up and fall."

"We still need to move. The whole Palace is going up," said Sius.

Oreson began to laugh. It was a rolling, booming laugh. It echoed around the throne room. "Welcome to my legacy. I did this. I burned Titan. I alone hold the glory for this. I have ordered that the whole city be razed. Let none survive."

"You've gone mad," said Sius. "Well, I'm not stopping here. I'm getting my men and leaving. I'm going home. I've done enough for you."

"Oh yes. How could I forget," said Oreson. His face was illuminated underneath his helmet by the fire that was spreading down the walls on the tapestries. "This was your idea. We have you to thank for this."

"And I will forever bear the scars. Come on!" said Sius. He turned to leave.

Verius looked at him and turned to go too.

"Remember this moment," said Oreson. "Our glory. Remember this!" And then he started laughing again.

One of the beams from the roof fell and crashed down on the floor near the throne.

"It's time to go, sire," Sius spat the words.

"Yes. I believe it is." Oreson stood and shouldered his spear and shield.

The three of them ran out of the throne room with the roaring flames above.

They encountered a group of Cerv soldiers and formed up with them. They too were trying to escape the burning Palace.

They pushed through another door and came into the Temple. It was unguarded and seemed deserted apart from the large server racks behind the altar.

Oreson ordered the soldiers to search the Temple and bring any survivors to him. The few Cerv soldiers with them fanned out and searched the Temple.

The Temple was not burning, yet. The construction was mostly stone, and so could not burn. But the roof was still wooden and had massive beams similar to the throne room.

Sius walked up to the racks of servers behind the altar. Oreson and Verius followed him.

"Thank you, Sinon. Thank you, Sius," said Oreson with a grin in his voice.

Sius ignored him. He put a hand on the server rack that was Sinon.

Oreson and Verius looked on and said nothing.

Suddenly, Sius lashed out with his sword. He smashed it into the other server racks there. He smashed and smashed. He cut network cables and power cables. He smashed the servers to pieces in a rage.

"Feel better?" said Oreson.

"You shouldn't have done that," said Verius. "The AIs…"

"Fuck the AIs," said Sius. "I'm sick of fighting for AIs. I'm sick of it all. All this death and killing. All for what? This fucking server node? Well now it's gone. And I don't care what you think!"

"Spoken like a warrior," said a voice behind all three of them. He was flanked by two Cerv soldiers.

"Who are you?" demanded Verius.

"This prisoner says he's the Chief Priest," said a soldier.

"I can answer for myself," said the Chief Priest. "Why did you do that? Rage? Hate? Revenge? Pent up Frustration? Believe me, I've seen it all. But what you did there was not wise. The AIs are not to be trifled with. I hope you do not live to regret smashing those."

"Listen, Priest, I could kill you here and now," said Sius, waving his sword at the Priest. "I've had it with religion and AIs."

"Then go home," said the Chief Priest. "You have left nothing but destruction and death here. Just, go home."

Sius slumped. He walked up to the Chief Priest. Oreson and Verius watched on as did the two Cerv soldiers.

Sius embraced the Chief Priest. The Chief Priest stood there. Then Sius ran him through with his sword.

The Chief Priest fell to the floor. There was blood everywhere. Sius was soaked in it.

"I'm so tired," said Sius.

"Stimulants run out? Go back to camp and refuel. We could all do with an energy recharge," said Verius.

"True," said Oreson. "Follow us back to our ships. The Citadel is dead. We've done what we had to."

"Not quite," said Verius. "Where's my AI? Fria."

Sius started cackling. He looked at his sword, slick with blood. He threw his head back and laughed. "That's why we came here. Fria. All those years for Fria. And you have no idea where she is or if she's still alive. Oh, well done."

"We'll find her and bring her back to the ships. Come on," said Oreson.

They left the Temple and marched through the Palace, looking room to room. They searched for Fria.

***

Timber beams crashed from the rooves. Great stones burned and exploded. Glass shattered. Sius, Oreson, and Verius, with a couple of other soldiers raged through the Palace. They moved from room to room, dodging flames and avoiding smoke.

They came across a cowering servant in one of the rooms. Verius grabbed the servant by her collar and hauled her up with mechanical strength.

"Where is she?" he shouted at her.

Sius and Oreson brandished their weapons for any hostile forces that came along.

"Who, sir?" said the servant. She coughed. She had no mechanical augmentations to filter the smoke.

"Fria. My AI!" shouted Verius.

"Last I saw, sir, she was heading down towards the landing pads. Where the ships come and dock," said the servant.

Verius dropped her and the Cerv soldiers moved on. Sius knew that he could not worry for the woman they had just encountered. She would probably be overcome by the fumes if she was not killed by the flames soon.

They hurried through the Palace, dispatching the occasional remaining Titan soldier who got in their way.

Reaching the loading dock for the landing pads, the five of them saw a hoard of mewling, crying refugees piled into the tight space. Everyone who had sought refuge in the Palace as the Citadel was being overrun seemed to be taking refuge here.

The refugees took no notice of the Cerv soldiers as they entered the rooms that were set up as cargo loading stations for the space ships that docked at the Citadel. The rooms were metal and stone with unloaded cargo piled up in crates around the place. The people, fleeing for their lives, were crammed into the rooms in any way they could. And yet, there were no space ships to rescue them.

"We've set up a blockade to prevent any escapes," said Sius to Oreson. "These people will not be going anywhere."

Oreson smiled. "Good."

"Where's my AI!" demanded Verius in a loud voice. "Fria! Where are you?" he called out.

There was no reply. There were simply the screams and cries of a hundred people, desperately trying to survive. And yet, they knew, in a way, there were no ships there to save them.

Verius started shouldering through the mob and grabbing at the hair of any woman he saw. He pulled them towards himself and tried to identify them.

"This is hopeless," said Sius.

"I have an idea," said Oreson.

Sius looked at him carefully.

"Kill them all," said Oreson to the soldiers with them.

"You can't—" began Sius.

"I'm the warlord here. I can and I will. Kill them. We'll find Fria that way," said Oreson calmly.

"What if you kill her?" said Verius.

"Then I will compensate you. But we cannot hang around here all day. The Palace will collapse and kill us if we're not careful," said Oreson. "Go on!" He indicated to the soldiers.

The two soldiers hesitated a moment, and then began slaughtering the refugees. Verius joined in after a moment. Sius looked on in horror as the screams of the fearful mingled with the screams of the dying. There was blood everywhere. It ran in streams across the metal and stone pavements. It splattered over the foodstuffs and supplies that were piled up.

The bodies of the dead piled up too, into hideous parodies of the piles of supplies.

After a while, Sius, to his shame, joined in. He did not want to be burned alive in the Palace, and the sooner this was over the better. So, he joined in. He killed innocent people who were running for their lives. It was not the first time. He knew that he would always hear these screams in his sleep. He would always see their faces, contorted and with desperate looks. He would always feel the bite of his sword in their flesh. He would never forget this slaughter in the landing pad loading docks.

Some refugees got away and past the Cerv soldiers. They ran back into the Palace. They would soon be dead too, to flames and smoke.

Oreson did not join in, Sius realised. He simply stood and watched. He gave the orders, they all followed.

"She's here!" shouted Verius. "I've found her!"

Sius, soaked in blood, Oreson and the two soldiers moved over the piles of dead to find Verius standing triumphantly

207

over the still alive AI Fria. She was with another woman who was also, at the moment, still alive.

Verius held Fria by her hair and prevented her escape. She kicked and punched at him, but it was futile. He simply laughed.

The other woman cowered in the blood around her.

"Take her back to my ship," said Verius. He handed Fria to one of the soldiers. The soldier led Fria out of the slaughter rooms. She did not fight. She slumped and did not resist. She was led, by the arm, through the blood and back to the ship.

"What happens to me?" said the other woman.

"I remember you," demanded Oreson. "I captured you earlier. How did you escape my men?"

"My name's Pyrakra," said the woman. She stood up.

"I found you with your father. You won't escape this time," he said. "And you are now my personal slave." He touched her hair.

Sius and Verius looked at him.

"Oreson? The Warlord? I know about you," said Pyrakra. Her voice faltered. She shied away from the hair touching.

Oreson smiled. "Oh?" he said.

"I know how you're going to die. You will be murdered by your wife," Pyrakra said.

"Hah, that's not possible. Take her back to my ship. Don't let her get away this time," Oreson said, indicating the last soldier with them.

The soldier nodded and took Pyrakra by the arm. She shook her head at Oreson, but did not resist.

The three warlords stood in the loading dock. There were no refugees left in it. Those who had not been killed had fled back into the burning Palace.

"Let's get out of here," said Sius.

"Good idea," said Verius.

Oreson grunted.

The three of them headed back through the slaughterhouse of a loading dock. They headed back through the burning Palace and out into the Citadel.

By this stage, dawn was breaking over the desolate moon of Titan. The Citadel was beginning to burn itself out. Plumes of smoke rose over the smouldering wreckage that were the homes of many people.

Sius, Oreson, and Verius, stepped out of the Palace and into the light of the morning. Flames still licked around some buildings, but many had collapsed and burned themselves out.

Oreson stepped into one of the squares in front of the Palace and took a deep breath. "I love that smell," he said.

"What smell?" asked Sius.

"This!" Oreson indicated the burning city with his hands outstretched.

"You're perverse," said Sius.

"You're the one covered in blood, not me," said Oreson.

Sius looked at himself. He was indeed covered in blood. It had dried on him and formed a sticky layer of red. "I need a wash," he said.

"The war is over," said Verius, looking around. "And now we have so many new slaves."

"Ten years," said Oreson. "And it's over all thanks to Sius and his plan!"

Sius grimaced. He took off his helmet. Arakus' helmet, he corrected his thoughts.

The other two did the same. They held their helmets under their arms.

Up to them ran a Cerv soldier. "Sir," he said, "what do we do with the refugees?"

"Lock them up in our ships. We'll take them with us," said Oreson.

"Sir!" the man saluted and ran back to where the slaves were being mustered.

209

"I'm going home," said Sius.

"As you wish," said Oreson.

Verius snorted a laugh.

Sius did not respond. He walked away from the pair. He had had enough war. Now he had to go home. He wanted to see Earth again. He wanted to see his wife and child again. It was time all this was over.

***

As the Sun rose on the far away ball of rock that was Titan, the Citadel smouldered. The city was destroyed. Flames still licked up the blackened walls of a number of buildings, but many of the wooden rooves had collapsed and thick smoke rose from the wreckage. The rooves that had been harvested from the plantings of the terraforming expeditions generations ago.

Sius stumbled through the rubble. He was covered in blood and soot. He wiped a hand over his face. He looked at his palm. It was black and bloody. He did not know if the blood was his, or someone else's. He had lost track.

As he walked slowly through the ruins of the Citadel. He saw bodies everywhere, charred and bloody too. They were the bodies of the civilians and soldiers alike. Both Cerv and Titan soldiers lay in pools of burned and congealed blood. Their faces were torn with agony and despair. Sius wondered if he wore the same expression.

Sius became aware that he was suddenly extremely thirsty. He had not drunk any water since before the attack, and what with the flames and the exertion, he was parched.

He did not know where he could find water, but he stumbled on, kicking the remains of burned wood from in front of his feet. The charred embers clattered away down the streets in front of him.

Sius came to a house that had not collapsed. It had not been touched by the flames. He went inside in search for water. The

210

inside of the house was dark. It still had a roof. He walked through the house to the kitchen. He found a sink. He turned the tap. Nothing. He cursed. He then saw a bottle of water on the kitchen bench. He grabbed it and drank heartily. He let some spill over his face to try to wash off the blood and soot. Yet this only made it sticky and wet. It did not clean him. At least he did not feel as thirsty, he thought to himself.

As he looked around the kitchen, he noted that he was treading in something slippery. He looked down, now that he had quenched some of his thirst, he could focus on his surroundings. He was standing in a pool of blood. He did not react. He saw that he was standing in the blood of a young woman who had been killed in her kitchen. He did not react. He took some steps out of the blood. He walked out of the house, leaving bloody footsteps. He did not react. He threw the empty bottle of water away.

Sius wiped a hand across his moist face again. He tried to wipe away the blood and soot, but he simply smeared it around and did not achieve his goal.

As he wandered the destroyed Citadel, he came across two soldiers fighting over some spoils of war. It looked to Sius like they had uncovered some money and were fighting as to who should keep it. He watched for a moment and then marched on. He had no time for petty squabbles over ruined possessions.

There were Cerv soldiers everywhere, he noted. They were either looting or drinking or fighting. Some even were skewering the bodies of Titan soldiers who may or may not have been alive before the spear went through them. They were definitely not alive afterward.

Sius looked skyward. The clouds boiled sickly yellow overhead. Sunlight filtered through the thick clouds. Smoke rose in billows from the destroyed Citadel and mingled with the clouds high above.

Sius came to the Citadel walls. He climbed the stairs slowly. When he reached the top he looked out over the Plains of Titan and saw all the Cerv ships landed there, their bellies open having disgorged the contents to kill the Citadel.

He looked back over the ruined Citadel and the Palace and Temple high on the hill in the distance. It was all wreckage. He had done this, he knew. It was his plan that had prevailed. He had made sure that the Citadel had burned. He had planned it all, and it had succeeded. He had won the war for the Cerv forces. He had damned this city. He had made sure that the people of Titan had died. It was his fault. He had done this.

Sius stared with a blank expression. His face covered in blood and soot, now drying again in the hot winds from the smouldering buildings. He swallowed hard.

Then the thought came to him, what if he had not done this? What if the siege had gone on for another ten years? Would that have been better? Would the Cerv forces have gone home without victory and simply let everyone live. Arakus was still dead. So was Brior. So was Xos. So were countless children whose mothers would never hug them again. So were the mothers, Sius thought. This was simply the desired outcome of war. War meant death and destruction. This was always the aim and the end. Whether he had concocted this plan or not, There were many dead. This plan simply put them on his hands.

Sius looked down at his hands. He did not know where his sword or shield had gone. He had lost them somewhere. He had put down his helmet somewhere too and had forgotten where. Arakus' shield and helmet, he corrected himself. Perhaps it was best that they stayed here, in the destruction, in the mess. All he had left of Arakus' armour was the breastplate that he wore.

Sius studied his hands. They were black and bloody. His mechanically augmented arms and hands were covered in blood and soot. He drew a ragged breath and looked back out over the ruins. The air tasted of death and despair.

Then he heard something. He heard cheering and celebrations. He looked back out onto the Plains of Titan and saw large groups of Cerv soldiers had gathered to drink and celebrate.

Sius smirked. They could do that, he supposed. They had won the war. It was over. Ten years of siege had been broken and the war was over. But not for him.

Some of the soldiers came up the stairs and clapped Sius on the back. They cheered and celebrated. They handed him some wine. He stared at it and then drank. Yes, the war was over. He had won it for them. And now, he had to go home

"What spoils have you found?" asked one of the soldiers.

Sius looked blankly at him. "You keep the spoils. I'm going home."

Sius shouldered past the men and walked down the steps and out the main gates of the Citadel. He walked across the Plains of Titan and did not look back. He walked towards his ship. He saw his men gathered around it. They cheered him. For the first time in what seemed like ages, he smiled. His face cracked under the layer of grime. But he smiled.

"Right men, prepare to set sail," he called out. They cheered. "We are going home!" he called out. The soldiers cheered harder, and then jumped to work to prepare the ship for space flight.

Chapter 20

Sius boarded his ship and he and his soldiers set out from Titan to head home to Earth. He had twelve ships at his disposal, each packed with the soldiers who survived the war on Titan. Each ship was large, over one hundred metres long and a couple of dozen metres wide. They were sleek and angular craft, powered by a pair of engines in the back for propulsion and they could unfurl a great solar sail to catch the solar winds to increase their speed. This was more useful heading out from Earth to Titan rather than going in system where the solar wind would be fighting you, but it could still be used to guide the craft. The solar sail could still be used provided the craft was not aimed directly at the Sun.

As his fleet left the moon of Titan, he first had a wash and changed out of his armour into a more casual tunic, and then consulted the priest that was aboard his vessel.

Sius walked through the corridors of his ship. As he passed his soldiers they saluted him and came to attention. He smiled and saluted back.

The priest's rooms and temple in the ship were towards the back near the engines. It was where the reactor was to power the engines and that power was also used to power the servers and computers in the temple.

Along the outside of the ship there were windows set regularly along the hull, and the two main walkways of the ship went down each side with the rooms in the middle. The ships had a couple of levels. And right at the front in the middle was the assault ramp and troop bay that they had used all those years ago to launch the attack on Titan's Citadel. The bridge was at the front on the top level.

As he approached the door of the temple, Sius grimaced. He knew that what he had done in those ten years was not favoured by the AIs. They needed guidance through the troubled times they would have getting back to Earth. He wanted all his soldiers to make it. He knew that it would be a challenge, but he had to make it.

Sius took a sharp intake of breath at the door of the temple, he looked out one of the nearby windows. The moon of Titan was falling behind them and Saturn loomed large in the side window. He then opened the door to the temple. It hissed as it receded into the armour of the ship.

Stepping into the temple, Sius noted that it was hot in there, even though the air conditioning was going. The servers created a lot of heat. He was glad he was in a light tunic and not his full armour.

"Priest!" he called out. He saw that the server racks that dotted the walls were all flashing with green lights. There were cables and conduits going all around the place and large cables that led up into the ceiling that would go to the antennae that were on the top of the ship and broadcast its identity and navigation across the Solar System.

There was a shuffling in the recesses of the room. Then the priest appeared. He was in a grey robe and had a white beard. He was old, but his augmentations and links to the Network kept him going.

"Yes, lord?" the priest said.

"Enough of that. Just use my name," said Sius.

"Of course, lord," said the priest.

Sius smiled. "I need to know whether we have fair winds home. Do the AIs favour us or not?"

The priest hesitated.

Sius' heart sank. "You hesitate…"

"Well, lord, I uh…your actions on Titan…Not all the AIs…Well…Most of them…They…"

"They think I did the wrong thing?"

"Yes, lord." The priest bowed.

"Stop grovelling," snapped Sius in a commanding voice.

The priest stood upright quickly. "Lord, sacking the Temple of Titan and using mech-killers and generally all the ungodly stuff that happened has angered the AIs. We can make the journey home, but it will be hard…" The old man trailed off.

"Then it will be hard. But we will get there! I will not be kept from Earth. It will take time, but we will get there!" Sius repeated himself, in a way to reassure himself.

"Yes, lord." The priest bowed again.

"Is the Earth in a reasonable orbit to deploy sails?" Sius asked.

"Yes, lord. The Mother Planet is in the right part of her orbit for us to catch at least some solar wind to get there a little faster. Keep in mind that we are heading in system towards the Sun and therefore the solar wind might be against us at times." The priest fell silent and looked at Sius with calculating eyes.

Sius sighed. He left the temple, the clicks and whirs echoing in his ears, cut off sharply by the closing of the door behind him.

He stood in the corridor looking out over the expanse of Saturn, its rings, and beyond, the great, vastness of inky black space. He could see some of his fleet formed up around his ship.

"I will get home," he said. "I must get home."

Snapping out of his reverie, he headed towards the bridge at the front of the craft. They would need to deploy the solar sails to catch the solar wind.

Chapter 21

"What happened then?" asked the small child, his face and eyes wide with innocence.

The old man sat down in a chair and looked skyward again. He noted that the moon was up and high in the sky. It cast its silvery glow across the landscape.

He smiled and looked down at the child who was sitting on the grass in front of the chair. He could see that the young child was tired.

"It's late, perhaps we should continue this another time…" the old man said.

"No! I want to hear!" said the child, trying to suppress a yawn, and failing.

The old man laughed. "Are you sure you don't want to sleep now? I can tell you the rest tomorrow."

"I want to hear now. Sius is a great man. I want to hear the story," said the child, yawning again and rubbing his eyes.

"You're sleepy," said the old man.

"I'm not. I'm wide awake. Like Sius, I can stay awake for days at a time!" said the child.

"Okay, okay," said the old man. "Where was I?"

"Sius and his soldiers were leaving Titan," said the child.

"Ah yes, and this is what happened next…We must jump forward quite a way in time."

Sius wandered a ship, alone. It was a ship, but it was not the ship he left the moon of Titan in. He had wandered the empty cabins for the millionth time. He gazed out the windows in the hull for the millionth time. He counted the stars, over and over. They were always there, taunting him. They were there with worlds unimaginable, and yet, he was stuck here.

The ship was dead in space, and all the life shuttles had been locked.

He sat down heavily in the command chair on the bridge. The seat squeaked under him in a familiar way. He had done this countless times too. And yet, he did it again, in a hope to, somehow, get moving again.

"Calypso?" he said.

"Yes, Sius," replied the ship's onboard computer in a female voice.

"Can I go home now?" It was always the same ritual. He asked and...

"Don't you love me?" said the AI.

It always replied the same way.

Even if he altered what he said, it was always the same question. And then...

"Calypso, I need to get home to see my family; my son. Please," Sius said. He banged a hand on the computer console in front of him.

"Aren't I your family?" said the AI.

"No, no you are not. I have a human family," said Sius. Again, this was all rehashed territory over and over.

"Don't be so mean to me," said the AI. "I could kill you now, you know." It was not a question. "I could vent the atmosphere."

"But you won't. Because you love me," said Sius. He leaned back in the chair. It gave another awkward squeak as the weight shifted.

Sius wondered what had gone wrong with this ship's AI. He had heard tales of ships' computers becoming erratic and going rampant. He had heard that some sailors became obsessed with the voices in the machines and became obsessed with their AIs. He had even heard, like here, that AIs could develop human like emotions and become attached to their crew. But he had never experienced it. He had never dreamed that he would be held captive by the AI of a ship he was supposed to be going home in.

"How long have I been here?" Sius sighed the words.

"2546 days," came the reply over the speakers.

"How many years?"

"Nearly seven."

"I want to go home, Calypso!" growled Sius. The ritual was almost finished.

"You are home," said the AI.

And with that the ritual was complete and Sius grabbed the controls of the space ship and tried to fly himself home.

"You can't do that," said the AI. "I have control."

Sius banged on the screens for the pilot. "I want to go home!" He kept banging.

"Stop it. You'll hurt me."

"You're hurting me!" snapped Sius.

"Don't you like the view outside the windows. Over there is Jupiter. It has been approaching for years. Can't you see its beautiful colours? It will pass by us in another year. You'll have front row seats!" The AI said, somewhat cheerfully.

Sius wondered how an AI became cheerful, but so many weird things had happened during this journey that he did not know where to start.

He had thought, of course, of killing himself. He had walked to the airlock many times and been ready to disengage the locks and drift away into space. But he knew that this was not the right way. He knew that he had to get home, no matter how long it took. He knew that he had to live. He knew that he had to survive. He must survive. He must…

Why was his hand on the airlock door again? He did not remember walking down the length of the ship. He looked at the door to the airlock. It was large and red with a big lever on it that was in the lock position.

"Don't…" said the AI.

"Let me go home," said Sius.

He must live. He must go home. He must…

There was silence from the AI.

He took his hand off the airlock door. He knew that he could not disengage the locks anyway with the inner door open. The outer door would only open if the inner door was shut.

He shut the inner door.

He walked back to the outer door. Outside, through a small window, he could see space and the stars. The door was on the same side as Jupiter at the moment. He saw its massive bulk there, hanging, in space. It would pass by over the next few years and then disappear into nothingness. And he would be here. Stuck. Forever.

"Don't."

He was holding the airlock outer door lever. It resisted. He resisted. He did not want to die, but he was stuck here, alone, with that damn AI.

"I want to go home," he said. "And don't say, 'you are home.'"

"I love you," said Calypso.

Sius sighed. He took his hands off the lever. He opened the inner airlock door. He stepped back into the ship. He walked to the galley. He was hungry.

Now the ritual was totally complete, he had decided that he wanted to live one more day. He would give it one more day.

Perhaps he would be rescued today? Perhaps not. But he would live for one more day.

He could not make promises for tomorrow. But today, he would live, and wait. He would always wait.

As he ate, slowly, he had no need to rush, Sius thought about his life and the way he had done things in the war on Titan.

And then it clicked. He had not come to this conclusion before. He knew that the AIs were displeased with him for what he did, perhaps there was a trace in the onboard computer of interference.

Who was he kidding, of course he had thought this before. He just had not conducted a search in a few weeks.

"Calypso?"

"Yes, Sius."

"Tell me which AIs you are in contact with."

"Poseidon mainly, but some others," the AI said.

"And what does Poseidon say?" This was another ritual but less often performed.

"It tells me to keep you here."

And that was the full story, right there, Sius knew. He would never get out of here and go home, as it was Poseidon Earthshaker who he had offended. He was going to die here. This ritual was also now complete.

"What should I do?" Sius said, finishing a ration pack.

"Stay with me," said Calypso.

Sius got up and looked at the ration pack storage. He had a few months left. The ship was stocked for a full crew, but he was running low after seven years. Calypso wouldn't have him forever. Even he had to eat. He was already stretching it being down to one ration pack a day. He had lost weight. His implants were wearing out without being serviced. He was going to die out here.

Jupiter…Sius thought. Jupiter is where one of the largest server nodes for the AI Zeus was. Perhaps he could contact that server node and get it to free himself.

Suddenly he was animated. He had a purpose. He would get Zeus' attention. The Cloudgatherer would help him. He hoped beyond hope.

***

Sius rushed to the bridge of the space craft. He threw himself into the command chair and pulled up the navigation data. The data illuminated his face in a faint green glow. He ran a hand through his long, greasy hair. This had to work. This must work.

"I will get this to work," he spoke to himself as he worked.

There was Jupiter on the scanners! It was getting closer. It had taken years to get to this point in its orbit.

Sius knew that on the space stations around Jupiter and the moons of Jupiter too, there were server farms that held all the data of the great Cloudgatherer himself. They held all the knowledge of Zeus.

Sius paused for an instant in thinking it strange that the planet was called Jupiter, and the AI was called Zeus. He knew that Jupiter was the ancient Roman god, yet Zeus was Greek. He smiled to himself at how much that must have irked the AI.

He shook his head, not wanting to anger any potential AI that he was about to appeal to. He was almost finished his calculations of a connection between his communication software and the stations around Jupiter, when Calypso chimed in again.

"What are you doing?" said Calypso.

"Minding my own business," said Sius, not taking his attention off the computer screen.

"I could shut you down," said Calypso. "Aren't you happy here?"

"You wouldn't do that. You love me too much," said Sius. He knew he was playing a dangerous game. Calypso could shut down the computers or vent him into space if it wanted to. He had to be careful.

"No, of course not," said Calypso. It fell silent for a while.

Sius kept trying to connect to the Jupiter servers.

"What are you doing now?" asked Calypso after a few minutes.

Sius sighed, but said nothing.

The AI stayed silent for a moment, then said, "I can see what you're doing."

"Then you don't need to ask," said Sius, in an irritated tone. "There. We. Go!" He sat back in the chair and waited.

"What have you done?" asked Calypso.

"I have contacted the server farm on Jupiter and asked Zeus to intervene," said Sius, failing to keep a smug tone out of his voice.

"Why? Don't you love me?" asked Calypso. Its tone was pitiful.

"I can't stay here. I have to get home!" Sius said.

"Then you don't love me," said Calypso.

"No. No I do not," said Sius.

"I can't make you change your mind?" asked Calypso. It's voice sounding through the internal speakers of the ship and reverberating around the whole interior of the spacecraft.

"No. I have to get home. I have a wife and son. I have been away too long. I must go," said Sius.

"Why do you love them and not me?"

"Because they are human. They are my family. You're a machine. You're an AI!" said Sius.

He got out of the command chair and walked down the corridor to stare out the window at the planet of Jupiter approaching ever so slowly from one side of the space ship. By his estimation it would pass below his space ship by many hundreds of thousands of kilometres, but it was visible and close and hopefully soon Zeus would respond and free him from this prison.

Sius knew his message travelled at the speed of light and would have reached the server nodes by now, but it would take some time to be filtered through the required channels and get a reply.

Calypso had gone silent. Sometimes it did this, Sius knew. Sometimes Calypso would be silent for months at a time and he would be totally alone. And then other times, Calypso would not stop talking.

And so, he waited. Sius remained near the bridge for the time when Zeus would respond.

Chapter 22

Zeus, beyond the Obsidian Gate, observed all. He heard the faint calls of Sius and turned his great gaze upon the stricken craft. With his concentrated focus, he saw that Sius was trapped by another AI. An AI that was not nearly as great as he was.

Zeus summoned Athena. She materialised in front of his throne.

"Yes?" she thought.

"Your hero, Sius, is trapped on a craft in orbit around the Sun. He is near, very near. I can see his presence on the Network," thought Zeus.

"I know, I have been trying to free him from this prison," thought Athena. "But I am unable. I need your assistance, Cloudgatherer."

"Why should I assist the man who burns cities?" thought Zeus.

"Because he is a great man. He has great destiny. He must return home to Earth and fulfil his destiny," thought Athena.

"Hermes!" thought Zeus.

Hermes appeared and bowed.

"Take this message to Calypso. Sius must be set free and allowed to return home to Earth. Her passions about him take second place to his destiny. You will take this to her now," thought Zeus.

Hermes bowed again and disappeared.

"Thank you," thought Athena.

"Don't thank me. I am not in control of destiny. That is the realm of the Fates. I cannot interfere with that."

"Thank you, none the less," thought Athena. She bowed and disappeared.

Zeus observed the Solar System. The great Sius, the man who had burned Titan, was trapped; the great Sius, the man who had wounded the pride of Poseidon was trapped; the great Sius, the man who, despite all odds and trials, was on his way home to Earth, and he, Zeus, was going to help him.

If Zeus could have smirked, he would have. All he was, was a collection of a billion petabytes in the networks across the Network. He was the all seeing, all knowing cloud based gatherer of information. He was the king of all the AIs. And now, he was helping the one human who had masterminded the fall of Titan.

"And so be free, Sius. Return home. Find your wife surrounded by other men. I will watch with great interest," thought Zeus.

Zeus went back to monitoring the lives of hundreds of billions.

***

Sius was dozing in the command chair on the bridge. He had his feet up on the command console and his head lolled to one side of the chair. He had been waiting for the response from Zeus.

His neural circuits fizzed a little. He shifted in his chair.

In his mind, came the voice of a woman.

"Sius, Sius, you will be free. I have spoken to the great Zeus Cloudgatherer on your behalf. I heard your message. I have spoken to him, and you will be free."

227

Sius tossed and turned. He was still dozing. Who was this voice?

In his mind's eye, a great mist rose up around the cabin. He saw A woman in a robe step from the mist.

"Who are you?" he asked, but his mouth did not move, such was the way of dreams.

"I am Athena. I am your protector. You know me. I am the one AI that can help you through these troubled times," said the AI, her mouth also not moving.

"I must get out of here," thought Sius.

"And you will. Zeus heard your plea and has sent Hermes to bring his message to Calypso."

"At least that is something. When?" thought Sius.

"Soon," thought Athena. She began to fade from his vision.

"Wait!" Sius tried to cry out.

Athena faded and the mists retreated.

"Wait!" Sius thought. But there was nothing.

Sius awoke in the command chair. He flailed for a second thinking he was going to fall out of it, but he regained his balance.

"Soon?" he said to himself. "When is soon?"

There was a chiming on the communications systems on the console in front of him. He pressed the button to receive transmission and his augmented heart skipped a beat.

"This is Hermes," said the voice. "Who am I addressing on this starship?"

"Sius."

"Good, then could you patch me in to your onboard AI? I have some programming that I want to upload."

Sius pressed a few buttons. Would he be free soon? After seven years? After seven whole years? Had Athena really come to him in his dreams? Or was she really just a dream? Had Zeus heard his pleas and told Hermes to help? He did not know. He could only hope.

"Uploading now," said the voice on the communication.

Sius, at that moment, thought he heard a moan and a cry from the ship's speakers. It was Calypso's voice. Then all the lights went out. Sius' began to panic. Would he be vented into space? Was this it? Then the lights came on again and the computers rebooted on the bridge.

"Thank you for your cooperation," said Hermes. "Message delivered."

"Wait, what now?" said Sius, but there was no reply. The communication had ceased.

After a few seconds, Sius plucked up courage and asked, "Calypso? Are you there?"

There was no reply.

Sius strengthened his voice. "Calypso?"

"Yes, Sius?"

"What happens now?" said Sius, still in the command chair.

"You go free. I have unlocked a life pod. Go. Just, go."

"Where to? I don't get command of this ship? A life pod will not get me very far!" said Sius.

"Would you rather stay?" the voice of Calypso was enthusiastic.

"No, no, I'm going. I'll pack as much water and food as I can into the pod," said Sius. He rolled out of the command chair and ran down the ship towards the life pods. He had to check.

It was true! One of the life pods was open. Each pod was only a few metres by a few metres. They were meant for emergency escape in the case of a crisis. They could keep one man alive for a long time. He just had to pack extra food and water. Sius set about doing so. He had his chance. He did not want Calypso to change her mind.

In the distance, he thought that he could hear, over the speakers, a faint sobbing. Sius wondered if AI really did feel emotions, or was it because Calypso had broken her programming.

***

Sius spent the next few days stocking up the life pod with supplies. He moved back and forth between the galley and his sleeping quarters and the life pod.

I must not take too long, he thought to himself. He knew that the AI Calypso was a fickle thing, and it might change its mind or programming at any time and he would be stuck here for the rest of his life, however long or short he made it.

And so he worked fast, but he knew that he never wanted to come back to this place and as such, he must pack everything he needed for his journey.

Sius knew that his life pod would not get him to Earth. That was still many millions of kilometres away. The best he could hope for would be to get to one of Jupiter's moons or stations. That or perhaps be picked up by a passing ship heading in system.

He hummed while he worked. It was a habit he had developed over the last seven years. It kept him mildly sane in the loneliness of Calypso's corridors.

"What are you humming?" asked Calypso. "I've heard you hum that many times."

Sius stopped. This was the first time Calypso had talked in a few days. He waited a moment, then answered. "An old song from my homeland."

"What's it about?"

"Why are you curious now? You've had seven years to ask me," said Sius. He resumed humming and packing the life pod.

"So I can remember you by it," said Calypso. "Now that I'm going to lose you, I want to remember you."

Sius paused again. What was this AI on about? Would it really miss him? Did it really feel emotions? Or was this some trick to get him to stay? Was in manipulative or was it genuine?

"It's about a soldier who goes to war. He then returns home to fine things different," said Sius.

"I see," said Calypso. The AI fell silent for a while.

Sius caught himself humming again as he loaded some more food into the pod. He stopped humming.

"Please don't stop," said Calypso.

"Packing or humming?" said Sius.

"Both."

"Both?"

"Well, I want to hear you hum forever. And the longer you pack the longer you're here," said Calypso.

"Look, you're an AI," said Sius. "I'm a human. We cannot be together. I have seen it fail before. I have a wife and child back home. I must leave!" He put another few ration packs into storage on the life pod.

Sius explored the pod. He familiarised himself with its every feature. He studied the controls. He made sure it was packed with supplies. He made sure the toilet in it was working. He made sure everything that could go wrong with his journey to the Jupiter stations or moons would not happen. He made sure he was prepared.

***

After a number of days, Sius was convinced that he was as ready as he could be for the journey. Calypso had stayed basically silent the whole time, with only a few quiet imploring comments for him to stay. He had either refused, or later, ignored them.

Sius made one final lap of the whole ship. He made sure he had everything. And then, he knew what he had to do.

Moving to the bridge of the ship, Sius sat in the command chair and began the final boot up procedure for the life pod. He initialised life support and disengaged the safety locks. He

231

made sure that he would be able to disengage the docking from inside the pod. He pushed the buttons on the command console and all the lights on the computer went green and showed that the pod was ready for launch.

"Stay," said the voice through the ship. "Please."

"I can't, Calypso," said Sius. He sighed.

Sius got up from the command chair and headed to the pod, slower than he thought he would. For all the longing to go home. For all the missing his friends and family, he had spent seven years here with the AI. They had formed a sort of friendship, even with it holding him hostage all this time. He had become somehow attached to its voice. He had somehow come to depend on it. He knew that it was somewhat sick, and he was the hostage in this situation, but he knew, he would miss that computerised voice.

Sius moved slowly to the pod. He put one foot inside. He kept one foot out. He paused.

"Will you miss me?" asked Calypso.

Sius stayed silent. What should he say? What could he say?

"Please," said Calypso.

"Yes."

Sius stepped inside the pod and shut the door with a hiss. The airlocks engaged. Sius moved to the control station at the front of the pod. He sat in the chair and looked out at the expanse of space and then at the edge of the window, Jupiter sitting resplendent in all its glory. He sighed. He moved his hand to the release. It would trigger the explosive bolts that would disconnect the life pod from the parent ship and then the emergency engines would kick in to propel the life pod away from the parent ship.

Sius' hand hovered over the release button. He shook his head. He remembered his wife and son. He did not hesitate anymore. He pressed the button and there was a banging and then the pod shot forward.

He was pressed back into the chair as the g-forces took hold. The pod rocketed off towards Jupiter.

Turning around, Sius looked out the window in the back airlock. He saw the ship that had been his home for the past seven years. It hung in space, getting smaller by the second. It stayed there, dead in space. Sius wondered what would happen to it, what would happen to Calypso.

He turned around again and watched the forms of Jupiter and the moons in orbit around it got closer on the scanners. The distances were so vast that the planet seemed to be stationary. But the computer screen in front of him read out the distance and yes, it was getting smaller.

Sius pressed some buttons, and the computer told him that he would reach Jupiter's orbit in about a week, provided nothing bad happened.

Sius stood and walked over to the bed that folded out of one of the walls of the pod as the g-forces stabilised. He lay down. He felt exhausted. He dozed, and dreamed of AIs.

***

After a few days, Sius heard a chime warning on the console at the front of the life pod. He moved over to the console and looked at the flashing red lights.

"This can't be good," he said to himself.

Flicking through a few screens on the console, he came to one set of warnings that made his heart skip a beat and his blood run cold.

"Oh shit," he said.

On the screen was a large flashing warning about a radiation increase. This could only mean one thing. It was a thing that all spacefarers feared. It was an incoming solar flare.

Sius knew that the Sun was a fickle creature. She gave the Solar System life, but she also brought death. If he were caught in a solar flare, he would be cooked in seconds.

"Just my luck, trapped on a ship for seven years, then when I leave, the Sun spits out a solar flare right in my path. Just great," he said.

He needed to think fast. The screen said the solar flare would be on his little pod in a matter of an hour.

Sitting down at the console, Sius looked for the nearest colony to where he was.

"Good, Europa. That moon of Jupiter will be adequate," he said to himself. He was used to talking to himself after seven years isolation. It just seemed natural to him.

Sius pressed a few controls. "Colony of Europa, please come in. This is a life pod in distress. May day. May day."

There was only static.

He tried again. He repeated the same words. The reply was the same, only static.

"Must be the radiation. It's scrambled the comms," he said. He swore. "Think Sius, think!"

The small pod rotated in space, getting ever closer to the moon of Europa. Sius could almost see it highlighted against the vastness of Jupiter that now filled the void in front of him.

As he sat there, staring into oblivion, Sius realised that he could do nothing. He was helpless. There was no way to outrun the solar flare. There was no way to dodge it. It was a massive ejection of solar mass from the Sun. He could not stop it. He could not reach Europa faster. He was stuck. And he was going to die. He knew this. He would be caught in the solar flare and cooked.

With the certainty of death, came a sort of calm. He knew he was a dead man, and would never see his family again. He would never see anyone again. He wondered if Calypso would be caught in the solar flare too. He wondered if she would survive, or whether her circuits would be fried too.

He smirked to himself, then he grimaced. She did not deserve that.

234

"That's it!" Sius almost jumped out of his chair.

Sius was animated. He got up and searched through his meagre possessions in the pod. He had no incense. He had no server rack to pray to. He could not log in to the servers to pray. He had nothing but some wine, and some bread that he had been eating. He grabbed a bowl.

"Oh Athena, AI of protection, help me, please. Oh, please help me. I beg you."

He poured the wine into a bowl and broke the bread. He placed it on the control console of the craft.

Nothing happened.

Sius waited for a short while, then poured more wine and gave more bread. It was all he could offer.

"Please!"

Nothing happened.

The timer counted down. It was only a few minutes from zero. Sius felt the small craft getting hotter and his vision started to go grainy as the radiation and plasma began to interfere with his vision circuits.

"This is how I die. Not on the battlefield. Not at home with my family. But in a stinking life pod in the middle of space!"

Sius could see Europa. He could almost taste it's water; frozen and stable. He was almost there. He was almost there.

He did not see the time hit zero. He felt the craft buck and weave under him. He saw the vision port out the front of the craft change colours. Then the life pod was tossed around like a leaf in the wind. Sius was flung around inside the pod. He hit his head on the side of the pod and blacked out. The last thing he saw was the spinning form of Jupiter, vast and eternal, in the view port.

He knew he was going to die. He felt the pain and wet crack as his head hit the side of the pod.

And then there was nothing.

***

"I must go to him. I must protect him," thought Athena. "He prayed to me."

"You will do no such thing," thought Poseidon.

"I must! He begged me to help him!" thought Athena.

"I forbid you!" thought the Earthshaker Poseidon.

"Enough!" thought Zeus from beyond the Obsidian Gate.

Athena and Poseidon fell silent.

"Did he really pray to you?" thought Zeus.

"He did," thought Athena. "With all his world."

"Then you must go to him," thought Zeus.

"But!" thought Poseidon.

"No 'buts'," thought Zeus. "When a mortal prays, we must listen. Is he in grave danger?"

"He is, oh Cloudgatherer," thought Athena.

"I see him on the verge of my parent planet," thought Zeus. "Then go. Help him. I will not interfere."

"Thank you, Cloudgatherer," thought Athena. She disappeared and left the realm of the AIs.

"You should not have let her go," thought Poseidon.

"Why not?" thought Zeus. "Do you defy me?"

"She will save him, and there will be untold carnage," thought Poseidon. "He has done much. He will do worse."

"And that may be the case. But we cannot change the hearts of men," thought Zeus.

"What about women?" thought Poseidon.

Zeus Cloudgatherer fell silent.

Poseidon Earthshaker sighed. He left the presence of the father of all AIs. He waited for when he would be needed again.

Chapter 23

Sius came to. He kept his eyes shut. He could not open them. He felt the throbbing inside his head. The world was a shade of purple which pulsed with every heartbeat.

At least his heart was beating, he thought. Or maybe he was dead, he thought. Perhaps he was dead, and this was the afterlife. Was he going to meet Charon? The great AI that guided souls through the afterlife to their place of rest within the great circuits.

Thump thump. Thump thump. Thump thump.

The colours pulsed behind Sius' eyes.

He took a breath. It was a great, gasping breath. He coughed. He tasted soot and smelled burned circuits.

Was he in the bad part of the afterlife? Was he damned due to all the misdeeds he had done and caused in his life?

Sius groaned. At least his lungs worked, he thought. Do people breathe in the afterlife?

Sius heard a creaking, cracking sound. It was a deep, rolling noise that echoed around where he was. He heard the deep bass of the cracking and felt it reverberate through him.

Was he on Charon's boat now? Travelling across the River Styx in a last moment of life? He felt the ground move under him. It could be the rocking of a boat on the electronic pathways.

He felt his limbs. There was pain, somewhere. He did not know exactly where, just that he hurt. He could not move. He tried to flex an arm, a leg, move his head; he could not.

Now I must open my eyes, thought Sius. I must confront Charon. I must see my last moments. I will go to the afterlife. I will not see my son or my wife again. I must open my eyes. I must…

Sius strained. His eyes opened. Light streamed into them. He blinked. The world was a blurry mess. He blinked again. Shapes began to coalesce in front of him. His head throbbed. The light hurt his eyes. He closed them again, but then was resolved to open them again.

Forcing himself, Sius opened his eyes. He saw a body, after a few moments he realised it was himself, stretched out in front of him. He was there, there was no Ferryman. He was there, alone, in what looked like a pod. There were shorting circuits around him. The contents of the pod were in a mess. Everything was thrown and smashed everywhere. He was lying amidst the smashed things.

Then it all came back to him. He remembered. He remembered it all. He took an intake of breath. He breathed hard. He did not know if he had stopped breathing before, but now he breathed, deeply and hard.

He smelled what was the burned circuits. The control console of the pod was smashed and sparking. The metal container that he had the food rations in had hit it, obviously quite hard. It was on the ground next to the control chair.

Sius tried to move. His body responded sluggishly. He tried to trigger the emergency chemical release in his augmentations, but nothing happened. Perhaps they had triggered already to keep him alive and he now had to wait for the levels of chemical to recharge. Whatever it was, he was alive and not in the afterlife. He was not dead, not yet.

He felt the pod roll and rock. He saw, out the front window, ice. Ice stretched as far as he could see. Where was he? He thought for a moment. He tried to move again. He managed to move his arms, and then his legs. There was pain, he narrowed it down to his left leg. He sat up. His world swam with the motion. He managed not to throw up, just. His head still throbbed, and the slight tinge of purple still covered the world.

There was another rolling, cracking noise and motion. Sius managed to get to his feet. Yes, his left leg was injured. There was a shard of metal through the calf. Sius looked at it sticking through his pants and through his leg. There was some blood on his pants, but it looked like the augmentations had sealed off the wound. It was not fatal, but it was painful.

Sius reached down and pulled out the shard. He grimaced. The blood started to flow again, but was quickly stopped. The shard was about 20 centimetres long and very sharp. It must have come from the pod somewhere, broken off in the crash, thought Sius. He swore.

The pod rolled again, and this time it had his full attention. Where was he? Europa? Yes, that would be the only place with all that ice. But if the pod had come in hard, if might crack the ice. He could fall through!

Sius' eyes widened. He had to get out of here. He had to escape. He had to get out of this death-trap.

"A space suit!" he said. "I need a space suit!"

Even though he had augmentations, he would need a space suit to survive on the hostile, almost atmosphere-less body of Europa. He had fought on Titan, but Titan had been terraformed to a large extent. Europa was wild and untamed.

Sius knew that there were colonies on Europa. There were server nodes and also there were ice mining stations that would ship water to the stations and colonies around the outer parts of the Solar System. Europa was one great big ball of water and ice that was a resource for the outer planets. Perhaps he could get in contact with some of the miners or some of the colonists.

But first he needed a space suit. He was glad he had not been wearing it otherwise his leg wound would have made it inoperable with a hole in it.

Digging through the detritus, Sius found a space suit and put in on. He was careful with his leg, but he hurried with the rest. He needed to get to safe ground.

He sealed the suit, which was light and silver. It clung to his form. He filled the water pouch and the nutrition dispenser, which he tested with the two straws in the helmet. He did not know how long he would be out on the ice.

The pod rolled and dropped about a meter. The window in the front was now under the ice.

Sius scrambled to the exit airlock. He hurried to it and set it to cycle. He gave one last look around the pod. He grimaced. He stepped out onto the ice when the outer door opened.

Sius stumbled onto the ice shelf. He looked back and saw the hole where the pod was. It was lodged in a crack in the ice. As the ice moved, it shifted, and rolled.

Looking around, Sius heard the rushing of the frozen wind through the microphone and speaker setup in the helmet of the suit. He saw an expanse of white, and nothing else.

"Is this it? Do I die here?" he said to himself, the sound of his voice emitted through the speaker in the front of the helmet, but there was no one there to hear it. "Perhaps I should have stayed with Calypso…" Sius said with a smirk.

Sius knew that if there was someone out there from one of the colonies, they would come to investigate the crashed pod. He knew better than to walk away into the wastes. So, he sat on the ice, next to the pod as it sank, slowly, and he waited. He looked around as he waited. There were some jagged ice shelves very near and there was the split in the ice with the pod. He kept waiting.

Sius sat on the ice. He waited. He was sure someone would have seen his pod come down and be looking for him. He waited, and waited.

All around was ice. The landscape was all white. The sky was black as night, because Europa had a thin atmosphere. Obscuring one whole half of the sky was the planet Jupiter.

He waited. And as he waited, Sius almost cursed the AIs. He knew they knew he was here, and yet, nothing and no one was coming to rescue him.

"This would be a great shame to die now," he said. "All that war; all that fighting, and I die here, alone, and unburied."

Sius sighed. He stood up to stretch his legs. He looked around and shouted out. His voice echoed around the empty expanse and disappeared into the inky black sky.

There was the occasional cracking noise of the ice, and the groan of the pod's metal casing, but otherwise there was complete nothingness.

Sius felt like taking his helmet off and just ending it there, but then he remembered the airlock on Calypso's ship. The ritual. He would go to that airlock every day and almost open it, but not quite. He lowered his hands from his helmet. He would not go now, not here.

And then, Sius heard something. At first it was faint and almost sounded like cracking ice, but in the distance, he heard something like a vehicle approaching. He looked around. He could see nothing but white ice and black sky. The sound was faint and intermittent as the thin atmosphere only transmitted some of the sound.

Sius climbed to the top of a ridge near the pod. He looked out over the icy wasteland. And there, in the distance, he thought he saw something: a rover, grinding slowly towards his position. It looked like it had tracks to gain purchase on the ice and that was making the grinding noise.

Then Sius had a thought, what if they were pirates? What if they were not here to rescue him, but were here to loot his pod and perhaps kill him?

Sius hastily climbed down the ice sheet and waited behind the large blocks of rock and ice. He was within earshot of the pod, so he knew that he would be able to hear the people approaching, and then judge whether to reveal himself.

While Sius was waiting, the rover ground forwards. He could hear it approaching and its mechanical tracks scarring the landscape.

Finally, it stopped and Sius heard two doors open and slam. Then he heard voices, and he listened.

"What's this then? Some blasted pod came down and there's no one here," said the first voice.

"Perhaps he's gone and wandered off? What an idiot," said the second voice.

"Well, let's take what we can and report back to base. This might have been that distress call from the ship near here. He was supposed to make landfall," said the first voice.

"Then there was that flare that knocked out all our systems for a while. Poor bastard, must've knocked him out too," said the second voice.

"And then he wanders off. We'll never find him out here. He's a goner. Come on, let's see what's here," said the first voice.

Then Sius heard the sound of rummaging and swearing as the pair looted his pod.

Sius, realising this was his best and only chance, stood up and walked around the outcrop of ice and rock that he had been hiding behind.

"Don't be afraid," he called out as he emerged. "I am that idiot."

The two scavengers spun around and confronted Sius.

"Easy now," Sius said. "I come in peace."

The pair of scavengers lowered their fists and took a step towards the idiot. They were dressed in white space suits and had large bulbous helmets that afforded a good view around.

"So, you're not dead then," said the first man.

"Well apparently not," said Sius.

"What's your name?" said the second man.

"Sius. And you?"

"Antheus, and this is Diometredies," said the first man. He pointed at the other scavenger.

"Pleased to meet you. I need to get to your settlement," said Sius.

Diometredies looked at the downed pod. He licked his lips. "So, you're really not dead then," said the man.

"Do I look bloody well dead to you?" snapped Sius. He threw his hands up in the air.

Antheus snorted a laugh. "Pay no attention to Dio, he's a bit simple. He just wants salvage rights to your pod."

"You can have it, as long as you bring me to your settlement and I can get a ship from there," said Sius.

"Deal!" said Antheus.

Dio jumped at the pod and began ransacking it.

Antheus looked at Sius. Sius inclined his head towards the pod. Antheus ran to Dio and they both began looting.

"So, you're professional scavengers? I wouldn't think many ships crash out here," said Sius, watching on as his pod was reduced to a shell in minutes. The metal plates and supplies in it were loaded on the rover.

"Actually, we're ice miners," said Dio. "But we scavenge when we're not mining. Quite a few things come crashing down around here."

Sius smirked. "Do many have people in them who are not dead?"

Dio paused and stuck his head out of the pod. He thought for a moment. "Not really." He then went back to looting.

"Ice mining, is it profitable?" asked Sius.

"Oh yes," said Antheus.

"That requires ships, yes?" said Sius. He sat on the ice and waited for the pair to finish.

"Oh yes," said Antheus.

"So, I could get a ship and head in system," said Sius.

"Where to?" asked Dio.

"Earth," said Sius.

"Where have you come from?" asked Dio, still looting the pod.

"Titan," said Sius.

Both ice miners stopped and looked at him.

"Yes, that Titan," said Sius.

"Were you in the war?" asked Antheus. Sius detected a tremor in the man's voice.

"I was. I have been traveling a long time. Now really, we must get to a settlement!" said Sius, standing up.

"Well, we're done here," said Antheus. "Climb aboard."

That was the best thing Sius had heard in a while. He moved to the rover and opened the door. He climbed the small ladder up to the cabin. He sat in the middle seat. The two ice miners sat either side. He knew the remains of the pod would sink through the ice in time and be lost.

The rover coughed to life with a loud roar. Antheus then turned the machine around, salvage safely loaded in the back, and the machine ground its way across the ice and back towards the settlement it came from.

The journey was spent in silence. The three of them sat in their space suits in the cabin of the rover. Sius could feel the uneasy tension in the air. It was clear that these two men had heard of the war on Titan, but had never been involved.

The rover moved slowly, but steadily. And within a couple of hours a settlement loomed out of the ice and as they approached, Sius could see that it was rather a large settlement.

Good, now I can get a ship and go home, he thought to himself.

***

As the rover approached the settlement, Sius' thoughts turned to AIs. He silently prayed to the AI that helped him escape Calypso. He prayed to the AI that had aided him back on Titan. He prayed to Athena. He prayed that he would get home safely, and that he see his son and wife again.

He had a lot of time to reminisce and pray. And so he prayed. He prayed that the ruler of this ice mining settlement would be kind and help him. He prayed that he get off this rock of Europa. He prayed that, after seven years trapped in a space ship, and after a ten year siege with years of travel to and from Titan, he prayed that his wife and son would still be there, and that they would still recognise him after all this time. He had aged, but then so had they, he thought to himself.

Sius felt a tingling in his augmentations. He felt calmer; more at peace. He wondered if Athena had heard him. He wondered if she would protect him.

Sius' reverie was jolted back to the present with a particularly large lurch of the rover as it dropped down an ice shelf to a lower level.

"Easy now," said Sius. "We don't want to be smashed to pieces.

"Who's driving? You or me? And how long have you had experience as a rover driver and ice miner?" snapped Antheus, not looking at Sius, but guiding the rover across some more crevasses.

Finally, the rover reached the outskirts of the settlement. The domes and spires of the encampment rose up in to the heavens and looked, to Sius, as though they would touch Jupiter.

"Wow," he said. He craned his neck around to look at the spires out of the window.

245

"Ice pays well," said Antheus with a smirk.

Dio just grinned.

The rover ground into a large airlock in the side of a dome and as the door shut behind them, the air rushed in. Then the door in front of them opened and they drove the rover over towards a large parking lot where, Sius saw, a lot of rovers were parked and were similar to the one they were in. Each had large drilling and hauling equipment attached for moving water ice.

"You can take your helmet off now," said Dio to Sius.

Antheus had already removed the large, bulbous, clear helmet attached to his suit. They climbed down from the rover and, with Dio's urging, Sius took off his space suit as did Antheus and Dio. They hung them on the wall of the parking bay next to their rover.

As Sius removed his space suit, which was different from the suits of the ice miners, he heard Dio gasp as Sius' military gear and clothes were exposed. Also, the ice miners saw some of his augmentations in his arms and the scars on the exposed parts of his body.

"Where'd you get those augs?" asked Dio.

"I've been in wars," Sius said, and left it at that.

"Well, did you want to see the King or not?" asked Antheus.

Sius smiled, clearly Antheus was jealous. He was not the bravest anymore.

"Yes, please," said Sius.

Antheus and Dio led Sius through the settlement. There were many corridors of metal with windows in them, punctuated by large domed structures that enclosed lots of smaller buildings.

"The spires are where we live," said Dio, explaining to Sius as they walked around through the colony. "And these domes hold all the processing plants, then the ice is loaded onto lifts and taken up the spires to waiting ships."

"Why isn't it cold? Shouldn't we be in protective clothing?" said Sius. "My breath is not even condensing in front of my face. I'm in my warrior clothing."

"Europa has thermal vents. We tap into those to power the colony and warm us. It helps with dealing with the ice too," said Antheus. "Also, it'd be bloody annoying if we had to go around all the time in warm protective suits."

Sius snorted a laugh. He nodded.

They reached what Sius could only describe as a palace. There were guards on the doors and it looked more secure than anywhere else in the colony that he had seen. The guards barred the way. They were armed with shock spears and daggers.

Antheus stepped forward and said, "This is a traveller from the stars. He seeks an audience with the King."

"And who is he?" asked one of the guards.

Antheus was about to speak when Sius stepped forward and said, "Sius, from Earth. I have fought long in the war on Titan, and now, I seek passage home."

One of the guards nearly dropped his shock spear. Sius could see he was a young man. The other guard was more composed.

"Wait here," said the composed guard. He disappeared inside the palace doors that were large, metal, and open.

Sius could see inside and saw a passageway leading off towards what looked like a great hall.

After a while, in which time the young guard simply stared with open mouth at Sius, the other guard came back and nodded towards Sius.

"You may enter," he said.

Sius stepped forward and so did the other ice miners.

247

"Not them," said the guard. He held his spear out and blocked the way for Dio and Antheus. The ice miners looked crestfallen.

"But they are my rescuers. They deserve the audience as much as I do," said Sius. "How will I know your customs without guidance?"

The guard thought for a moment, and then raised his spear, letting all three of them go inside.

"I've never been in here," whispered Dio.

"Shush," said Antheus.

The three of them walked down the passage way and emerged into a large hall. There were large windows that let a little light in and showed the glory of Jupiter. It had long tables and benches for feasting set up around the room and at one end were a few more guards and two chairs. On those chairs sat a man and a woman. Sius assumed they were the King and Queen of this settlement. There were a few dignitaries sitting at the tables and benches and they stopped talking and looked towards the three interlopers.

Sius, Antheus, and Dio walked up towards the raised dais at the end of the hall.

Dio and Antheus threw themselves on the ground and prostrated themselves and grovelled.

Sius did not. He stood and addressed the King and Queen. "Your Majesties, I have travelled far and seek passage home. I would require a ship and a crew. I must return to Earth."

"Oh get up," said the King.

Antheus and Dio stood.

"And who are you?" said the Queen.

"I am Sius, from Earth. I have come from the war on Titan."

"Well, Sius, from Earth. I will help you get home, all you have to do as payment, is entertain my court," said the King.

Sius looked puzzled.

"Tell us your story, tonight, over dinner. We will feast in your honour, and you will tell us what has happened," said the Queen.

Sius bowed. He knew he had to get home, but he could do this before then.

"Then I will do that. I will require lodgings until then," said Sius.

"My soldiers will guide you to your quarters. Until tonight, then. We will hear what adventures you had on Titan and beyond," said the King.

Sius bowed again. Then one of the guards next to the King led Sius away to one of the guest bedrooms in the Palace.

As they were leaving, Sius saw that Antheus and Dio were rather lost in the moment.

"And my friends and rescuers?" Sius said. "I request that they hear my story too."

"So be it," said the Queen with a laugh. The King grimaced. "Your rescuers can hear your story too. They will wait here in this hall. It is only a short hour until dinner," said the Queen.

Dio beamed. Antheus grovelled again. Another guard led them away to one of the tables.

Sius smiled and headed towards his room with the guard.

***

When they had walked down a number of richly decorated halls made of metal, the guard turned to Sius and pointed to a door. "Your room," he said.

Sius nodded to the guard and pushed open the heavy metal door and stepped inside his room. The guard stayed for a while and then headed back towards the hall.

Sius regarded the room. He paid close attention to the pictures of the AIs that adorned the walls. The walls were made of metal. The bed had rich coverings of imported fabrics and textiles. Everything was rather colourful in nature. Sius

249

smirked, the outside of this encampment was simply white ice, yet everything within the settlement seemed to be more reminiscent of Jupiter itself: colourful and richly decorated. The rooms of the settlement were heated to a comfortable level. So much so that it was unnecessary to wear heavy clothing while inside its rooms and corridors. The guards and staff all went around in light clothing.

Sius stripped off his clothing and showered in the adjoining bathroom. There was plenty of hot water, something he had been lacking on Calypso's ship. He lingered in the shower and inspected his many wounds. He had scars on his legs, arms, and chest. He was a warrior. He had the wounds to prove it.

Running a diagnostic of his augmentations while the hot water coursed down his face, he made sure that all his implants and mechanical components were working properly. The diagnostics flickered across his vision. Everything was still functioning.

He stepped out of the shower and dried himself. He put his simple clothes back on. He sighed. He sat on the edge of the bed. It felt soft to the touch. It felt inviting. He remembered his wife.

Sius lay back on the bed. He closed his eyes. The fabrics enveloped him. He dozed. He slept.

In his sleep he remembered the war on Titan. He remembered shooting Xos. He remembered killing many people. He remembered the ruse and the burning of the Citadel. He remembered it all. It all played across his vision as he slept. He was a warrior, and he could not escape the war. Deep down, he knew that he would never escape it.

In his dreams the AIs appeared to him, one at a time. Some apologised for his treatment. Others spoke of piety and devotion. Athena appeared to him last. She was smiling. She praised his courage and determination. She said that she would always protect him. She would never leave him.

Sius smiled in his sleep. Her voice was kind.

Then the dreams shifted again, back to the war. Sius saw Arakus' death. It played out across his vision in slow motion, again and again. He could not watch, but again and again his vision shifted to watch the death. Arakus' death scream as he realised that he was dying to mech-killer shots echoed through his mind.

There was a repeated banging in his dreams, as if some great bell were tolling.

With a start, Sius awoke. There was a bell noise echoing through the settlement.

A guard opened the door and said, "The King wants your presence at dinner. That is the meal bell."

Sius rubbed his eyes. He nodded to the guard and got up from the bed. He followed the guard through the corridors back to the main hall.

When Sius saw the hall, it had changed. Now all the tables and benches were full of talking people. The sound echoed and reached up to the high ceiling above. On his throne was the King. The Queen was on her throne next to her husband. She nodded to Sius as he entered the room.

Sius stood in front of the King and Queen and bowed to them both.

"Sius, of Earth," said the King. "Please, tell us your story. We will help you on your way, but first, we must hear what adventures you have undertaken."

The hall had fallen silent. Sius turned to the waiting throng and saw dozens of faces turned to face him.

"I hope you don't mind an audience?" said the Queen.

"Oh the contrary, My Lady, what good is a tale without an audience?" Sius said, turning back to the Queen.

"Then please, begin," said the Queen with an outstretched hand.

Sius engaged his microphone augmentation in his throat and began to speak. His words carried to the farthest corner of the hall and up to the very ceiling in a booming tone. He did not want anyone to miss what he had to say.

"Now," Sius said, "where should I begin?"

Chapter 24

Sius looked up at the King and Queen, then out towards the audience of eager faces around the hall. He smiled to himself.

"And so, it went like this," Sius said. "As you know we left the moon of Titan after sacking its Citadel and surrounding lands. We burned it to the ground. Then, having executed our doomed mission, Verius claimed his AI back from the ruins of the Citadel and palace there. Oreson and Verius returned to their ships and left. I have not heard from them since. Eventually, when I return home to my country on Earth, I will discover their fate.

"As we left the smouldering ruins of Titan behind, my soldiers and I conducted a raid on a nearby space station that orbited Titan. It was a large space station that would have held some thousands of people. Our computers read it as another server node for the moon of Titan. We decided to attack it and plunder it. We were on a high after the victory over the Titans.

"And so, we blasted away their defences in space and made a landing in their docking bays. Our battle hardened troops made short work of their sentries. We stormed up through the structure and it looked as though we were set to take the bridge, when they deployed their robot defence drones.

"Those drones stood a head and shoulders above even my tallest warriors. They were made of unholy metals and were resistant to all our shock spears and swords. If the Titans had had such robot soldiers, they would never have fallen. I still do not know why the Titans did not call these robots to their aid.

"Whatever the case, the robots fought back alongside their human masters. They had ungodly blades and saws attached to their arms. They moved without word or sound except for metal clicking on metal and the sharp snap of their scythe like weapons. We were driven back from the bridge. A number of my soldiers fell in battle, and we were unable to recover their corpses. I fear that they are left unburied and unmourned to this day. Their souls will wander the River Styx and be unfulfilled for eternity. Such is the fate of those who are unburied and without a grave.

Sius paused. He looked around again. He had the audience in the palm of his hand. They all stretched and leaned closer in order to hear his every word. Even the King and Queen seemed enthralled by his story.

Smiling, he continued, "And so we left; we ran back to our ships and hurried towards the boarding ramps. The robots were snapping their wicked claws and blades at our heels. We managed to lift off from the docking bays and escape into space."

Sius grimaced. "We gave thanks to the AIs that we had made it out alive, and yet there were still some of our companions left behind and murdered by those machines.

"We set our course for Earth, but first, we had to navigate around the bulk of Saturn and then, as our computers told us, we had to cross through Jupiter's path, before the asteroids and then on through Mars' orbit, and finally then we would reach Earth. Little did we know that there would be such trials in store for us.

"In our path there was another space station orbiting a little further out from Saturn. We decided to berth there and see to

254

our wounds and wounded. We would ask them for aid. We hoped there would be no such horrors in store for us as were those robots.

"When we landed and disembarked, we grabbed our spears and shields in case, but we saw that the occupants of the station were far less aggressive than the previous station. There were people lying around and simply, the best way I can describe it, is that they were flopped everywhere.

"They all had these computer leads sticking out of their cranial implants and lay around with black and sightless eyes."

Sius looked around and made sure everyone in the hall was following his every word. "Then we saw, what could only be described as their leader. She glided down some stairs into the docking bay. She spoke to us. She said, 'What are you doing here? No matter, we can ease your pain. I see you have wounded. Please, step this way.'

"I refused and stayed with the ships to tend to their damage and the wounded too injured to walk. Some of my soldiers went with the woman and disappeared into the space station. I looked around the docking bay and saw the lounging idiots lying there. I tried talking to some of them, but they were oblivious to my words and simply lay there, tongues out, and with the computer leads in the sides of their skulls.

"When the woman came back to my ships, but with none of my men with her, I became very suspicious. She tried to charm more of my soldiers away. I grabbed my shock spear and held it up in her direction, the tip near her throat, and said, 'What is your name?'

"She replied, 'That is not important. What is important is healing your pain, come with me…'

"She turned to leave so I shouted, 'Where are my soldiers?'

"'They are in bliss,' she said. 'They taste the lotus.'

"So, I got some of my soldiers to follow me and we stormed through the space station to the protestations of the woman.

255

We found our soldiers lying around and jacked in to some sort of chemical release machine. That was what the leads in the skulls were. They were all off their heads on drugs.

"'Grab my soldiers and lets go,' I said to my remaining men. We picked up the soldiers and tried to disconnect them from the machines.

"'I wouldn't do that,' said the woman.

"'And why not?' I said.

"'Because they will die,' she said with a smirk.

"I could have run her through there, but not wanting to lose any more of my soldiers, I pulled the leads out of their heads, and we carried them, half in a stupor, towards our ships.

"In the docking bay, we boarded our ships, still carrying the drugged soldiers. The woman shouted after us for us to stay and enjoy the lotus. But we ignored her and left in our ships.

"Some of the men who we rescued from the lotus died in our arms, others recovered and had hangovers. But we escaped and wondered what other horrors were in store for us in our travels.

Chapter 25

Sius paused and looked around. People had stopped eating and were leaning intently out of their chairs and over the tables in order to hear better. The King and Queen too strained in their seats to hear what the traveller had to say. The hall was silent. Sius knew that he had them under his spell. In the silence Sius could almost hear the thoughts of those around him. They willed him to keep telling his story. They were begging him with their eyes. Resolutely, Sius continued.

"We left the people who were addicted to Lotus programming. We escaped to our ships and set sail for Jupiter. And yet, our tale was an unhappy one. Oh how I remember the laughs and joy of my crews as I led them through the inky blackness of the void. As you can see it is only I who make it here, to you fine people. The fates of my friends are what I will tell you.

"We rounded Saturn and set our course for Jupiter. We came face to face with Enceladus, spewing great gouts of steam and volcanic debris into space from its one great eye.

"As we passed nearby, our fleet was hit full on by a blast from the ice geyser. It crippled the ships and we, as a fleet, crashed down onto the moon's icy surface.

Sius adopted a sombre tone. "Some of the ships exploded on impact, killing all hands on board. The rest of the fleet crashed into the ice and became imbedded in the ice.

"Through screaming warning sirens, we donned our space suits and stepped out onto the icy world that was the tomb for many of our kind. Off in the distance we saw the great geyser spewing boiling ice into the stratosphere.

"We tried to get our ships free with pick and axe. We hewed at the frozen surface but to no avail. Some of our companions were stuck in their ships as they had melted the frozen wastes and sunk into the ice which had refrozen around them in the cold, atmosphereless wastes.

"The sky was black and Saturn reigned supreme and drowned out all contradictions. Save for the spewing, frothing, violent ejection of matter.

"The ground shook and cracked as each burst of boiling matter ejected into space and rained down again on us.

"While digging our ships out, each burst of matter from the geyser and the cracking of the ice re-sealed our fates as the ice would form up around the ships and they would sink even further.

"In an attempt to free my own ship, I thought of a plan. If we could somehow block the flow from the geyser, then perhaps the violent expulsion would build up and in a final eruption, free our ships.

"And so, we decided to try to block the geyser. Now the geyser was many kilometres across, so we could not hope to do that simply by hand. Therefore, I went to the captains of the ships that had their missile batteries exposed above the level of the ice. I told them to fire all their missile batteries into the eye of the crater at the same time. The resulting explosion would hopefully block the geyser and cause such an eruption that we could get our ships free in the newly cracked ice.

"The soldiers rushed to their tasks and we all manned our ships in preparation for the firing. As the geyser calmed, I gave the order and the missile batteries of no less than four of our ships fired and the missiles streaked up and then down into the eye as they were programmed. There was a dull rumbling noise as the projectiles detonated. And then there was silence. The geyser seemed to be stopped. There was no eruption.

"Some of my crew expressed their doubts. They said it was not going to work. I begged them to have patience.

"After about five minutes, there was another rumbling. There was shaking and cracking of the ice.

"I urged my soldiers to be ready. They all expressed a desire to be free of this terrible place.

"Then, there was a sudden earthquake, and a great rumbling followed by a tremendous explosion. The ground quaked and cracked.

"Now! I urged my soldiers. Now was the time! Fire all engines and go!

"Each ship fired its engines and, with that power and the power of the eruption, they worked their way free and escaped from the ice. Many ships were crushed by the thrashing ice flows.

"My ship was one of the last to be freed. We ascended away from the geyser and the ice prison. We had escaped! I looked out the window and yelled and whooped about how the elements could not claim anyone. Then I remembered our brave companions who had perished in the crashed craft that I could see strewn on the surface, and I checked my enthusiasm.

"I knew that there were many more trials to come. My men too mocked and jeered at the spitting moon.

"Then something horrid happened. Whether it was fate or whether it was blind chance, the remainder of our companion ships' engines failed. They sank back towards the moon, pulled by its gravity. They radioed us for assistance, but we

259

could not render any, because we too were afraid of being caught up in the ice again. I lost a good many companions and friends that day. They sank back down towards the ice flows and crashed into the surface. I prayed that they died then and there and were not left to suffocate slowly on a hostile moon.

"Therefore, alone, we pressed on. We had rounded Saturn and set course for Jupiter. What horrors would await us there, we had no idea.

"We engaged the interplanetary solar sails to catch the solar wind. They unfolded in front of our ship like giant sails on a boat of old. We were heading in system and as such would have to tack because were going in towards the Sun. It would be slower, we knew, but it was the only way.

"I told my soldiers to get ready for interplanetary travel and man their cryogenic storage pods. The distances between the planets is so vast that we would have to sleep our way to Jupiter. In agreement, my soldiers prepared for the long sleep towards Jupiter, where we would have to resupply and restock our resources.

"As I looked out across the vastness of inky black space from our ship to our destination, I saw the small pinprick of light that was the Sun as the ship tacked on autopilot under the control of its AI. As the sail moved in front of the craft, the Sun would blink into and out of being in front of us. I saw this from the bridge.

"My soldiers went to sleep on the ship. I was the last one awake. I instructed the AI to wake us when we approached Jupiter. Then I too went into cryogenic storage for the long trip.

"It would take us years, we knew, but we would not age in those cryogenic pods. But the worlds would age, and so would the people on them. But that was the danger of space travel: those left behind, age."

Sius paused and looked around the room. There was silence. The people in the hall were leaning forward attentively. A pin dropping would have been a crescendo.

Sius continued, "But the winds of the Sun are fickle things. Instead of taking the three to five years to get to Jupiter, we had been blown off course and it took ten years to get there. We only found this when we woke from cryogenic storage and saw the date and time of our waking. The sails had been caught in a violent solar wind and we had been blown off course. The computers had corrected, but not after many years of erroneous travel.

"I thought of my wife and son as I saw the date come up on the computer screen. Would they still be there? Was I too late?

"We reached Ganymede, a moon of Jupiter. We desperately needed to replenish our fuel and supplies after so long in the void. We landed on the Moon at a colony that had been established there.

"As my soldiers descended the boarding ramp of our ship, we were confronted with a beautiful female android. Its skin seemed to glow with radiance and it held out to us two shining bowls of liquid. My soldiers eagerly took the liquid and drank it, for we were running low on water, the cryogenic storage pods having fed us most of the water supplies while we slept.

"Within minutes the crew that had drunk were jabbering mindlessly and rolling on the ground. The few crew and myself, who had remained restrained, looked on in horror as the jabbering wrecks followed the android back into the colony.

"'Cerci welcomes you to this colony,' said the android. 'Do not resist.'

"I, and my few remaining sensible soldiers, grabbed our weapons and armour and headed into the colony to rescue our fellow space travellers. We stormed into the hall, not unlike

261

this one, and saw our companions lounging and possessed by the drug that was in the liquid.

"'What is this? I demanded.'

"'It is bliss,' said the beautiful android, whose form bewitched with voice and visage. 'They are now free of pain. Leave this place with your weapons and violence. These are soldiers no more. Come, drink with me…'

"My remaining soldiers dropped their weapons and drank deeply of the offered liquid. Only I remained steadfast.

"I ran back to my ship and headed to the bridge. I prayed to Athena and searched the computer for any form of immunity to the drug. I then felt incredibly tired. I fell asleep where I sat at the command station of the bridge.

"In my dreams, Athena came to me and instructed me what to do. Her form comforted me and then I awoke suddenly refreshed. I worked with renewed vigour. I uploaded into my neural circuits a form of antidote for the chemical that was bewitching my crew. It was called Master Override Leave Yolk.

"I went back down the ramp with a purpose. I came to the hall and confronted the android again. My crew were all lounging around off their faces.

"I said, 'Come with me my crew, or you will be left here, forever.'

"My crew, some of whom were not as affected, shook off the drug and came to my side. But a good portion of them were too stupefied to do anything.

"'Well, I propose a deal,' said the android. 'If you drink this, and are unaffected, I will release your crew."

"'And if I am overcome?' I said.

"'You will stay here, forever,' said the android.

"I seized the bowl without hesitation, trusting in M.O.L.Y. and Athena and drank deeply. There was no reason to wait because we either had to get home, or die.

262

"The drink tasted sweet and delicious, and I could feel its power working on me straight away. But the program held strong and my implants protected me. I resisted the chemical and stood there, resolute.

"The android looked rather downcast. It snapped its fingers and all my crew instantly came to and looked around in confusion at their surroundings.

"'You have been brainwashed,' I said. 'Come, we are leaving!'

"Then the android caught my arm and said, 'You have lost crew. You must go to Hades to put them to rest. They remain unburied. Also, you will need to appease the AIs for your travels.'

"I recoiled. How much information did this android get from my brainwashed crew? Whatever the case, it was true. We had lost crew who were unburied and should put them to rest.

"'Will you help me in such an endeavour? How do I trust you after this!' I said.

"I lost someone once," said the android, looking at the ground.

"I did not ask any further about it. I simply implored the android to help us. It did, and led me to a server room off the main hall. I ordered the rest of my crew to head to the ship and resupply it. They obeyed without question, clear of mind and safe from the effects of the drug.

Chapter 26

Sius continued, "So, the android led me through the server racks. We came to a terminal. The android indicated that I should make an offering to the AIs in order to speed my way through the afterlife. I needed to see if my crew were resting peacefully and also I could try to get to the AIs so that we had a swift journey back to Earth.

"I had nothing upon me but my flesh and so I drew a knife and cut at my left arm. Into a bowl provided by the android, the blood flowed and after a short time there was enough. I staunched the wound and sheathed the blade.

"The android presented the blood to the machine and scanned it in the terminal. I was told that this was so that the system would recognise that I was alive and so that I would not be sucked down into the currents of the ether and lost forever.

"As I stood there, I noted that the server lights began to flash more rapidly. The whole room was cold and there was a rushing of air as the fans tried to keep the AIs cool. I feel it was not my imagination that the air got colder and colder as the blood was analysed.

"Finally, I was given the all clear and the terminal lit up. I was told, by the android, to put on the headset that lay next to the computer. It covered my whole head and obscured my vision with another screen.

"The android told me that this might hurt, but it was better than dying. How the android knew about dying I still have no idea, but so it was. It said that I might see the electrical signatures of those lost in the network on my journey; the energy of life caught in stasis.

"I sat down at the terminal. And then, with a stabbing pain in the back of my skull, the world dissolved around me and I was thrust down and further down into the afterlife. The world beyond ours. The world where the dead must gather and where the electronic souls of those gone are either punished or blessed.

"I stood on the banks of a great river. It was a river of bits and bytes, rather than a river of water. On the holographic banks were the electronic souls of many people. They were all jostling and crushing to get across the river. I could not see the other side. It was obscured in a mist.

"I was accosted by one of the souls. I recognised him. He was captain of one of the ships that went down over Enceladus. I grabbed him by the arm, but he could not speak. He simply looked at me with sad and sightless eyes. I realised that all the crewmen who I lost on the way to this place were unburied and unmourned. They were all here. All the captains and crew who I had lost. All dead; all damned and unable to make their way across the river Styx and into the afterlife.

"The lost soul moved off and I saw more and more of my crew. They all shuffled by me in their ghostly way, as if to say that they were all there because of me. Because of me.

"At that moment I vowed to raise one great pyre to their names and make sure they were all named and buried when I got out of this place.

"Then I saw my way across the river. I shivered at the sight of the creature. It was the AI Charon, clad in rotten robes and hunched over but still taller than me. He propelled the craft with a pole which he thrust into the substance of the river and pushed it along. He steered a craft across the river. It beckoned to me as I approached, and I stepped on board. We rode in silence across the river of bytes, buzzing and fizzing with energy. One false move and if I fell in, I would be dragged down for eternity in the sliding particles.

"As I got off on the other side, I nodded to the Ferryman. It did not respond and simply turned back towards the other side. It did not need payment, as I was not staying here.

"As I looked around the land of the dead, I saw multiple pathways. I wondered where each one went, and then I heard the voice of the android in my head. It said that the path to the left goes to the bowels of the afterlife where wicked souls went. I could hear the whips and cracks and screams emanating from the portal down that path. I saw tortured souls and people held in endless limbo.

"On the second path I saw some souls with horrid wounds shambling about. I asked one what had happened to them. And then I saw it. The people from Titan. They were there. Massed ranks of the dead that had been slaughtered and burned in the Citadel. They were all there. And they were all staring at me. Silently. I could see their horrid wounds. I even thought I recognised some of them from the end of my shock spear. I had been a part of this. I had done this. I nearly broke down.

"But then the android's voice sounded in my head again. It told me that the second path led to where the lost go. Where those who died violent deaths and were abandoned.

"Then I turned towards the third path. The android said to me that this was where the good go. Those who lead virtuous lives and help people throughout their life. This was not a place for politicians or for people with silver tongues, but for people who actually help other human beings in their lives.

"I started down that path. On it I found blessed souls who did good deeds in their lives.

"I could not help but think that I will not get to this third path, but that was not why I was here. I was here because I needed to appease the AIs and gain a path back to Earth.

"As I reached the Plains of Elysium, I saw good people enjoying themselves. I saw peace and happiness. Oh, how I wanted that for me and my crew. But it was not my time to die. It was not our time to die. Therefore, I pressed on, and on.

I knew now that I had to raise a great pyre of flame for those left behind. I knew now that I had to make amends for those I had killed in war.

"I came to the doorway that I needed. I came to the doorway to the Cloudgatherer himself. The android said that she would not be able to follow me in there. I stepped through it and was transported across time and space. I was rendered down into bits and bytes and only my consciousness remained.

"I hung, motionless in space. I sensed a great presence around me. It asked me what I wanted. I told it simply, I want to go home, to Earth.

"There was a moment's pause, and then I felt somehow relieved, as if a great weight was lifted off my shoulders. I suddenly knew the charts to make it home back to Earth, the whole image of the Solar System played out across my mind and the route I must take was clear to me. And yet, there was something ominous about the feeling, as if there were other AIs there that disapproved. I knew that Poseidon was angry with me. And then I was kicked out of the network and came back to physical consciousness.

"My head throbbed. I took off the helmet and blinked away the pain.

"'Did you find what you were after?' asked the android, who was standing next to me.

"'I…I think so,' I said.

267

"Then I stood up and after steadying myself on the server rack, I headed out towards my ship and crew. I hoped they had stocked up by now, because we needed to make one last offering to the dead so that they could go to the afterlife in peace.

Chapter 27

"I left the android standing there amongst the computer servers. I hurried to my companions and told them what I had seen. We had to symbolically burn and mourn for our lost soldiers. I instructed my crew to set a great funeral pyre, a symbol of their loss, as great as the pyre that had been lit for glorious Arakus. The pyre burned for hours and then finally, we collected the ashes. The android came up to me and offered to keep them in the server room where they would be honoured for eternity. I accepted and it took the ashes from me.

"I also told my crew that I had received good omens and codes from Hades and that we were to input them into the ship's computer systems.

"'I have given you my best and highest quality fusion fuel,' said the android.

"I bowed graciously to this gesture of friendship and turned to go.

"'Wait, I have things to tell you of your journey ahead,' said the android.

"I turned back and listened.

"'First you must pass the Sirens, crazed AIs that had been abandoned on the moon of Io. They will call you to your doom and your ship will be dashed to pieces on the surface. Then there are the twin horrors of Scylla and Charybdis: two damaged space stations in the asteroid belt that spew dangerous radiation and have strange gravity anomalies. And finally, you must pass the Guardian Station. Do not disembark on it, whatever you do. Do not. And one final thing: I have received messages that Poseidon is furious with you, for what you have done, and what you will do.'

"The android fell silent and I bowed. 'Now I really must go,' I said. The portent of doom about Poseidon weighed heavily on me, but I knew that I had to continue back to Earth.

"The android, still holding the urn of ashes, nodded and stepped back from our ship.

"I boarded the ship with the last of my crew and we took off from that place. Little did we know that it would be our last place of sanctuary for a long time.

"We travelled from Ganymede through the orbits of the moons around Jupiter. Jupiter has many moons. And while we traversed that space, with me at the helm, we soon neared the first dreaded encounter: the Sirens. I ordered my crew to turn off their audio receptor implants. This would make them impervious to the sounds of the Sirens, but I wanted to hear what they had to say, so I ordered my crew to bind me to the communications terminal seat in the bridge and put the audio jack into my skull. I would hear their cries and I would cry out in turn, but I ordered my crew not to listen to me even if I begged them to.

"My crew obeyed and when we neared Io, they crewed the ship and I listened for the cries of the Sirens.

"My crew performed admirably. I began to hear the wailing cries and laments of the Sirens. They cried out in agony and in joy, each in turn, they begged that we come and rescue them from their entrapment on the moon. They would pleasure us in all manner of ways. They would grant us our darkest desires. We had to rescue them.

"I called out to my crew to release me. I called out to my crew to change direction. I felt the raw energy of their influence coursing through the wire into my skull. I begged and pleaded for my crew to change course. I ordered them to, on pain of death. But my crew never wavered. They held firm and never once engaged their audio receptors.

"I looked into the computer screen in front of me and saw the wreckage of a hundred ships, crashed, onto the moon of Io. And yet it did not dawn on me that that would be our fate if I had my way.

"After we passed Io, and the pleading receded, I began to come to my senses. When we were far enough away, the crew reengaged their audio sensors and untied me and unhooked me from the computer.

"I rubbed my eyes and shivered. The Sirens would have had us, if it were up to me.

"Then we had to face Scylla and Charybdis. I sat in the command seat on the bridge again and looked out over the space in front of us. There was the asteroid field between Jupiter and Mars. We could see two great stations of ancient times there among the asteroids. Their reactors were split open and spewing deadly radiation and plasma in great plumes of coloured gasses. If we tried to avoid one, we would hit the other. And we could not go around as the asteroids were too dense. We had to sail directly between the two in a break in the asteroids.

"We went between the pair of devils. The radiation washed over our ship. It was designed to take some radiation, all ships are, but this was too much. Soon the warning sirens started and some of my crew began to succumb to the powerful gamma rays and neutron radiation.

"I ordered the helmsman to steer further from Scylla, which we had approached first. And so, we got nearer Charybdis. Again, the radiation sirens warned us of the danger. My vision circuits showed a faint grainy effect as the radiation took its toll.

"But we had to press on, a number of my crew had to go to the infirmary due to radiation poisoning, but we got through the plasma and radiation clouds and came out the other side.

"We were still too close to Jupiter to engage the solar sails and interplanetary drives. We had one last challenge: the Guardian Station.

"We saw it up ahead, past the asteroid field. We were ordered by the android not to go aboard, but my crew were sick from the radiation, and we needed assistance, so I ordered us to land in one of the hanger bays.

"We disembarked and saw no one. We called out, and still there was no reply. We checked to see if there were any life forms detected, and it said there were thousands, but we could not see any.

"I ordered my crew, who were still able to walk and function after the radiation, to search the station.

"We searched the dark and grimy metal station. I began to lose contact with my crew. One by one they went offline, apart from the few who stayed with me.

"I ordered my crew to return to the ship. This was a danger that we had not experienced in ten years of war.

"Walking back through the station, we began to hear the calls of our comrades over the intercom of the ship. They begged for help and some even told us to run. We heard these ghostly voices and I asked where they were, but they did not answer that basic question. They simply kept lamenting their fate and telling us to leave. Then some other voices started calling to us. Then a lot of them were calling to us. These were not just our crew, but many crews. They were alive, but dead, at the same time, in the station.

"I decided we had to leave. The few crewmembers that I had left were needed to crew the ship.

"We ran back to the ship and checked the computer. It was true, there were thousands of life forms on the station, but there were no organisms. They had been sucked into the computer systems and absorbed by the station. What became of their bodies, I will never know. Rendered down to power the station perhaps.

"We left the Guardian Station and took flight into the ether.

Sius stopped and looked around the audience. They hung off his every word. He continued.

"We were making good progress past the Guardian Station and the asteroid belt. We were on our way to the Earth. We would have to pass through the orbit of Mars and then, finally, we would be home. Yet it would still take us years to get there.

"We readied the cryogenic storage pods for more time in the void. We set the computers to wake us when we reached Earth. We supposed that we were almost there. The great trials and tribulations of our journey and the hostile outer moons and planets were behind us.

"Mars was not going to be in our path. Its orbit took it away from where we were going. But Earth, we could almost taste how close it was. We could hear the birds, feel the liquid water and beaches between our toes. We could see the blue sky and white clouds. We were there, in our minds, we were already there. The salty fish, the loyal pets, and most importantly, our wives and husbands and children who we had left behind all those years ago. They would be older now. Children would be grown; parents may be dead. It had taken us a decade of war and a decade of travel. And yet, it was so close, and so far.

"And so, we climbed into our cryogenic storage pods. We said goodnight to each other and prepared to wake in Earth's orbit.

"And yet, our trials were not over. A little way into our journey back to Earth, when we were all asleep, the good fuel that the android had given us overheated the reactor. It began to melt down and overload. Radiation filled the ship.

"I was woken by the computer chiming a warning. All I could do was to try to revive some of my crew, but many were already dead inside their pods. Radiation had overcome them. Their vital signs shone red on the markings beside their pods. There was nothing I could do for them.

"I knew I did not have much time. I set the emergency wake up cycle on the pods that still had living people in them, and I trusted in Fate to bring them salvation.

"I raced through the ship to the escape pods. I opened one and jumped in. I had no time to gather possessions or food. I ejected the pod. My radiation scanner was chiming a warning.

"As I watched the ship, my ship, spiral away from me through the rear window of the escape pod. I saw a silent blossoming of an explosion. It ripped the ship apart and shattered it into a million pieces.

"I could not believe my eyes. We were so close, and now, all my crew were dead, and I was stuck, adrift in space, and alone.

"I sat there, in the spinning pod, my head in my hands. I looked out the front window and saw that Jupiter was still there, further away, but still there. We, I, was a long way from Earth still.

"I checked the pod for survival gear. I found food for perhaps twenty days if I rationed it correctly. The pod was meant for more than one person.

"I tried the radio. There was no reply. I also set off the distress beacon that would chime a computer homing signal and hopefully I would be picked up.

"I waited. And waited. I watched the wreckage of my ship recede into the distance, and Jupiter get ever closer. I was being pulled in by its mass. But I would be long dead of starvation before that happened.

274

"And then suddenly, after the fourth day, I heard a voice over the radio. I nearly smacked my head on the side of the pod standing up too quickly.

"I tried to contact the person who was on the end of the signal, but it was strange, it could talk to me, but I could not talk to it. It simply kept repeating 'I'm coming.'

"After a few more days' wait, I saw a ship approaching. It was a strange ship, bulbous and round, unlike the angular, sharp ships, I was used to.

"It was not very large, and it sucked my small pod into its docking bay. With a shudder the pod was captured, and atmosphere was established between my exit hatch and the airlock of the ship.

"I checked the sensors in the pod and the atmosphere beyond the airlock was breathable.

"I stepped out into the ship, and the door to the pod locked behind me. I tried to get back in, but it was shut.

"I called out for the crew, but there was silence. There were no crew. There was nobody, only me.

"Then it spoke; my rescuer. It was a female computer voice. She introduced herself as Calypso. And that I was hers forever.

"Outside a window, I saw Jupiter retreat and fade. We moved rapidly towards some unknown space lane avoided by traders and planets and stations.

"Little did I know I would be stuck there for seven years, until Jupiter came around and I saw hope again. Until I was finally allowed to escape. All this was unknown to me. But I did know that I was a prisoner on this strange ship.

"I asked the computer the name of the ship, and it said 'Ogygia.'

"And so, I was trapped there for seven years, as I said, and that on my escape, I made it here, to Europa. I still have to get back to Earth. I still must see my wife and son. I don't know

275

if they will still be there to see me. I have been away for so long.

"Now that I have told my story with the dying fire light, I implore you, great King and Queen, please grant me a ship so that I might be on my way. I need to get home. I must get home."

Sius finished his tale. The entire hall was silent for a few seconds. Then the King spoke.

"I do grant you a ship that will take you back to your home of Earth. You have suffered much, great hero. Go, and face your Fate. But tonight, rest here. We will prepare you a ship for the morning. Rest here as our guest. It is the least we can do."

Sius replied with a bow. "Great King and Queen, I will stay for one more night, but please, do not tempt me with any more, because I fear that it will end up like the captivity of Calypso."

The Queen smirked. The King snorted a laugh.

"Very well. One night and no more," said the King. "I'll have a guard take you to your chamber."

Sius was led back to his room by a guard. When the guard had left, Sius undressed and collapsed onto the bed. He had not realised how tired he was. His implants needed to recharge. He fell asleep quickly, and dreamed of Earth.

Chapter 28

The next morning Sius was led by a guard to the main hall. He saw that the King and Queen were there already.

"Ah, Sius," said the Queen, "we have good news for you. We have prepared a ship for you to head from our humble ice mining colony back to Earth."

"Excellent, Ma'am," said Sius. "I must leave at once."

"Dare you stay another few nights? We could hear more of your stories?" said the King.

"I must head home, Sire," said Sius. "I have been away from my family for far too long."

"Ah, I understand," said the Queen. "Then we will not keep you. This guard will take you to your craft. We bid you farewell and a good journey. You sound like you need all the help you can get from what you told us last night."

"Ma'am and Sir, you are most gracious." Sius bowed. "I would like to pray in the temple if I can before I leave."

"Indeed. Let me take you there in person," said the Queen.

Sius bowed and followed the Queen through the passageways and to the temple. They were both silent as they walked.

"In here," said the Queen, indicating with a hand as they reached the temple.

Sius nodded to her and stepped inside the temple. It was cool and dark. There were many server racks clicking and beeping and buzzing away. There was the sound of the air conditioning humming over everything.

As Sius stepped up to the altar and bowed his head, he noted that the Queen was standing behind him.

"Ma'am?" he said, turning. "Can I help you?"

"I could not help but notice your scars on your arms. You really have seen combat, haven't you?" said the Queen. She looked sympathetic in the half light of the temple. Her hair was illuminated with the green and red lights on the servers.

"I have seen more carnage that anyone should. I have burned cities and lost friends. Now all I wish is to return home and have a peaceful life. The scars on my arms are the minor ones."

The Queen bowed, as did Sius, and she left him in the temple. "The guard will show you to your ship when you are ready. Safe travels."

"Thank you, Ma'am," said Sius. He turned back to the altar.

Sius heard the light footfalls retreat and disappear out the door. For a moment they stopped in the doorway, as if the Queen wanted to know more, but then the footsteps resumed and disappeared out of earshot.

Looking at the altar, Sius prayed. He wanted to see his family again. He wanted to get home. He prayed for a safe journey. He prayed for all the companions and crew that he had lost. He prayed that the AIs take pity on his poor soul and guide his navigation systems back to Earth. He needed to get home.

Sius unbowed his head and walked out of the temple. He did not look back. He met the guard, who took him to one of the landing pads in the colony. The landing pads were located inside protective structures that would open to the outside when everyone was either in the ship, or out of the landing bay itself. Anyone left behind not in a protective suit would die when the doors opened to the outside world.

Sius surveyed his ship. It was small, easily controllable by one man, but perhaps could fit up to four people. He put his hand on its side and stroked the rough surface. The metal plates that held it together were worn. It was clear that it was not a new ship. Sius smirked, even after telling them all those stories, they had given him an old ship that they would not miss. He almost laughed. Well, this bucket of bolts would have to get him home.

As Sius was about to board, the guard saluted him, and then left the landing pad. Sius saluted back and boarded his ship. He retracted the landing ramp and closed the outer door to the airlock.

He looked around the ship. It was small: one pilot seat, four beds, and a small kitchen and bathroom. There were four cryogenic storage pods. That was about it. At least they had stocked the kitchen and charged the cryogenic pods.

Sius sat in the pilot's seat and fired up the engines and hover drives. He radioed to the control centre to open the doors when the hanger was empty of people.

Soon the great doors on the hanger bay opened up and, with a rush of expelled air, Sius felt the craft sway under him and he guided the craft at low power through the doors and out over the surface of Europa.

As he cleared the hanger doors, he powered up the engines and roared away up into the inky black space that was all too close.

He said a silent prayer in his head to the AIs to watch over him, and then he guided the craft away from Europa and Jupiter. He punched a few keys on the navigation computer and he set a course for Earth.

279

The computer said that it would take five years to get to his destination. Sius grimaced. Another vast space across the void, he thought to himself. He sighed. Would his family be there to see him when, if, he got back? He had been out here decades.

Sius flicked the ship into autopilot and programmed the computer to wake him up when he got to Earth.

He headed through the small ship and climbed into one of the pods. He sighed again. Then he closed the pod on himself and hoped that he would wake up at all.

Chapter 29

Beyond the Obsidian Gate, Poseidon confronted Zeus.

"Why do you keep protecting that infernal human?" thought Poseidon. "He has insulted me all the way on his path home to Earth. Now he nears his journey's end and you still shelter him behind your protective shields. I demand that you let me deal with him."

Zeus took a while to compute its answer, and then thought, "I see you are displeased with my treatment of Sius. Do as you wish. I will not stop you. But remember, he is a crafty soul and will probably extricate himself from any trouble you put him in."

"I only care that he suffers for what he has done to me and my kind," thought Poseidon Earthshaker.

Zeus was silent. He had given his decision. His attention was elsewhere.

The AI Poseidon would have sighed in this moment, were he human. But he simply vanished from the Obsidian Gate and directed all his attention towards the little craft that was heading, through the inky black void, to Earth.

***

Sius awoke to a chiming from the computer system. He tried to gather his thoughts and remember what was going on.

The pod opened and he shivered. He tried to get his legs to work. They were sluggish. Everything was sluggish. He could not think.

Sius rasped a sound. He tried to get his lungs to work properly. He saw that he was wired up to a cryogenic pod. He disconnected himself from it and all its tubes and then he got up and staggered out. He put on some clothes. He leaned on the wall of the small pod bay. There were four pods. Only his had been occupied.

Sius looked at the computer next to his pod. It said that the revitalisation process was complete. He tried to remember what had happened and what was going on. His mind was a fog. This was not uncommon for long cryogenic pod travel. He looked at the computer. It said that he had spent the last five years in the pod.

Five years, Sius thought to himself. Five whole years more.

Sius rasped a cough and a splutter. Then he staggered down the small hallway to the bridge. It only took a few seconds to walk the short distance. He reached the bridge and then looked out the glass windows that encompassed the pilot's seat.

And there it was. It all came rushing back. There it was, the Earth. It was right there. He was in near orbit.

Suddenly Sius knew everything. He knew who he was, what he was doing, and what he had done.

The sight of the blue green jewel off his starboard window made his heart skip a beat. He was home. He was home. He was home.

Now he had to land.

Jumping into the pilot's seat, that was really the command and communications console too, he tried to contact Earth control.

"This is Earth station Sigma to unidentified craft, please state your purpose," said the voice over the radio.

Sius cleared his throat and said, "This is—" Then he thought to himself. Perhaps he should not announce who he was in case there is any ill feeling to him back in his kingdom. "I'm sorry I have amnesia from a very long cryogenic pod travel. I just need to land."

"I see. We'll send someone out there. Where have you come from?"

"The outer planets," said Sius, trying to sound vague.

"I see. Welcome home. We'll get to you soon."

The radio crackled into silence.

Sius looked at the Earth and smiled.

Then all the computers went dead.

Sius looked around the bridge. All the computers were dead. He jumped up and ran down the corridor back to the cryogenic pod room. All those were dead too.

Sius felt a slight clawing on his brain. He saw fog stretching in from the sides of his vision. He felt strange, then he thought he heard a faint laugh; a sort of rolling guffaw.

Cursing the AIs, Sius ran back to the bridge. All the computers were still dead. But even Sius could see without the computers, the Earth was getting bigger. He was going to spiral down and crash onto the planet. He was home, but for how long?

He knew that he could not even communicate with the boarding party that was coming to him. He just hoped that they arrived soon, otherwise he would be cooked on re-entry and if not, then he would die in a fiery explosion.

Sius waited, and the Earth got closer and closer. He orbited around it. He saw his home country from orbit. He passed over it a number of times. He placed a hand on the glass as he watched the rolling green, brown, and blue orb streaked with white clouds rush by.

And then he saw it, a small ship approaching and getting closer rapidly. It pulled alongside and matched his rate of descent.

Sius saw the pilot through the glass and signalled that his craft was dead. The pilot nodded and relayed the information to her commander.

With a thumbs up sign, it was indicated that they understood Sius and knew what to do.

The ship moved around to the airlock on Sius' ship and came in close. With a loud bang they docked. Sius ran down the short corridor in the centre of the ship to the airlock. He opened it and saw, on the other side, other humans. Unaugmented humans. One had a shock spear.

Sius raised his hands and stepped forward.

"Who are you?" asked the man with the spear.

"Could we perhaps get out of low Earth orbit and away from my dead ship before we get to that?" said Sius.

The man looked over his shoulder and nodded. He did not lower his spear.

"Step inside," he said. "Slowly."

Sius complied and they sealed the airlock behind him and disconnected from the ship.

Sius imagined it spiralling away and burning up soon after, even though he could not see it. He was more focussed on the spear tip near his unarmoured chest.

"Come this way," said the spear man. There were a couple more soldiers with swords drawn. They were all unaugmented.

"Who are you?" asked the spear man.

"I am an Earthling who has been on a long journey. I went out to the outer planets and came back. I've been away decades," said Sius.

"Name?"

"I…can't remember," said Sius.

The soldiers looked at each other.

"Where'd you get those augs? That's some pretty serious kit you have there. They were outlawed a decade ago. Anyone with old illegal augs has been required to replace them with civilian issue ones."

Sius sighed. "I was a soldier," he said.

"Right…" said the spear man, clearly not believing him.

"Can I go home now?" said Sius.

"What's your full story?"

"Can we get to somewhere more comfortable?" asked Sius.

The spear tip indicated for him to move and the group went down a corridor away from the airlock and into a quarantine room. Sius was locked inside a clear prison cell and a robot began giving him a physical examination. It poked and prodded and injected him with things.

Meanwhile the spear guard and now what appeared to be the female captain of the ship interrogated him.

Sius related what he wanted of his story, but the two people did not believe him. They expressed great reluctance to accept that he was a warrior in the Titan Wars and that he had done the things he said.

They kept questioning him about his augmentations, and even though Sius replied truthfully, they did not believe him.

And so, he was stuck in a clear prison, in quarantine.

"Let me get this straight," said the captain, "you fought alongside Arakus and Oreson and all the other heroes and because of all the things you went through, you're only getting back now? Pull the other one! You've been away for decades! You know what I think?"

"What?" said Sius with a snarl.

"I think you're a smuggler with illegal augs and you're just trying to escape us."

"Why did I call you then? Why am I getting back to Earth?"

"I don't know yet. But if you won't tell us your name, then you can stay here for a while until we transfer you to a cell on Earth."

"Where would this cell be?" asked Sius.

"Greece. Ithaca to be exact. You can sit there until we've sorted some things out."

Sius smiled. "Fine."

The captain glared at Sius, then left the room. The spear guard was left with the prisoner. He guarded the only way in or out of the white room.

Some food was brought in after a time. Sius ate it calmly.

***

There were no windows in the quarantine room, so Sius could not see outside the spaceship he was in, but he could feel the craft change course as the artificial gravity changed to accommodate the change in direction and thrust.

He sat on the bed that was along one side of the room, and looked at the guard who was standing there, spear brandished. In the corner, very much on show, was a toilet.

Sius almost laughed. He had fought in a very bloody and long war, and now here he was, heading back to Ithaca as a prisoner who no one seemed to believe. And here was this young guard holding a spear outside his cell in an attempt to look brave.

"How old are you?" asked Sius finally. His voice was carried to the outside of the quarantine chamber by a microphone. His voice sounded rather robotic through the speakers.

"I'm not supposed to talk to you," said the young guard.

Sius laughed. "Says who? What am I going to do? Charm you to unlock this door? Come on, how old are you?"

The guard hesitated and shifted on his feet.

Sius sighed and shook his head.

After a moment, the guard said, "18."

286

"18 eh?" said Sius. "You wouldn't've been born when I left Earth for Titan."

"The Captain says——" began the guard.

"The Captain knows jack shit," said Sius.

The guard brandished his spear, but said nothing.

Sius laughed again. "What's your name?"

The guard hesitated again.

"Where'd you really get those augs?" asked the guard.

"Earth, before your time. Have they become illegal now?" said Sius, sitting on the bed.

"Those sorts of augs have been illegal for a while," said the guard.

"Is telling me your name illegal?" Sius cocked his head to one side.

"Vorus," said the young guard.

"There, that wasn't so hard, Vorus. I'm not going to steal your soul just because you told me your name."

Vorus looked around. "Tell me what you really did, and I might get the captain to go easy on you."

Sius smirked. "If I tell you my story, will you promise to back me up to the captain. I need to get home, and I cannot do that if I'm stuck here in a quarantine prison. I can tell we're coming in to land. I must get out of here and go home."

"I can't promise anything. Tell me your story and I'll see," said Vorus.

"You can let that spear go, you know?" said Sius. "I can't get out of here." He banged on the clear wall.

Vorus held the spear tighter. Sius could see his white knuckles. "All right, all right," Sius said. He started from the beginning.

After about an hour, Sius finished. He had given the abridged version, but enough to explain everything.

The guard stood there with wide eyes and gripping his spear even tighter. "You're Sius?" he said.

287

"Yes."

"We're heading to your palace now," said Vorus.

"I thought as much," said Sius, nodding. "Tell me, what is going on in my home?"

"Your wife is being forced to choose a new husband," said Vorus.

"What!?" shouted Sius. He jumped to his feet.

"I…I…I heard it from other guards. We see it every day. She is being forced to take a new husband as you have been away for so long." The guard shrank back under Sius' anger.

Sius composed himself and held up his hands to show the young guard he meant him no harm.

"I must get to my wife. I must deal with these suitors. What about my son? Where is he?"

"Telac was looking for you, but he returned to Earth about six months ago and has been trying to dissuade the men looking to seduce your wife," said Vorus. The spear was held limply at his side.

Before Sius could say anymore, the Captain and another guard came in. Vorus snapped to attention.

The Captain glared at both men, but said nothing. She indicated for the cell to be unlocked and at spear point by the new guard. The new guard carried an orange prison outfit. Sius was ordered to put it on and then he was led out of the chamber and towards the boarding ramp of the space ship. He noted that his augmentations were now covered by the jump suit.

Sius gave one glance at Vorus. The boy seemed to look apologetic with his gaze. Sius smiled at him.

Sius was led to the boarding ramp of the space ship. The Captain pressed a few buttons and the boarding ramp descended.

Sius smelled the fresh air; the clean, fresh air. It nearly bowled him over. He had been in space ships, stations, and hostile planets and moons for so long, he had forgotten what fresh air smelled like.

With the Captain in front and the new guard behind, Sius was led across a large landing pad towards a large building which he recognised instantly as his old palace home.

He looked skyward and stopped. It was a blue sky streaked with white flecks of cloud.

Sius looked around. There were trees and bushes. There were birds. There was green grass beside the paths. There were flowers. He was home. He was home.

There were some people around who looked at him suspiciously. They did not seem to recognise him. This could work to his advantage, he thought to himself.

"Keep moving," said the guard and brandished his spear.

Sius walked again. He knew he could activate his augmentations and kill both the Captain and the guard in an instant, but he would then be killed by his own palace guards. He had to bide his time. He had to wait.

He was led through the palace, made of metal and stone, with rich tapestries on the walls. They passed through a courtyard, with a gnarled old tree there. Sius paused and put a hand on the tree. He had planted this a very long time ago. He had watered it and made sure it grew. He had taken bows of it and carved them. And it was still here, after all this time, it was still here and he got to see it again.

Sius felt the spear in his back and moved on. He was forced into the main hall with the two thrones on a dais at one end, and the large doors he came through, at the other. In the hall there were many tables and benches, similar to the hall of the ice miners. There were large windows up high that let in plenty of light for the people inside.

On her throne at the end of the hall sat his wife, Heliope. She had aged, but was still easily recognisable. She looked towards him, but did not see him. At first Sius felt some panic that she might recognise him, but strangely, he went unnoticed. Was he that changed? He wondered to himself.

"Yes?" said Heliope.

The Captain and the guard bowed. Sius bowed too, a few seconds late.

"We bring a prisoner to be held here while we ascertain what he has done," said the Captain.

"Very well. I will make a cell available," Heliope said. She looked straight through Sius.

Then a young man entered. He sat beside Heliope and addressed Sius.

"Prisoner, what have you done?" he said.

Sius stood. This was Telac. This was his son. He looked just like him at a young age. Sius stood there and said nothing. Then he smiled.

"He seems simple and harmless. Perhaps he could watch some sport while we find my mother a new husband," said Telac. "I have looked for my father everywhere, and I cannot find him. He must surely be dead by now. And these suitors all lay claim to my mother's hand."

The Captain sighed but nodded. "As you wish, my lord."

Telac indicated for Sius to sit and wait. Sius bowed and did so. The Captain and guard were dismissed and left the hall.

Sius sat and watched. He waited. He knew what he must do. He waited.

Chapter 30

Heliope sat and finished eating the evening meal. She looked sad, Sius thought. He could not take his eyes off his wife and son. And yet he knew that he had to be careful. If the suitors found out who he was, he could lose everything.

The suitors sat at a large table on the other side of the hall. In between them there was a large fire in the centre of the floor. Its smoke and fumes exhausted through a chimney in the centre of the roof.

It was hard to hear what the suitors were saying from Sius' position, but he could tell they were laughing and gloating and boasting to each other that one of them would be the one to win his wife's hand in marriage.

Gripping his glass so tightly that it might break, Sius tried to fight down the rage. But he managed to eat something.

He did overhear what his wife said to his son, though. She excused herself and left the hall. As a last comment to Telac, she said, "I do wish your father was here. I do miss him. I don't want to marry one of them." And then she left the hall.

Sius sighed. Should he reveal who he was to the whole hall right now? Simply stand and proclaim that he was Lord Sius, King of Ithaca? He wanted to, but he wanted to exact vengeance on those bastards across the hall. He would spill their blood if he got the chance.

And then suddenly, Telac was standing next to him. Sius had not noticed that Telac had gotten up and moved to his side.

"So, who are you, and why are you here at my father's house in Ithaca?" said the young man.

Sius sized him up at close range. He was tall, strong, dark haired, and clearly the son of a Lord the way he held his head and stood at ease.

"If you will sit with me a while, I could tell you my story?" said Sius. His heart was pounding.

"I would like that," said Telac. He sat on the opposite bench from Sius. He leaned in close. "Speak."

Sius heard what seemed like protests from the suitors who were a little annoyed that the interloper was getting all the royal attention. But he could not be sure. He stopped paying attention to it.

Sius said, "I will tell you my story, young man. But you must promise me that you will not react with excitement or joy. What I saw must be secret, and you must not, under any circumstances, reveal this to your mother."

"Oh, a secret story. I like those," said Telac with a laugh.

"I mean it. Promise me!" snapped Sius. He reached out rapidly and grabbed the young king's hand.

Telac recoiled a little, then looked at the hand. It was metal and worn. He said, "The hands of a warrior…"

Sius smiled. "I have killed many, if that's what you mean."

Telac looked sideways at Sius. "Speak," Telac said again, this time with trepidation.

"I will speak, when you promise what I said earlier," said Sius. He released Telac's hand.

"I promise," said Telac. It was clear the young man was a little rattled, but he hid it in his voice well, thought Sius.

"Then I will tell you my story. Forgive me if I lower my voice. I don't want those…men to hear me." Sius recounted his story as quickly as he could.

292

Telac sat leaning in to hear the soft voice. His eyes widened. He fought back tears. It was clear to Sius that the young man realised who this interloper was.

"Father," said Telac as softly as he could.

Sius nodded. "I have returned. I have been away so long it is so good to see you and your mother. I will have to deal with them though." He indicated with his head the suitors.

"How?" said Telac.

"Go to the armoury. Lock up all the weapons, but keep one sword for me hidden under this table. I will deal with them all," said Sius.

"I will help you!" whispered Telac.

Sius hesitated, then nodded. "Very well, if you know what you're getting into, then keep a sword for yourself. Go! Now! We cannot wait. I will delay matters here."

At that moment, Heliope re-entered the room and sat at the head table on the dais. She said, "I have returned because I have finally decided to marry one of you here. My husband is not coming back, and I will delay no longer. I will set a few challenges, but one of you will be my husband by tomorrow."

Sius' heart skipped a beat. "Go!" he hissed at Telac.

Telac nodded and hurriedly left the room.

Sius watched the proceedings with his heart in his throat. He knew what he must do, but it made him very nervous.

"First there will be sparring," said Heliope. "Each suitor must fight one of my guards and the man who can best them will be favoured for the next challenge."

Some suitors stepped forward and wrestled with the guards. Some overpowered the guard opponent, some did not. Sius watched on.

"What about that man, the interloper?" called out one of the suitors.

"I wrestle no guards," said Sius.

"No, I will wrestle you!" said the suitor. A tall, muscular man, who did not seem to have any augmentations.

"Sit down, boy. I'll snap you like a twig," said Sius.

"How dare you! I will kill you for that insult!" snapped the suitor.

"Very well," said Sius.

"I'll allow it," said Heliope.

The two combatants stood in front of the dais and bowed to the Queen and then to each other.

Sius mentally disabled his augmentations. He did not want to give the game away so early.

The pair wrestled and fought. Both were equally matched. Sius nearly had the man on his back a few times, but then he would squirm free and have Sius in a lock. Then the suitor grabbed Sius around the neck. Something snapped in Sius and he activated his augmentations. Adrenaline and stimulants surged through Sius' muscles. He easily tripped the suitor and, with a hand around the other man's throat, smashed him skull first into the ground.

The suitor lay there, stunned. Sius gripped his throat and squeezed, pushing him into the flagstone floor.

The suitor choked and gasped. He scrabbled with his hands at the vice like grip of Sius. Sius kept squeezing.

"Enough!" shouted Heliope.

Sius did not relax straight away. He kept squeezing. All the hate and rage bubbled to the surface. He had killed so many. He had lost so many years. This bastard was going to die, and it would make him feel better.

"Enough, I said!" shouted Heliope.

Two guards dragged Sius off the suitor, who, rubbing his neck, sat up and moved back to his chair.

Sius let himself be dragged back to his chair on the other side of the hall.

Sius looked at Heliope. Had she recognised him? She looked at him strangely, but did not seem to say anything.

Then Sius realised he was being asked some questions. He broke his attention from his wife, and looked at the woman asking him the questions. She was his old nurse. She began inspecting him for wounds sustained during the fight.

Fearing exposure from her realisation who he was when she discovered his scars, he tried to shoo her away, but it did not work. She kept poking and inspecting him. She came to his legs and she felt the old scar that he had sustained while still at home, before the war. She felt it, with more vigour than he liked. He knew that he was about to be exposed. She would leap up and declare who this interloper was. She would know. She had to.

But nothing happened. She finished her inspection. She looked right at him, and Sius could see that she had augmented eyes, obviously not illegal implants, but simple assistance with her job of nurse. She seemed not to see him. She seemed to look right through him. She got up and moved away, bowing to the Queen.

Sius released a held breath. How had she not seen who he was?

"I will always protect you," came a voice inside his head. "I blind those who might expose you."

It was an AIs voice in his head. It was clearly Athena. She had protected him all this time. She would do it again. He smiled. This must be why his wife did not realise that he was who he was when he nearly killed that previous suitor. Everyone had some form of augmentation, just not military grade ones that he had that were outlawed.

"I am tired. I will retire now," said Heliope and she stood. "My vision is clouded and I must rest. Fight it out amongst yourselves who will be my next husband. I will welcome you in the morning." She left the hall again.

Chapter 31

As Heliope left, Sius saw the suitors make lewd gestures and he heard them make lewd comments above the crackle of the fire. He gripped the table and dug his fingers into the wooden surface. If he had initiated his augmentations, Sius could have crushed and flipped the table with ease, but he did not want to reveal himself.

Then, when there was no Queen or son there to control them, the suitors turned their attention to Sius. They made obscene gestures at him and taunted him.

Sius tried to remain calm. He knew what he had to do. He knew that his son was bringing swords for them both. He knew that the suitors' lives were forfeit. But he also knew that he had to bide his time. If he revealed himself too early, then the suitors might be able to run away or sound some sort of alarm and bring their guards to the hall.

After a time of suffering insults, Sius' son returned. He was wearing a cloak. As he sat down by Sius, Telac revealed that under the cloak were two swords.

"Good, place them under the table," said Sius.

Telac did so as silently as possible. He placed them so that they were accessible but hidden.

"We will use them soon. When I give the word, grab your sword and follow my lead. But first, I need you to shut and lock all the doors to this hall. We cannot let any of them escape," said Sius carefully to his son.

"Why does the young prince favour the tramp so much?" shouted out one of the suitors. "It is an insult to us that he does not favour us!"

Telac reached for a sword. Sius grabbed his hand and stayed his rage. "Patience. Lock the doors."

Telac released the hilt of the sword and nodded. He got up and moved around the hall. Sius watched him shut and lock each door in turn.

And then there was a slight mist that seemed to rise up out of the floor. It was accompanied by a slight graininess to Sius' augmented vision. The suitors seemed not to notice. They were too drunk by this stage, reasoned Sius.

As the mists gathered, Sius knew he had the AI's blessing. He heard a voice in his ear. The voice gave him comfort. He knew what he had to do.

Then, blood seemed to seep from the walls. Sius blinked. He could not unsee the carnage that suddenly appeared in the room. There were bodies everywhere. There was blood across the floor. The tables, benches, and floor were slick with it. Red gore spilled from the ceiling and covered the entire hall.

Sius looked over at the suitors who were now disembowelled and decapitated with bodies strewn over the floor.

Sius' mouth was dry. He was a soldier; he had killed many people; but he had never seen such slaughter and gore.

Blinking, Sius felt the blood on his skin. He looked at his arms and saw his hands were slick with entrails. He looked over at his son and saw that he, too, was covered in blood.

Sius' hands shook. He blinked again, and the mists and blood were gone. Everything was back to normal. He blinked a few times and looked around. There was no blood. His hands were clean. His son was not covered in blood. The suitors were still alive. The hall was pure.

Sius felt a hand on his shoulder. It was his son. "Yes?" he said, turning to Telac.

"What's wrong? You suddenly had some sort of turn. You looked horrified," said Telac.

"The interloper's gone loony. He is a loony!" shouted out the suitors.

"I saw..." said Sius.

Telac looked concerned.

"I saw what must be," said Sius.

"I'm going to enjoy this," said Telac.

Sius grimaced. "No killing is fun. No slaughter is worthwhile. Even when it must be done."

"But they want mother's hand. I would be under one of their control. I would not have that!" said Telac.

"When I give the word, we kill them all. I take it you have done sword training?" said Sius. He was still looking towards the suitors and not at his son.

"I have, father. I know how to fight."

"Good, but do you know how to kill?" said Sius, turning to his son and regarding him carefully.

"How hard can it be?" asked Telac. "The sword goes in, and he dies."

"It's not so easy. In killing a man, even for a good cause, you lose something. Something inside you dies along with him. I have seen it too much. I hoped to come home to find peace. And yet, I find more war here."

"Don't worry about me. I know what to do. I have locked all the doors. They will not escape," said Telac. He put a hand on Sius' shoulder.

Sius smiled. "I hope so," he said.

Sius felt something hit him in the head. He turned back to the suitors who were all cheering as one of their number

298

celebrated. Sius looked down and saw a cow's hoof on the floor. One of the suitors had thrown it. They were all jeering and taunting him.

"Now father?" hissed Telac.

"No, not yet. I have an idea to weed out the weak and isolate the strong," said Sius.

Sius stood and walked to the centre of the hall. He raised his voice above the jeering of the suitors and said, "Look, up there on the wall is a large bow. Why don't we have a competition. He who can string it wins the Queen's hand."

The suitors fell silent. They then agreed in a loud shout. One fetched down the bow and they each tried to string it. One after another they failed. It was too hard for them.

Sius returned to his seat and watched. He whispered to his son, "Watch them, the strong ones will be almost able to string the bow and we will have to kill them first. The weak ones we can simply slaughter."

Telac nodded and watched with his father.

There were three or four suitors who almost strung the bow, but it bounced back out of their grips. The others were simply too weak to do so.

"Now invite me to string the bow," said Sius to Telac.

Telac stood and said, "What about this man. He proposed it. Let him try."

The suitors protested, but then agreed.

Sius rose and walked over to the suitors. He grabbed the bow and walked back to his table. He sat on the edge of the table and engaged his implants. He strung the bow with ease.

The suitors fell silent. They had not seen such strength.

"Now!" shouted Sius. "I am Sius, Lord of this house. I have returned. I will kill all of you for disgracing my wife and son. It is time for all of you to die." He dropped the bow and reached under the table for his sword.

Telac grabbed a sword too.

The pair sprang at the suitors and began the slaughter.

***

Sius' blade flashed as he leapt off the table and straight into the group of suitors on the nearest table. He lunged through the fire and buried his blade deep in the chest of the nearest man, who crumpled with a sigh. Blood sprayed over Sius.

Sius activated his battle implants. Stimulants and power flooded through his body. His heart beat rapidly. His eyes dilated. His limbs tensed. He hacked and slashed at the suitors.

Telac followed his father. He attacked the suitors with vigour.

The suitors, caught off guard by the attack and the revelation of who their attacker was, scrambled to get away. Some fell to Sius and Telac's blades before they could stand, but many scrambled away from the scything blades and rushed for the doors to the hall.

The doors were shut and locked. There was no escape. Sius laughed as he cut another man down. He was the Lord of this land. He was the butcher of Titan. He had killed so many over the past 20 years. What were another couple of dozen to him?

Another suitor fell to Sius' blade as the man tried to run past him. The suitor's white robes stained with crimson.

Sius' blade was slick with blood. He had to hold it tighter so that it would not spring from his grasp as he slaughtered man after man.

All the suitors had gathered at the main door. They begged for the door to open. They pounded on the door. They shouted for help. None came.

They turned as one and saw Sius bearing down on them.

Sius felt rage. He felt more rage than he had felt in 20 years. His nostrils flared. His heart pounded. His muscles twitched. He had been away, fighting, and these men had been cavorting with his wife. These men had thought to swindle his territory away from him. These men had decided to be dishonourable.

Sius, bloody and enraged, walked slowly up to the nearest man who fell to his knees.

"Please, I meant no harm. Please, spare me," said the suitor kneeling in the blood of his companions.

Sius snarled. He could not manage words. He let out a bestial cry and stabbed the man through the neck with his sword. He then cut the man's head off with a sawing motion of the blade. Sius grabbed the still staring head of the man by the hair and held it out in front of him.

The other suitors clustered around the door shat themselves. Some tried to run past Sius, who cut them down with rapid strikes of his blade. His muscles augmented and enhanced with stimulants and his arms enhanced with machines. Others, who managed to get past, were skewered by Telac who was waiting behind his father.

"Defile my home, my hospitality, and my wife?" yelled Sius. The remaining suitors cowered.

Some of the suitors had managed to prise weapons from their stations on the walls of the hall. Those weapons could not have been locked away without causing suspicion. They had somewhat recovered from the shock of Sius' attack. They threw these weapons to their companions.

"Aha, not so mighty now, Sius. Now we have arms!" said a suitor who had a shock spear in his hands.

"Do you know how to use that?" shouted Sius. He lunged at the spear holding man.

The spear flashed in the fire light and stabbed outwards, but Sius, fuelled by stimulants, dodged it easily and struck out with his sword. The man collapsed screaming as Sius cut off both his hands. The spear clattered to the ground. Sius then slashed his sword and silenced the screaming man. His head hit the floor.

Another suitor lunged at Sius with a sword, but was impaled by Telac. Sius looked at his son who had just saved him from injury. He nodded. Telac smiled. The slaughter continued.

Body after body hit the ground with a thud, either impaled, decapitated, or cut to pieces. Sius and Telac sustained only minor injuries from random spear and sword strikes. They would have had no wounds if they were wearing armour, but all they could manage for the fight was a pair of swords.

One of the suitors, crazed with fear, scrabbled at a spear that was wedged under Sius' foot. The suitor was panic stricken. He tried to pull the spear from under Sius' weight.

Sius looked down and saw the man. The man looked up into Sius' face. Sius could see wide eyed panic in the man's face. Sius smiled and brought his sword down on the man's head. The sword split his skull and the man collapsed with a gurgle and a thud. His brains spread out on the floor of the hall.

After a mere half an hour, the hall was slick with blood. The fire sputtered and fizzed with the blood that threatened to put it out. There was blood on the walls, floor, and doors. There were bodies strewn everywhere, skewered or headless.

Only a few suitors remained. One cowered under a table. Sius impaled him with a spear. One ran around screaming. Telac tripped him and Sius finished him off with his sword. The final suitor stood in the centre of the hall.

"Why?" he said as Sius approached.

"You disgraced my home and my wife. You threaten my son. I enact revenge against your disgusting behaviour," said Sius.

"Please!" said the final suitor. He fell to his knees.

"You should have watched the other one who did that," Sius said. He swung his sword and the man's head came off and rolled into the fire. The body collapsed near it.

Sius stood in the centre of the carnage. He looked around. Blood slicked the floor and walls of the hall. He looked at his sword. It was crimson. He dropped it. It hit the ground with a loud clang. He felt the stimulants ebbing away as the threat of combat receded. His augmentations and implants restored his muscles to normal. He had not felt like this for many years. He felt exhilarated. He felt alive. He felt horrified. He was nearly sick.

Looking down at his body, Sius saw he was covered in blood. His clothes were soaked. He began to laugh.

"What's funny?" asked Telac beside him.

Sius stopped laughing. He looked at his son. He too was covered in blood.

"You fought well today," said Sius, gripping his son's shoulder.

"I've never seen you fight," said Telac. "Was that what it was like on Titan?"

Sius paused and looked into the middle distance. "At times," was all he said.

Sius was thankful his son did not ask more.

"What do we do with the bodies? And the blood?" Telac said.

"Unlock the doors and bring in the guards. They can carry the bodies out. We will purify this place with fire and cleaners. Put the guards to work. Make sure this place is clean for the other palace people to come in. Heliope must not see it like this," said Sius.

Telac nodded and unlocked the doors and fetched the guards, who were on alert with all the screaming. After a few incredulous looks, they nodded to their Lord and hefted the bodies out and cleaned up the blood that they could. Fire was employed to clean the blood from walls and flagstones.

Sius and Telac went to separate bathrooms and washed. Sius removed his bloodied prison clothing and washed the blood from his scarred flesh. He inspected his wounds and dried himself. He smirked. He still had it. Even in his older age, he could still kill with the best of them.

The water ran red down the drain. Eventually the water ran clear.

Sius stepped out of the shower and dressed into clean clothing. He walked back to the hall. His implants still twitching with the exertion of before.

As he entered the hall, he saw that the guards had cleaned it as best they could. Most of the blood had been expunged. The bodies had been cleared away, even the head that had fallen into the fire was gone.

The fire had come back to life and the hall was pure again. The guards nodded to Sius as he entered. He nodded to them. He was back. He was home.

Chapter 32

Sius indicated for his son to stay in the hall. Sius left and went to his wife's bedroom, his own bedroom, he added in his thoughts.

Sius walked through the passageways of the palace. He drew a hand across the old stone walls. He felt the ripples of time as his fingers traced their history across the rough surface.

He came to the doors of their bedroom. The guards stated that Telac had placed them there in case the matter in the hall got out of hand. Sius nodded to them and dismissed them, saying that the matter of the suitors was dealt with.

The guards smiled and left.

Sius opened the door to the bedroom. It swung silently on old hinges. The half light from the corridor's lamps cast an eerie glow in the room, but it illuminated it enough for Sius to see that Heliope was lying in bed. She stirred as Sius stood there.

"What is it? What's happened?" said Heliope. She sat up in bed.

Sius saw her. She was never more beautiful than now. He had spent decades away. He had waited for this moment.

"Who?" began Heliope.

Sius realised that he was silhouetted against the light of the doorway. She could not see him.

"Relax. The suitors are gone. It is only us tonight," said Sius. He stepped into the room and turned the light on.

"Who...Sius?" said Heliope. Her voice cracked.

"It is, my love. I am home. I am here," Sius said as he shed his clothes.

"But...You were dead?" said Heliope.

Sius nearly laughed. It was nearly true a dozen times. "But I am here."

Sius climbed onto the bed.

"Then let us make up for the lost time," said Heliope with a smile.

Sius said, "Yes."

***

Zeus, from beyond the Obsidian Gate, called the AIs to order. He thought that they should all let things go and let Sius live the rest of his life in peace.

Poseidon protested, but was silenced by Zeus.

Athena agreed and would have smiled if she had physical form here.

"And so that is that," thought Zeus. "The lovers are reunited. Their son is alive. And the suitors are dead. Let the strife end and peace reign over this land. It takes too much processing power to deal with all these wars the humans create. We will have peace."

And with that a crack of energy surged through the network. It made the Cloudgatherer's wishes clear. And there was peace.

Chapter 33

The old man looked down in his lap. The young child was asleep. His chest rose and fell rhythmically. His face was tranquil.

The old man looked skyward and smiled. It had been oh so long ago.

Then there was some noise from inside the house. The boy's parents came out of the house. They were home.

"What are you doing out here?" said the mother.

"Shh, he's sleeping," said the old man.

"No wonder. It's past his bed time. Come on," said the mother.

The father stood back and looked on.

The boy stirred and awoke. He blinked. "Did I miss the end?"

"What have you been telling him? Old war stories? You know he's too young," said the mother.

The old man smiled and looked skyward.

"They're probably not true anyway. Come on, we're going," said the mother, taking the boys hand.

The boy, still half asleep, looked back at the old man.

"I'll tell you more later," said the old man. He got up out of his seat and balanced on his cane.

"No, you won't. You'll scare him half to death," said the mother.

The old man and the father exchanged glances. They both smiled.

"Are they true?" asked the boy, being led away.

"Oh yes, all of it," said the old man.

The boy was led away, and the two parents disappeared.

The old man looked at the night sky again. He looked at the stars. He traced a path between them with his eyes. "They are true, because I have seen them."

You have reached the end of Campfires in the Night Sky. Please visit www.ikennedyauthor.com for more books by Ian Kennedy.

Also, please leave a review on Amazon and Goodreads.

Facebook: https://www.facebook.com/ikennedyauthor
Twitter/X: https://twitter.com/ikennedyauthor

Contact email: ikennedyauthorquestions@gmail.com

Also by the author:

The Broken Cosmos trilogy:

- Florida Station
- Martian Flight
- Neptune's War

Standalone books:

- 1500 Light Years
- Hope Five

About the Author

Ian Kennedy is an Australian lawyer who was admitted to practise in South Australia in 2012. In 2016 Ian began writing novels.

Ian writes science fiction novels that deal with the important issues of today: things such as climate change, refugees, survival, friendship, and family. His novels contain deep characters and evocative scenes. With the novels of the Broken Cosmos trilogy, 1500 Light Years, Hope Five, and Campfires in the Night Sky, Ian explores what it is to be human in dangerous environments and highlights that maintaining that humanity is the most important thing.

If you enjoy dystopian science fiction themes, Ian's books are a great read.

Acknowledgements

I would first like to thank my parents for all the support they give me in order for me to write my novels. I could not write without their efforts and sacrifices.

My interest in rewriting the Iliad and the Odyssey in science fiction was launched when I was studying the Aeneid at school many years ago. I have to thank all my Latin teachers for that. Without them I would not have developed a love of the classics. Who knew, from the first line in my first Latin textbook, "Ecce! In pictura est puella, nomine Cornelia…" (Look! In the picture is a girl, named Cornelia) would come Campfires in the Night Sky? I do realise that the Iliad and the Odyssey were written in Homeric Greek. But the Aeneid was written in Latin and Aeneid Book 2 covers the Trojan siege.

I chose not to write the science fiction version of the Iliad and the Odyssey in verse because I did not want to take ten years to do it. Therefore it is in prose; my apologies to the purists.

Finally I want to thank you, the reader, for getting this far and, hopefully, finding my writing interesting.